mare's war
tanita s. davis

B
A
C
A
d
o

E

EMBER

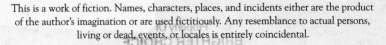

Text copyright © 2009 by Tanita S. Davis
Cover image copyright © 2011 by Glow Images

All rights reserved. Published in the United States by Ember, an imprint of Random House Children's Books, a division of Random House, Inc., New York. Originally published in hardcover in the United States by Alfred A. Knopf, an imprint of Random House Children's Books, New York, in 2009.

Ember and the E colophon are registered trademarks of Random House, Inc.

Visit us on the Web! randomhouse.com/teens

Educators and librarians, for a variety of teaching tools, visit us at randomhouse.com/teachers

The Library of Congress has cataloged the hardcover edition of this work as follows:
Davis, Tanita.
Mare's war / Tanita Davis.
p.   cm.
Summary: Teens Octavia and Tali learn about strength, independence, and courage when they are forced to take a car trip with their grandmother, who tells about growing up black in 1940s Alabama and serving in Europe during World War II as a member of the Women's Army Corps.
ISBN 978-0-375-85714-0 (trade) — ISBN 978-0-375-95714-7 (lib. bdg.) — ISBN 978-0-375-85359-3 (ebook)
[1. Automobile travel—Fiction. 2. Grandmothers—Fiction. 3. African Americans—Fiction. 4. United States. Army. Women's Army Corps—Fiction. 5. World War, 1939–1945—Fiction. 6. Sisters—Fiction. 7. Family life—Alabama—Fiction. 8. Alabama—History—1819–1950—Fiction.] I. Title.
PZ7.D3174Mar 2009
[Fic]—dc22
2008033744

ISBN 978-0-375-85077-6 (tr. pbk.)

RL: 7.0

Printed in the United States of America

11 10 9 8 7 6 5 4 3 2

First Ember Edition 2011

Random House Children's Books supports the First Amendment and celebrates the right to read.

For all of us, lest some of us
be forgotten

1.

NOW

It's just a sporty red car parked across our driveway, but when I see it, my stomach plummets. It's my grandmother.

Already, I hate this summer. Usually, I laze around with my best friends, Eremasi and Rye, for the first few weeks until it's too late to get a job and then find a babysitting gig or two to keep my parents happy, but this year, my parents jumped in and planned my summer for me. Yesterday was the last day of school. Last night, Mom pulled out the suitcases and made us pack. We're going to some kind of a reunion—with my grandmother. Today.

My grandmother isn't at all normal. She doesn't read mystery novels, or sing in a church choir, or knit, or sew. She doesn't do the Jumbles in the newspaper, and she hates crosswords. She isn't at all soft or plump, doesn't smell like cinnamon, pumpkin bread, or oatmeal cookies. My grandmother, Ms. Marey Lee Boylen, is not the cookie type.

She wears flippy auburn wigs, stiletto shoes, and padded push-up bras. Once, when we were little, my sister, Talitha, and I found a pair of panties in her bathroom with a fake butt. (We kept snickering, "Fanny pants!" at each other and busting up all afternoon. My mother finally made us go sit in the car.)

My grandmother has long, fake nails and a croaky hoarse drawl, and she's always holding a long, skinny cigarette—unlit, otherwise my dad will have a fit—between her fingers. She's loud and bossy and she drinks bourbon with lemon juice at dinner. She has a low-slung red coupe, and Dad says she drives like a bat out of hell. She's over eighty, and she still lives by herself in a town house stuck on a cliff near the Golden Gate Bridge. She takes the bus so she can avoid parking tickets and walks everywhere else on strappy high-heeled sandals.

Our journalism teacher, Ms. Crase, would say that my grandmother is colorful, like somebody from a book. I say my grandmother is scary, mostly because I never know what she's going to do next.

She talks to strangers. She asks questions—totally nosy ones—as if just because she's old, she can afford to be rude. She says what she thinks, she changes her mind every five minutes, and she laughs at me—a lot. She and I are completely different types of people.

I like predictability. I like maps, dictionaries, and directions. I like lists of things to do, knowing the answer, and seeing how everything fits. My grandmother is definitely one of those people who thrive on chaos and instability. She's what my mother calls free spirit and what I call completely random.

She can't even go by a normal name. No one calls my grandmother Grandma or Granny or even Nana. When my parents got married, she said she didn't want anyone calling her a mother-in-law. When my sister was born, my grandmother told Mom she didn't want anyone calling her a grandmother, either. They finally decided that the grandchildren were supposed to call her Mare, and that's what we all call her now, even my dad.

Mare. *Mère*. Like the French word for "mother." Which is just another example of how Mare is completely bizarre— I mean, we're not even French. And she's not our mother.

So going with her to a reunion is bad enough, but to make matters worse, we don't even really know where we're going. Mare has some whacked idea that it's more of an adventure if we just get in the car and drive east. And yeah, I said "car." See, since 2001, Mare won't fly—so we have to drive ALL THE WAY ACROSS THE UNITED STATES.

In the middle of the baking-hot summer.

My grandmother, my sister, and me, all trapped in one car.

I'm not the only one who hates this idea. You should have heard my sister.

"What? *Us?*" Tali's voice had climbed. "Why do we have to go, Mom? They're Dad's relatives."

"They're your relatives, too," my mother reminded her. "And, Talitha, it's a long drive back east. It's not something your grandmother should attempt alone, and you know your dad can't take the time off of work until the end of June."

"Can't we just fly?" I groaned.

Mom shook her head. "You know Mare doesn't trust planes. She wants to see her people, so she's going to get in her car and drive to them."

"Oh, nice," Tali sighed. "This is just how I wanted to spend *my* summer break. With the slow and the dead."

"Talitha Marie," my mother had said in that dry-ice voice she uses. "Enough."

Tali had given my mother one last look and then yelled for Dad. But no matter who she whined to or argued with, the end result is the same: in an hour, my sister and I are starting out on a 2,340-mile drive across the United States to somewhere in Alabama.

So much for summer vacation.

I'm not eager to see Mare, and neither is Tali, judging from the way she's sitting on the front porch with her backpack.

"Hey, what's Mare doing here already?" I ask, dropping my bag of library books on the step next to her. "Didn't she say we weren't leaving till eleven-thirty?"

Talitha shrugs, busily sending a text to one of her best friends, either Suzanne or Julie. "Don't know, don't care."

"Why are you waiting out here?"

"I'm not waiting. I'm texting, duh." Tali keeps her eyes on her cell.

I push up my sunglasses. "Well, if Mare wants somebody to wash her car, it's your turn."

"Fine. Last time she paid me twenty bucks."

"What?! She's *never* paid me anything!"

Tali glances up, her dark eyes barely visible above the edge of her blue-tinted sunglasses. "So? You should've asked."

Before I can answer, the front door swings open. "Girls, why are you outside? Mare's here." My mother has a line between her eyebrows and looks a little tired, the way she always does when my grandmother comes over.

"We're still not leaving for another hour, right?" Tali looks up, brushing a hand through her short, dark hair. Last week she dyed the tips the same fiery auburn as Mare's.

My mother sighs. "Talitha. You'll leave when your grandmother's ready, all right? You've seen Suzanne every day for the last six months; the least you could do is spend a little time with your grandmother without complaining. God knows you won't have her around forever."

"That sounds bad," I say nervously. "Is she acting sick or something?"

"Yeah, did she think the UPS guy was a burglar and mace him again?" Tali grins.

My mother ignores both of us. "Look, you're not going to spend a whole year at this reunion. All you have to do is spend a little quality time with your grandmother on vacation. It won't kill you. Look at it this way—you'll finally get a chance to know her."

"Mare?" I frown. "Mom, we already know her."

"Hello, she's been around since we were born," Tali reminds her, flipping the phone closed. "We've had dinner with her the first Sunday of the month since forever. We know her, all right."

My mother shakes her head. "There are parts of her you won't know until you take the time to *get* to know them. I wish I'd gotten this kind of opportunity with my grand-mother before she passed."

Tali rolls her eyes and heaves a sigh.

Mom taps Tali on the arm. "Listen. Drooling at the life-guards at WaveWorld is something you can do every sum-mer for the rest of your life, if you so choose. But this summer, you'll spend some time with your grandmother, without com-plaint, thank you. You won't have her forever, girls. Don't forget that."

Tali groans. "Mom, don't do the guilt thing, okay? Acting like Mare's going to die any second is so not fair."

"Yeah, you're the one who always says she's 'a tough old broad,'" I add.

My mother is quiet, looking across the street at the neighbor's sprinklers. "She is a tough old broad," she says fi-nally. "You know, girls, the world is different now than it was when Mare was growing up. In the South, women of color worked cleaning houses or tending other people's children or sharecropping on their farms. If Mare wasn't such a tough old lady, she wouldn't have left home; she'd have stayed on your great-grandmother's farm and probably would never have left the state, never bought herself a nice car or done anything, really. Aunt Josephine always says that running away from home was the best thing Mare ever did. Your grandmother changed the world."

"Whose world did she change?" Tali asks skeptically. "Not the one I live in."

My mother shrugs a little, then smiles. "Maybe she'll tell you sometime."

"Manipulative, maybe?" Tali scoffs. "Mom, what you're not getting here is I'm going to be wasting my summer driving around when I could be working, saving up for my car. You could at least make it worth my time. I mean, if I go, couldn't you buy me a car or something?"

"Buy you a car? When your grandmother is covering all of your expenses and has offered you girls spending money to boot?" My mother's voice rises. "Don't start with me about a car, Talitha Marie. You'll get one when you need one, and I don't want to hear about it again."

Mare's paying us? While Tali does kind of have a point, getting paid for vacation when my other choice is getting a job cleaning up dog doo at a vet's office like my friend Eremasi? I don't have to think twice.

"I'm in, especially if she's paying us," I say.

My sister glares at me. "Of course you are, Octavia, because in your pitiful little world, anything looks good. I, on the other hand, have a life," my sister continues, glaring at my mother now, "which you are totally ruining."

She pushes past my mother and stomps into the house, leaving me to trail behind her, feeling dumb. My mother rolls her eyes and shuts the door.

I used to really like Tali. Since she's two years older than I am, it's not like we have all the same friends and interests, but it used to be that she didn't mind me so much. She'd let Eremasi, Rye, and me read her magazines when she was done with them, and she didn't get mad if we borrowed her CDs, as long as we put them back in order. She let me tag along with whatever she was doing, sometimes even with her friends, and I took it for granted that nothing would ever change.

And then it did. Suddenly it's like she objects to me existing. I can't even look in her direction without her throwing a fit. *Octavia, buy another color. Octavia, go to another movie. Octavia, get your own friends.* Now that she's going to be a senior, it's even worse. Tali walks to a friend's house and catches a ride so people don't even know she's my sister. Tali and I might live in the same house, but it's like we're from different planets.

It would have been great to go on a vacation on the other side of the country this summer—by myself. Now not only am I stuck with Mare, my parents are making Tali go, too.

Like I told Eremasi and Rye, I already completely hate this summer.

✳ ✳ ✳

Eleven-fifteen. My grandmother closes the trunk with a solid thump and minces on her high-heeled sandals back toward the driver's seat, the last of a cigarette between her fingers. Dad is standing in the living room with his arms crossed, the screen door a flimsy barrier between us. Mom has already kissed us twice and gone back inside to pack up a few things for a snack, but Dad's fidgeting. Even through the screen, the tension rolls off him in waves. He's told us to be good now about six times, to watch the speed limit, and to make sure the car doesn't overheat. He's finally finished telling Mare the best route to get to I-5.

"You girls be good," Dad says to us again, and my grand-mother groans. She takes another drag on her cigarette, and Tali coughs loudly, instantly diverting my father's attention.

"Mama, you're not going to smoke in the car with the girls, are you?" My father's voice has that edge that means he's not really asking a question, and Mom's not here to tell him to be cool.

My grandmother sighs deeply, drops the cigarette on the driveway, and grinds it out with her sandal. "Goodbye, son," she says pointedly, and turns away.

"I'll just get you something to pick that up with," my fa-ther shoots back, and vanishes toward the rear of the house.

Mare mutters something under her breath and turns to-ward Tali. Tilting down her enormous sunglasses, she stares down at my sister.

"Talitha, you're not going to be a pain in my behind this whole trip, are you?"

"ME?" Tali huffs, offended. "I'm not the one blowing smoke on people." She replaces her headset and turns up her music, hunching into her hooded sweatshirt and closing her eyes.

Mare tugs an earphone out of Tali's ear. "Don't put that thing on when I'm talking to you. You've had something to say from the beginning—first it's my driving, now it's my cig-arettes. Tali, I'll tell you what—you keep those earphones out of your ears, and I will keep my cigarettes in my purse."

"*Whaat?*" Tali squawks, indignant. "Forget it. Me listening to my music is totally not like you poisoning me with your cigarettes. I mean, I'm not making you listen to it. It can't be bothering you."

"Oh, it can't?" Mare's brow rises. She reaches into her pocket and fishes another cigarette out of her pack. "It bothers me. You put those things in your ears and you're dead to the world." Tali tenses as Mare lights up again and drags in a deep, poisonous breath. "You think you know everything, and you can ignore anyone you don't want to hear. Those headphones are bothering me, all right."

Last week, when Tali had tried for the ninth time to get out of going on this trip, she'd claimed she didn't feel Mare's driving was safe. So Dad told Tali she was in charge of half of the driving, and Mare agreed not to drive more than six hours a day and not after dark. But then Mare said we'd have to be up every morning by six. "We have to drive early if I can't drive at night," Mare had insisted. Tali had gone to her room muttering about spending her whole summer waking up at the crack of dawn. Now she crosses her arms, looking sullen and sleepy.

"At least my headset isn't giving anyone cancer," my sister says. "Forget it, Mare."

My grandmother doesn't answer her. The silence stretches as Mare studies my sister, her unreadable expression making Talitha squirm. Finally, she jerks out her earphones in disgust.

"All right! Fine! I won't listen to my music right now, okay? Just don't smoke anywhere near me, either, and you have to turn on the radio, okay? I can't sit in the car all day without listening to something."

"No earphones where I can see them at all," Mare counters, "and we've got a deal."

"No earphones at all? Mare, that's not fair! Octavia has a CD player!"

"It's for books. I'm listening to books," I insist.

"You have music CDs, too," Tali accuses. "Don't lie."

Mare shakes her head. "I'm not talking about Octavia. I'm talking about you, Talitha. No earphones from you, no smoking from me. Deal?"

"Whatever." Tali sighs. "Let's just go before the summer's over, okay?"

My grandmother drops the butt onto the ground and puts it out deliberately.

"Girls?" Mom's coming down the stairs, holding a paper shopping bag. "I packed a few things for you to snack on." She glances down at the butts on the driveway. "Mare, you're going to give him a stroke one of these days."

My grandmother flashes her a conspiratorial smile and takes the bag. "Girl, what have you got in here? There's enough to feed an army!" She puts the bag into the car and gives my mother a hug. "We've got to get going, Thea," she says.

Mom hollers for Dad. "Phillip!"

My father erupts from the house with a whisk broom and dustpan and holds them out to my grandmother, who looks at them and grins.

"I'll take those," Mom says smoothly.

Dad sighs sharply but gives in, his shoulders slumping. He bends toward Mare to brush her cheek with a cursory kiss. "Have a nice trip," he says grudgingly. He won't forgive her for the cigarette butts anytime soon. He leans into the car. "You girls be good," he says once more. "I don't want to hear about you two fighting or—"

"Your father loves you," my mother interrupts, leaning in next to Dad. "Have fun, girls."

"Have fun," Dad echoes, looking sheepish. Giving Mom a sideways glance, he adds, "You give us a call if there's any trouble, all right?"

Then finally, finally, Mare settles in the car and snugs her seat belt around her waist. She checks her lipstick in the rearview and puts the car into reverse.

"Where in Alabama are we going? And who's going to be at this reunion anyway?" Tali asks suddenly. "Aren't Dad and Aunt Josephine your only relatives?"

"You know, Tali, you're working my nerves already. You remind me of a girl I knew when I was in Des Moines, Iowa."

"Iowa? Didn't you grow up in Alabama?" I interrupt, opening the map.

"Yes." My grandmother raises a plucked eyebrow in my direction. "And I grew up in Iowa, too. Stop interrupting me and wave to your folks so I can tell my story."

"Sorry," I say, annoyed. Tali snorts. Reluctantly, I wave and manage a smile as Mom blows kisses and mouths, "Have fun," in my direction. I catch my father's grim expression as Mare backs slowly out of the drive. He steps into the drive-

way and lifts his hand briefly before bending to sweep up
Mare's cigarette butts with the broom and dustpan he's
grabbed back from Mom.

"As I said," Mare continues conversationally, "Tali, you
remind me of a girl named Gloria. Now, Gloria was a pain in
my behind. She had something to say about everything, and
you couldn't tell her anything, just like some people I could
mention. . . ."

Tali whines, "Mare . . . you said you'd turn on the
radio. . . ."

So much for summer vacation.

I don't think I'm going to survive being in this car with Tali and Mare for three HOURS, much less three days. And Mare is driving so <u>slowly</u>. I swear we could walk a lot faster than she drives.

Mare's been telling stories. Not normal stories — I mean, they're not ones she made up, but they're family history, stuff Dad never told us about from when Mare was growing up. Did you know her family had so little money that she had to quit school? She had a full-time job plus a part-time job by the time she was fifteen! No wonder she thinks we're spoiled.

I think Mare and Tali are going to kill each other.

Wish you were here? :) Octavia

Mom
7519 Poppy Way
Pleasant Hill, CA 94523

2.

then

Around about six, just before it gets too dark to see, I pin on my hat, then shrug into my mama's felt coat and tie the belt. It is still her coat, though she don't never wear it. She hardly goes out after dark, but I do. Money is tight, and I am old enough to make wages on my own.

"You watch yourself, Marey Lee Boylen," my mama, Edna, must have said, but the words were garbled up around a mouthful of pins she was holding, stitching up another Christmas gift for her new beau, Toby.

"Watch yourself," is what Mama says every night, like I am a little old kid, not almost seventeen years old and knowing full well how to watch out for myself. "Watch yourself," she says, even though I watch out for myself better than she ever watches out for me.

I don't tell her none of that. Everybody know better than to argue with Edna Mae Boylen.

"Yes, ma'am," I say, tugging on my gloves. I grab my handbag and close the door.

I am tired, but I walk fast out here in the cold. If I don't get on to Young's Diner, where I work, Mr. Young will give my job to somebody else before I can say boo. At my other job I am the house girl for Mrs. Ida Payne. I dust and scrub the floors and wash up the kitchen there all day, make the beds and do the windows. Miss Ida got one of them fancy porcelain commodes, and I wash that out, too. Today was a heavy day: Miss Ida's friends came by for bridge, and she had a girl from the hotel come and serve. All afternoon I washed up and fetched and carried for her.

She leaves me a list: "Marey Lee, please see to the window in the guest room." "Marey Lee, please polish the silver and my good tea things." Miss Ida tells me I'm a smart girl. She is glad I read so well.

I am smart, smart enough to go to secretarial college, but Mama don't have that kind of money. Daddy up and died and left Mama with nothing but two babies to raise and the farm. Mama takes in washing and mending and has ever since I can remember, but there wasn't money enough. I had to leave high school. We have a garden, and we sell chickens, eggs, and hogs. We get by better than most, but Mama don't see no use for more school. If I can read and do sums, she says, what else do I need?

I could save my wages and go to school, but the closest colored college is all the way in Tuskegee, and I can't leave Mama and Josephine yet. Actually, it's Josephine—Feen, we call her—who I can't leave, not with Mama's new man around the house. Sister Dials at church say every colored man in five counties know Mama got a farm on her own. All kinds of men pass through, talking 'bout, "Do a little work around the place for you, ma'am," tryin' to talk sweet, all the while makin' eyes at Mama, hoping to get themselves a little land.

Mama calls the new hired man our "uncle" Toby. Mr. Toby has quick little eyes that slip around in his face. He told my baby sister, Josephine, her skin was like the color of honey, and he brought her candy every week like she was a real tiny kid when he was first here, courting Mama by being sweet to Josephine. Toby's always looking at us, bumping into us like he can't walk straight. Last week he told me I got hips like a boy.

Feen and me, we been through this before. Every time Mama takes up with a man, she gets forgetful of us. She play like she don't got no kids, and he play like he's our daddy till they get to drinking and brawling, then she runs him out. Me and Feen, we learn to stay out the way.

I told Mama she'd better watch herself, letting Mr. Toby come into the house like he is family, letting him help himself to our food and help himself to our beds. Mama slapped me in the mouth like I cursed her. You can't tell some people nothing.

My mama's a handsome woman. She's tall, big-boned, and broad like all her people, and she can butcher and smoke a pig just like a man. She makes her own whiskey, sews a neat seam, goes to church every Sunday and prayer meeting on Wednesdays, and can sing like an angel. Folks all up and down Bay Slough think well of her.

Used to be that mattered. Used to be Mama *cared* what

people think. Since Toby come, Mama giggles and laughs all the time, preening and flashing her eyes. Sister Dials at church say ain't no fool like an old fool got her head turned by some man.

Mama say Mrs. Betty Ann Dials best mind her *own* business.

Mama and Daddy bought this land; my daddy didn't do no sharecropping for nobody when he was alive, and he built this house with his own two hands and his own sweat and blood. Mama says I take after him, bein' skinny and all, but Feen takes after Mama, with that pretty long hair and her big old eyes. Feen's just like Mama, except she's a big old baby. Ever since Toby come, she been fussing, cryin' about, "Mama don't do this no more" and "Mama don't do that." Mama says we got to grow up now. She says I got to take care of Feen 'cause she's the baby. She been saying that since I was just about a baby myself.

We got a tin roof, not no tar paper like the real poor folks have. My daddy built us four rooms and a privy, and Mama taught us to keep it neat, like we got pride. We got a garden growing corn and beans, but we don't try to put in no to-bacco nor cotton like Daddy would, seeing as we ain't got no man around but Toby, and I hope he'll be movin' on real soon.

I wish I remembered my daddy. Aunt Shirley, Mama's sis-ter, is the only family we got, and she is up in northern parts. All we got around here is these "uncles," and not a one of them's no good, always bossin' us like they're the man of the family, talking about, "Girl, get me a plate a this or a glass a that," trying to eat up all the food and lay around. Don't none of 'em do a lick of work, and Mama just can't see what's right in front of her.

Josephine's in eighth grade, and if she can keep herself together, she'll graduate high school and get on up out of here. She could be a nurse or maybe even a teacher. For myself, I got plans—deep plans. One of these days, I am going to be gone. One of these days, I am going to shake free of Mama, Miss Ida, and this whole town. I'm going to get out of here, and I won't look back.

With the money I'm earning at Young's, maybe someday I can go to secretarial school and live in a city. In a city, they got movies and jazz clubs and places colored folks see and be seen. Up north they got writers and poets and folks who don't just work all day every day like we do down here. See, Mama thinks her girls are only looking to buy lipstick and talk to fast boys, but she's wrong—I aim to do more than that someday. One of these days, I'm going to get up out of little old Bay Slough, Alabama, for sure. I've just got to wait on Josephine, and then both of us be gone.

The bus is already at the stop when I get there, the driver slouched against its side, lighting up a nasty cigar. I nod to him, then step on, sliding in my token, and walk down the narrow aisle toward the back.

A man with a newspaper climbs onto the bus and deposits his fare. He slumps down, reading. Probably war news, which is all anybody ever hears since those Japs fired on Pearl Harbor. I hope they don't start that mess here in Bay Slough.

Two old women climb the bus steps, chatting, followed by a girl in a red quilted car coat and feathered felt hat, carrying a suitcase. Her brows are arched like Rita Hayworth's over big old green eyes and her lips flame red like store-bought cherries. She looks like a movie star going on a vacation to someplace like California.

The biddies put in their nickels, *click, click*. The movie star don't put a token in the till but strides halfway down the aisle, collapsing into a seat like someone cut her legs out from under her. I blink, a little surprised that she isn't going to get up and pay her fare. She sees me, but her eyes slide over me like I'm not there.

I turn away, look at my reflection in the window, my stomach clenching just a little. Somebody don't pay, there's going to be trouble. There is going to be some trouble.

The bus creaks in protest as the big-bellied driver climbs aboard. I hear the clink of the change as he checks the till, but my body still jerks a little when he speaks to me.

"Girl. You put a token in?"

"Yes, sir." I sit up.

The man grunts and checks the till again. "We're short." He looks pointedly at me, his small dark eyes like bullet holes in the fat white plaster wall of his face.

The old women continue talking, chattering like a pen full of hens. The man turns a page in his paper. The girl with the lipstick yawns and looks bored.

"Well?"

"Sir, I put my token in," I say, my eyes straying unwillingly to the girl in the hat.

"And I don't see it here."

"I—I put it in when I got on." I twist my hands in my lap.

"Maybe you just *thought* you did." The driver says his words real slow as if he were speaking to a small child or a fool. "I don't see it here, and we're short, so either you pay up or you walk."

I swallow. I reach for my purse. That girl got rocks in her head if she think I am going to pay for her.

"No, sir, I paid. I ride this bus every night. I always pay you."

The driver looks aggravated. "Girl," he begins.

"Oh, here." The girl in the red coat sighs. "Let's don't hold up the bus all night." She thrusts her hand into her coin purse, drawing out her token.

"Now, miss, you don't have to do that." The driver sounds all sugary and oily.

"Let's just go," she snaps.

"Why, thank you very much," the driver says politely. With a sharp glance at me, he heads toward the front of the bus.

I sag against the seat, breathing hard. Does that driver think I'm gonna say, "Thank you kindly," to the woman for finally paying her own fare? I glare at the back of her stylish head. What is wrong with white folks anyway? The driver catches my glance in his rearview mirror. I look down and stay very, very still.

Don't get uppity, Marey Lee.

✳ ✳ ✳

I am almost late to work with that nonsense and run to tie on my oversized apron to begin the task I most dread: draining fat. Mr. Young collects pork fat in old tomato cans like it was gold. It isn't just the families of the sharecroppers and poor whites who are scrimping and saving and planting victory gardens anymore. It's everybody; even folks like Miss Ida say times is tough. Mr. Young uses fat to flavor greens. Don't hardly anyone use more than a little meat.

The clatter and the routine of the kitchen at Young's calm me down some. Our cook, Samuel, is hollering out orders and flipping hash like his life depends on it. Betty King, an older woman from over Anniston way, is white up to her elbows, slapping down biscuits and turning them into the oven. Every once in a while, one of the other girls breezes into the back to grab some coffee. Mr. Young got no colored waiters, but we wash up and, if there's a rush, bus tables. "Order up," Samuel bellows, and slaps a plate of pork and greens on the deck. I slosh the last of the fat from the pan and wrestle it into the sink.

It is eleven-thirty when I scrape down the last pot and throw my weight behind the mop to wipe up the floor. Young leaves our wages in his office every week, and I pick up my $1.75. Mama don't understand why I got to go out and take up another job when I work enough at Miss Ida's, but I ain't trying to be nobody's house girl for the rest of my life. I aim to have something of my own someday, even if it takes all my blood, sweat, and tears.

"You ready?" Samuel jams his cap down on his head. I

nod and stumble out to his truck. I climb up into the back, watching out for splinters, and pull my hat down around my ears. Samuel drops off Betty and me every night so we don't have to wait on the bus. Back there in the wind, my face aches, but I am glad to miss the bus tonight.

✳ ✳ ✳

I can hear the air pushing out my sister's throat, wet and heavy in a silent keening. Josephine cries like a five-year-old, and she is near fourteen.

"You crying?"

There is nothing but the wet sound of Josephine's snuffling breaths.

"Feen, what is the *matter* with you?"

The floor creaks in the hallway outside our room.

I roll my eyes. Sure, I love her, but sometimes the girl ain't nothing but an aggravation. Feen cries at the drop of a hat. Always jerkin' and jumpin', scared of her own shadow.

The floor creaks a little more, then the knob rattles. Now I understand why Feen is crying. Toby. Like a bad wolf. All teeth and tongue and eyes.

"You scared of the dark, Feen? You know that's all that's out there. *Dark.* Anything else I got something for." I raise my voice a little, letting Toby know I know he is out there.

Toby got his nerve anyway, walking around this house at night. He got Mama doing for him, sewing up his shirts, doing his wash like he ain't the hired man. Sister Dials think he tryin' to be our new daddy. I ain't studying on having no new daddy around here just yet.

Josephine draws in a shaky breath. "Just had a dream," she mutters. "Nothing wrong."

"Go to sleep, then. You got school, and I got to put up with Miss Ida in the morning."

There is a listening silence.

"I can't go to sleep," she whispers. "He still there!"

"I'm up," I say.

"What are *you* gonna do?"

"Shut up, Feen. Go to sleep."

There are some long moments of silence before I hear the floor creak again. Toby went on, but it was a little while before I let my stomach loose itself. He didn't call my bluff tonight, but what if he had? It is time to make a plan.

3.

then

Tonight, while Mama was listening to the radio with Feen and Toby, I took the hatchet to the whetstone out back and sharpened it.

❋ ❋ ❋

Sundays are always the best day of the week. Sundays, me and Feen get up early, slop the hogs, and collect the eggs. We go with Mama to the African Methodist Episcopal church on Fourth Street. We wear our good hats. We step down the road, looking this way and that, seeing and being seen. On Sundays, the whole world is fine.

Even Josephine starched up a little this Sunday. Not only is it three weeks till Thanksgiving, yesterday Toby made some talk about how he had to see about his mother, so he had to get out of town. You should have seen the smile on that girl's face. Toby up and left just after dark.

He'll be back. But now I'm ready.

Last night before dinner, I made Feen slop the hogs, and I got the eggs myself, so Feen could stop crying about that setting hen that pecked her. I went into the henhouse, and Toby was there so fast I dropped my basket. He put his arm 'cross my throat and pushed me against the wall. He tried to reach down and pinch my privates, but I fought him like he was the devil. "Resist the devil, and he will flee from you," isn't that what the Book say? The chickens got riled and started cluckin' and Mama hollered I better stop fooling around out there. Toby sucked his teeth and grinned at me.

Mama uses the hatchet to take the heads off the chickens after she wrings their necks. It ain't big, but it's sharp like it's stropped. Last night, I slid it up under my bed.

Now I'm ready.

❊ ❊ ❊

At Bible study this Sunday, I heard tell that one of Saphira Watkins's boys is leavin' for the navy. Now she's braggin' that her boy's gonna "see the world" before he settles down. That Sister Watkins just about always got something to say. Mama says most likely her boy's gonna see a mop and a bucket to swab the deck, and that's all. At services, Reverend Morgan preached a sermon all about the prophet Deborah and how she prophesied to the general Barak that a woman would slay the evil tyrant Sisera, that the Lord would bring about His plan through the powerless and not the general and his army. Then, just like she said, Sisera ran away from the battle and came to Jael to sleep in her tent, then Jael nailed his head to the floor with a tent peg. What God says, He does—ain't that the truth? Then little Ananias Caldwell sang with the choir. Now, that boy has got a sweet voice. He might be famous someday. I'm gonna say I knew him when.

We came home for Sunday dinner, it being First Sunday and all. Mama made some corn bread to go with our beans, *and* she fried up a chicken, even though she was fussed that she couldn't find that hatchet. I scraped out some fatback for the corn bread, and it was good, good. Mama made us save half the chicken for Toby. She hopes he'll be back on Monday.

He'll be back. But now I'm ready.

Then Mama took a little rest with her bourbon, and Feen and me went to sew quilts for the needy with the Dials girls. While we was sewing, Sister Dials announced we having a Christmas social next Sunday. Sundays are always the best days of the week.

❊ ❊ ❊

Monday, Miss Ida's daughter, Beatrice, is home from her ladies' college, talking about she's going to Daytona Beach to join the U.S. *Army*. Now, this is a *women's* army, she tells Miss Ida. She's gonna be working with *women* to free up a man for the fight. It's her duty, she says. Well, sir, Miss Ida sure pitched a fit, said no daughter of hers was going to join no women's army like she ain't got no breeding.

"You know what kind of women they have there, Bébé," Miss Ida says, twisting up her face like she gone crazy. She still calls Miss Beatrice by her baby name.

Miss Bébé says it don't matter what kind of girls they got there, but Miss Ida shouted her down, talking about, "No child of mine!" Sent her from the table, too, like she was no more grown than a child. Miss Bébé blubbed worse than Feen, up there crying about how Miss Ida don't never let her do anything. She told me I should go, though, and she could go with me. Said all you gotta be is one hundred pounds or over, free of responsibilities, and twenty years old. Even Miss Bébé knows I am not hardly no twenty, but she says Mama wouldn't have to do nothing but sign and I could still go. Miss Bébé says she just knows *my* mama wouldn't hold me back from doing my "duty."

I ask her if colored girls going, and Miss Bébé said yeah, yeah, colored girls are going.

Huh. I'll just *bet* they got colored girls there. Got to have someone wash up and cook and fetch and carry for the women's army, same as for the men's.

❊ ❊ ❊

Feen got put in charge of the Sunday school Christmas play. She's been working every day after school, making robes for the Virgin Mary and sitting up working the treadle on the sewing machine all evening till I get home. Mama's been getting on her about how she's strainin' her eyes inside sewing all the time and she better get up and feed the chickens and not get too prideful about sewing for her play. Feen feed the chickens, all right, but she do it so early they haven't gone to roost, now. She do it real quick and get back inside, like she scared of the dark. Feen stay in the house right next to Mama, but she don't go to bed now till she see me home. She don't say nothing, but since Toby been back, she's been crying every night.

She sits in the front room with all the lamps lit. Feen thinks Toby won't do nothin' in the front room with the lamps on. She's smart, Feen is. Thing is, Toby ain't dumb.

That's all right. Marey Lee Boylen ain't dumb, neither.
This so-called uncle Toby keep messing with us, he's gonna
find out a thing or two about just how dumb it is to think he
can walk in here and take what he wants.

He's back, but now I'm ready for him.

4.

NOW

"You didn't tell your mother?" I blurt the question before I stop to think about it. Mare's story has made the hairs on my arms prickle.

"Sometimes folks don't want to hear things," she says shortly. "You can talk till you're blue in the face, but if you're not talking to the right person, it won't do you any good."

I think about this for a while, chewing the inside of my lip. If Dad died, no way would Mom not want to hear if some guy was bothering us. No way would any adult I told not believe me and help me. I look out the window and change the subject.

"You started working for Miss Ida when you were fifteen? Full-time? How come?"

Mare makes a face and pushes up her sunglasses. "Lot of girls my age had to work," she says. "Haven't you ever heard of the Great Depression? Mama needed an extra pair of hands to make ends meet. We needed every cent we had to pay the mortgage, and with the farm and all, we were better off than most. Folks did what they could those days to keep food on the table—"

"You couldn't have been *that* poor," Tali interrupts. "Dad always says we don't have any money, but we always do. It's just he doesn't want to buy me a car."

Mare glowers. "A girl your age ought to have had two jobs by now. What makes you think your daddy's got to buy you a car anyway? Why don't you get a job and buy it yourself?"

"I would," Tali says coolly, "but I can't work since I'm spending my summer with you. And anyway, I'm getting good grades, so I can qualify for scholarships. Mom and Dad promised they'd help with either college or a car, and I *need* a car."

Mare clicks her tongue in disgust. "You 'need' a car. You don't know what need is, Miss Tali."

My sister mutters something under her breath and looks out the window. I know what Mare thinks of us. I guess I never considered it, but I do have my own computer and my own room. Not only did Mare have to share a room with her sister, but when they were really little, they shared a bed.

Maybe Tali and I *are* spoiled.

Mare looks over at me. "And do *you* need a car?"

I bite my lip. I know the answer she wants me to give. "I don't have a license," I say finally.

"And you don't need one, either," Mare says with a kind of grim satisfaction. "You girls are too young to be riding around in anyone's cars. I know what kids get up to in the backseat."

"Mare!" Tali winces. *"Eew."*

"I don't even have a boyfriend," I protest.

Mare just shakes her head and continues poking along up the highway.

It's quiet for the next few miles, then Mare props her arm against the door and rubs her head like she has a headache brewing. A little pleat forms between her brows. "Octavia, get me another piece of gum, will you?" she asks.

I dig into the menthol-scented depths of her purse. I push aside her hoard of red and white mints, her bottle of mouth spray, her plastic-wrapped pack of cigarettes, and her reading glasses until I find what I am looking for. I take a piece of gum for myself as well and tilt the package in Tali's direction, but she waves it away.

Mare and I chew in silence for a while, me thinking and Mare creeping up the highway behind a truck belching exhaust and filled with cows. I can't keep my mind off of Mare's story. What she told us about Toby bothers me—a lot. I would have hated to work for somebody like Miss Ida, every day, just to have money for a farm mortgage and food, stuff that wasn't for me. I can't imagine Tali trying to protect me from somebody all by herself—or that she'd even try, knowing how she hates me these days. I don't know how Mare could do it.

Tali sighs loudly and slides down in the backseat. She isn't used to going so long without being able to shut out the sound of other people's conversations. She faked like she wasn't listening to Mare's story, but I know she was; she just thinks she's too cool to show it. Now she's flopping around in the seat like a hooked fish.

"Mare. If you told me where exactly we were going, I could just drive there. Do you want me to drive?" Tali asks suddenly.

"What?" Mare sounds far away.

"Tali," I hiss, twisting around in my seat. Her rudeness embarrasses me.

Ever since she started talking about the old days, Mare's been slowing down. First she just changed lanes so people could pass her, but now she's driving so slowly we're getting passed by trucks. Eighteen-wheelers. We're the slowest car in the slow lane.

At first, I thought it was because she and Tali were messing with the radio and she'd slowed down to argue over music—Mare thinks anything that isn't Ray Charles, Dinah Washington, Muddy Waters, or Fats Waller is playing fast and loose with the airwaves. But even after they settled on listening to one of Tali's music choices to two of Mare's, her driving still didn't speed up. The thing is, I think talking about the olden days bothers Mare. You'd think Tali would catch a clue.

"I said, do you want me to drive?" Tali glares back at me. "It's been four hours, Mare. Dad said I should do half the driving, so I think I should drive now. We can switch off later or something."

On I-5, the only thing in the slow lane other than us is huge RVs and trucks full of cows. It reeks, and there's hay and dust flying around everywhere. Right now I feel like I can walk faster than Mare is driving. I *would* walk, too, if it didn't stink so bad, but Mare driving slow while she's thinking is better than Mare driving fast any day. At least I think so.

"Why would I want you to drive?" Mare asks thoughtfully, as if she's just come back from someplace far away.

"Because . . ." Tali exhales an explosive breath and shakes her head. "Just . . . because."

Mare laughs, a guttural, machine-gun chuckle that makes me nervous. "Going too slow for you, Miss Lady?"

"Well, yeah," Tali erupts, and throws up her hands. "I'm sorry, Mare, but *old people* are passing and waving at me. I mean, do we *have* to be the slowest people on the whole freeway? At this rate, we're going to be in this car for days—"

"You're not going that slow," I interrupt, trying to soften the blow. "Tali's supposed to drive if you're tired, but if you're not tired . . ."

"I tell you what, Miss Thing, why don't you let me get from behind this truck, and I'll pick up the pace. Can't let any 'old people' get ahead of you now, can we." The car's engine whines as my grandmother's foot pushes toward the floor. "I told your daddy I'd listen to you girls about my driving, and I will. I surely will."

"Mare—" I begin.

Suddenly we're around the truck and diving into the next lane. Without signaling, Mare crosses two more lanes of traffic and cuts off a pickup truck. Tali yelps.

What's *she* whimpering for? *I'm* in the front seat, watching cars scatter and the man in the pickup gesture with his middle finger. I push up my sunglasses and slide down in my seat. My crazy grandmother is going to get us killed.

"Next stop, you ride shotgun, Tal."

"No way!"

Mare laughs, that machine-gun cackle again, and I grab on to the edge of my seat.

My grandmother took on a grown man twice her size to protect her sister. I have a feeling she could do it still, even today, if she had to. I watch as Mare expertly weaves in and out of traffic, feeling my stomach churn each time she changes lanes. She catches my eye and winks.

"Watch and learn, Octavia." She grins. "Watch and learn."

¡Hola, chicas!

I'm so bored I'm remembering Spanish class. Sad, huh? I may not survive this trip. My sister is on my last nerve already. I'd like to kick her out on the side of the freeway, but I'm afraid my parents might miss her. I saw her talking to some trucker guy at a rest stop. Can you believe her?

My grandmother totally drives like she's in NASCAR, but she tells Tali to shut up when she complains. Gotta love that! It's SO HOT already, and now Tali's whining that she wants to drive. If I kill her before summer vacation is over, come see me in jail, okay?

Wish you were here!
Octavia
:/)

Eremasi Sariki & Rye Preston
6 Waverly Place, Apt. B
Martinez, CA 94553

5.

then

When Samuel drop me off, the moon is low, but I can smell that nasty pipe Toby always be smoking and know he's out of doors. It is too cold to take much time in the little house out back, so I wonder what he's doing. My hand is on the door when I hear steps on the hard ground.

"That you, Marey Lee?" His voice is slurred.

"What do you want?"

"I'm waiting for my little girl to get home."

I say nothing and push open the door.

His laughter follows me in, and I know something in my bones. Toby's bad tonight, worse than I've seen him. Feen looks up when I walk in. "Get in the room quick," I tell her, picking up the lamp. I can hear Mama snoring from her bed. She sleep hard when she's been at her whiskey, but if Toby come and bother me, I'm gonna make a noise to wake the dead.

"Marey Le-e, why you runnin' from me?"

I can feel dread clawing up my spine. I close the door to

our room and push my sister onto the bed. "Feen. Get under, and don't come out till I say so."

Feen opens her mouth, and I know she wants to say something about, maybe, spiders or some such. But she shuts her mouth and obeys, for a change. She wraps herself up in a blanket and gets down on her knees.

Thump. Toby in the house. Josephine panics, and I can hear her trying to breathe quiet.

"Marey, what you gonna do? Call Mama. Call Mama!"

"Feen, you know we better not wake up Mama 'less somebody dying. I got something for 'Uncle' Toby if he come in here. Get under that bed.'"

"Marey Le-e! Josephine. Come give your uncle a kiss."

Feen slithers under her bed fast as she can. Good. I get down on my knees and take the hatchet out from under mine. I am surprised to see that my hands are shaking. I don't know why. I am ready.

Toby been bumping me, touching me, cutting his eyes at Mama when he thinks she don't see. He been talking filth to Josephine, and she been snifflin' and jumpy ever since he came. Feen try to talk to Mama, but Mama don't wanna hear nothing about nothing, seems like. Mama tell me to "watch yourself," and now I got to watch out for Feen, too.

Toby better not come in this room.

Then the door swings open, and even I am not ready. I scream. I scream long and loud like a baby, like Feen, and then Feen's screaming, too, and crying for Mama.

"Shut up! Shut up that damned noise," Toby growls,

launching himself across the room at me. He smacks me in the mouth before I can get my hand up. Feen hasn't stopped screaming, but I have. I tighten my hands on the hatchet.

"Get on out of here, you no-'count man. I'll call Mama. I will!"

"Your mama's asleep, and she ain't got no time for this nonsense. Y'all better hush up and stop acting like little children. I just want to visit with you, is all."

Toby backs toward the doorway, still trying to keep his voice down. He looks over his shoulder, toward Mama's room. He's thinking about her. He's still scared. I still got time. Toby ain't nothing but a low-down confidence man from Mississippi. Sister Dials say she seen his kind before.

"Get out!" I raise the hatchet, and when he sees it, a little sly smile come to his face. An ugly laugh come out his mouth, and weasel quick, he moves. He swings, and his big fist catches me from the side. Pain explodes in my rib cage, and I slam to the floor, a glimpse of Feen's frightened eyes as I land. Instinctively, I roll, stagger to my feet. My knees are shaking, and the hatchet has slipped from my fingers. I can feel it with my foot, but I don't dare take my eyes off Toby to pick it up. I'm still like a jackrabbit when a hawk flies over.

"Just tryin' to visit with you, and you get all uppity like you something special. I got a man's rights up in this house. Your mama *my* woman, and you girls is *my* girls. Keep snivelin' around like I ain't good enough to talk to"—he closes the door behind him—"and I aim to teach you better. Feen? Get out from under that bed."

Now, I know I don't have to tell Feen to stay put. Her squallin' is so loud she can't even hear him. She moanin' to Jesus, to Mama, to somebody to save us. What I know is this: God will surely help you, but you also got to help your own self. I put my foot on that hatchet again.

"Now, Josephine, I ain't mad. Get on out from under that bed and let your uncle Toby see you." He's talkin' sweet now, smiling that sly smile again, and I watch him lick his lips. He thinks Feen is his already. He's got another thought coming.

"Josephine, girl, get out from under that bed! Don't make me come and *get* you out."

I push the hatchet back some, behind me now. Toby should leave while he still got his life.

"Don't you move," Toby snarls at me, grabbing my chin. He shoves me back, then makes to bend down and get under the bed. "Jose*phine!*"

Mama said take care of Feen.

I grab for the hatchet and come up swinging.

"*Aww!*" Toby roars like a bull and twists, trying to reach his back. Dark blood stains his shirt. I pull on the hatchet, lift it again. Toby backhands me, clutching his side, and I fall against the door. I swing the hatchet as he comes for me again, but he grabs it, twisting my arm. I won't give it up.

"Get out! Get *out!*"

Feen is screaming, and I feel the bones in my arm grate. I know I have lost as Toby bends my arm up behind my back. He is pinning me against the wall; the honed blade of the hatchet has cut us both now and is slick with blood. I know he will hurt me bad.

"Run, Feen!" I scream, pain making my ears ring. My eyes are going dim, and Toby has his shoulder against my throat. I hear my heart pounding in my ears, and then Toby gives a hard jerk, and he has the hatchet. He pounds my head against the wall and I feel myself going under.

"Mamaaaaaaa! He's killing her! He's killing her!"

Toby's hands are hurting me, and then I hear a sound louder than thunder.

Boom! And that's all I can remember.

6.

then

There was blood on the floor, blood on my coat, blood on my hands, and smoke in the air. Mama had fired the shotgun, and a smoking hole gapes in the wall above our heads. Feen told me later Mama thought I was dead. When I can finally hear something, Toby is on his knees, begging Mama not to put him out. He say we all just misunderstanding him. Feen's still cryin' when the folks from the farm across the field bust in. They heard the shot, and knowing Mama is a woman alone, they came on a hustle.

Nobody believe his sob story, so they run Toby off. Don't nobody bother with the sheriff; the sheriff don't care what the coloreds get up to on their own 'less one of 'em look at a white girl wrong—*then* there will be trouble.

I can't get up, and I can't stop squealin' every time somebody try to touch me. My shoulder hurt so bad it feels like I'm burned. Mama don't call out no doctor; she looks me over and the neighbors help wrap up my hands. Toby didn't break my arm, but he twisted it out my socket so bad, makes me wish he had. Mama wraps her hands around my arm, puts her foot on my chest, and pulls. The neighbors help hold me down. It hurts so bad I can't even scream—and then it goes—a grinding, sick-making *pop*. I lay there and shake like I caught a chill.

I almost had him. I almost had him with my hatchet. He messed up my arm, but I am not dead, and neither is Feen.

Mama said to take care of my sister. I did all right.

We did all right, Feen and me.

It is a week past before I realize Mama ain't said nothing to me. She don't ask me what happened that night; she don't say a word. I want to tell her how it was, hear her tell me she sorry, so I stop one night before I go to Young's. Mama sitting in her chair, sewing like always.

"Mama," I say, "you know Toby—"

"Hush," Mama says. "Don't want to hear nothing about it."

"But Ma—" Something about the way she hold her mouth when she look at me says to let it go, so I do. But now she look at me like she don't even see me. I am at the bus stop before I realize she didn't even tell me to "watch your-self" when I left.

Feen, Mama, and me go on like we done before, only Feen stands up a little straighter, and Mama's face is hard, hard with pride. The gossips in Bay Slough have their day, but they know better than to say nothing to me, and nobody want to start mess with Mama looking like she gonna come out swingin'. Toby come back one day for his things, one day when Feen at school and me at Miss Ida's. I ain't said nothing to Feen, but I think Mama let him in. Mama still don't have nothing to say to me.

I wish she would just talk to me.

That's all right. I keep my hatchet nice and sharp. I nick my finger on it every night, just to check. Mr. Toby might come back this way, but I aim to be prepared.

✱ ✱ ✱

Thanksgiving Day, Mama butchers two hogs and gets the smokehouse ready for making sausages for Christmas. At Young's, talk is buzzing about the War Commission. Seems the newspaper say folks has got to work or fight. Since Uncle Sam is offering work, even colored folks are saying maybe they will join up now with the United States Navy, try to get out of this little no-'count town and get a little money now.

President Roosevelt says everybody need to help, and Feen tell me a lady from the women's army come talk at her school. I wonder if Beatrice Payne still want to get herself off to Daytona, but I don't give it too much thought. If Feen and me's gonna get up outta here when she done with school, I need to find us more money. I got to get more work. Maybe Mr. Young give me more if Samuel joins up with the service. Lord knows I can't expect nothing more from Miss Ida but words.

But after St. Valentine's Day, Mama gets a letter from one of her people and say Feen should pack up her things. Seems Auntie Shirley in Philadelphia lost a baby, and she got that woman's grievin' so bad folks are worried for her. Mama's putting Feen on the train to help her out and go to school there till Auntie Shirley is feeling all right. Now, I know ain't nothing wrong with Aunt Shirley that no little girl can fix, but Mama said go, so Feen going on to get packed.

I could be of more help to Aunt Shirley than little old Feen, but Mama don't even ask me to go. She can't spare the wages I bring to keep up the farm. But she don't say nothing to me. She just takes out the old cardboard suitcase Miss Ida gave her and makes sure Feen got clean stockings. I don't know what to say. Hasn't Mama been telling me all my life to watch after Feen? What am I supposed to do now?

What are me and Mama gonna do, rattling around this house like peas, without Feen there, talking her little talk about school and what so-and-so in her class said? Me and Mama don't got nothing to talk about, and that "nothing" has got two arms, two legs, and a name. Toby.

"Marey Lee," Feen whisper the night before she go. "You still gonna come get me when you get your place? Mama say I got to stay with Aunt Shirley till I get out of school. You won't forget, huh? You promise you gonna come get me?"

"Girl, don't bother me," I say, putting my arm around her and squeezing her good. "You know I will." But I got a bad feeling. Mama say Feen going to have opportunities in Philadelphia, maybe meet some city folk and find herself a *good* job. She says Feen has got to go while she's still in school, still young enough to learn—which Mama don't think I am, me being almost seventeen and hardheaded at that. Feen ain't gonna need no one to come after her once she gets up out of Bay Slough, but I don't aim to tell her that. And anyway, I know why Mama sent Feen off.

Sister Dials come by last week to tell me she's seen Toby back in town.

"I'll write to you when I get there so you'll have my address. You write back, hear?" Feen say at the station. "Don't forget me, Marey Lee."

"Don't you worry about me, girl," I tell her. "I'll see you before you know it."

Mama cries and carries on a little when Feen gets on the train, but I already done my crying. Once Feen walks up those stairs, I tuck my heart up tight against my ribs and put it on ice. I ain't got time for cryin'. My sister, Josephine, was holding me back, but soon as she's gone, I got nothin' to hold me in Bay Slough, Alabama, no more. Nothing.

Mama been saying for me to "watch yourself," and I am finished up with watching, biding my time, and waiting. Don't nobody need me at home no more. It is time for this girl to go.

***

My hands are shaking when I take the examination down at the post office. I show I can read, and I can write fine. I know I ain't hardly no twenty years old, but it is easy to slide a lie past the folks who don't know my mama wouldn't sign no permission letter. Probably lots of girls do it. Almost seventeen ain't much different than twenty anyhow.

In a day or two, I have my bus ticket. I pack my few things in a bag and I go see Miss Ida, like usual. I put on my apron. I whip up the mayonnaise; I cut the crusts off the white bread sandwiches Miss Ida wants for her ladies' club. I lay out the plates. I press out the napkins; I polish up the silver napkin rings and the big coffee service. It all looks real fine when I set out the white candles, and Miss Ida is some pleased.

One by one, the ladies come. They get to eating and talking and playing them cards. I serve and clear away, and then I clean. Afterward, Miss Ida tell me to help myself to the leftovers. I wrap up the silver, careful like I always do, and nod like I'm grateful.

Tonight, I am gone.

March 1, 1944

Dear Mama,

Miss Beatrice Payne say even colored girls can join the Women's Army, so I have got to go. I will send you some money for the mortgage when I get where I'm going.

I remember what you taught me, Mama. I know right from wrong. You don't have to worry about me none.

Marey Lee Boylen

Sister Dials's eyes get wide when I walk up to her door with my letter. She told me the truth about Toby, so I know I can trust her to do this, even though I also know she's going to gossip 'bout it soon as she got time.

Back home, I fold up my few things in a flour sack and tuck it up under my arm.

I am ready.

Sister Dials said she hope I know what I am doing.

Lord have mercy, so do I.

7.

then

It is cold gray dawn when we board that bus from Bay Slough to take us to the army place. Some girls look real cute, with new shoes and hats settin' off to the side of their heads like they are going on vacation. I don't have no new clothes; I wear my Sunday hat and hold on to Mama's coat. I feel bad taking Mama's coat, but she don't hardly use it none anyway; when it gets cold, Mama holes up with her whiskey, and that's all the warm she needs.

I am the only colored girl on this bus, and I sit in the back, my hands sweatin'. I sure hope Beatrice Payne ain't nowhere near here. I don't need nobody trying to talk about home folks with me. Some of the girls are quiet; some are singing and rowdy till they fall to looking out at the dry, hilly land. Then there ain't nothing to hear but the rattle of that old bus stretchin' out those miles and miles and miles. Some girls cry a little, but I do not. I got to hold on.

It is dusty when they put us out in Tennessee. We climb onto a passenger train, onto a coach just behind the engine,

where they pack us in like sardines. White girls ride in a car
further back, away from the soot and the noise. That train
rattles and shimmies something awful. It is too loud to even
talk, and we ride for hours: Tennessee, Arkansas, Missouri,
then Iowa. We eat dry sandwiches from the porters when
they pass through. It is a long, long time.

Can't see nothin' of Des Moines, 'cause it is pitch-dark
and raining when we arrive. We stand around in the cold,
waitin'. After a while, they send trucks for us. The colored
girls ride out with the white girls, and the white girls don't
complain. Everyone is too tired to care about anything, and
at every bump we bump each other and some girls try to grab
on to others. Some girls don't know nothing about riding in
a truck.

"Jump down!" somebody holler when the trucks stop. My
legs is stiff. I jump down fast as I can, but then somebody
shout, "Fall in," and folks looking around them like they
crazy. Fall? On this wet dirt? Some of the girls get in line, and
nobody gets on the ground, so I follow them other girls. They
send us to a different line than the white girls, then line us
up on our own side, two by two, and say, "March." We all
stomp real good over to a little metal house. I got my bag in
my hand, bumpin' up on my legs. "March," they say, and my
chest is bumping up into my throat. Lord Jesus, what am I
doing here?

In the little metal house, it is noisy with voices, bellowing
loud. Girls in there hardly can make a sound for the women
in uniforms hollerin' out orders. The sign says Women's

Army Corps, and we are in receiving, and they say we got to get to processing. They give me two sheets, a pillowcase, and two blankets. I got to sign my name for everything. Then we got to stomp back in line and stomp some more over to our house, carrying all that stuff. I got a pillow in my face, and I can't see nothing but the top of the head of the girl in front of me. They can't let me put my bag down fast enough.

"This is a barracks," they tell me. "You in Company Twelve. This the Third Platoon."

Now, that don't mean nothing to me 'cept that I finally got somewhere to sit down. I sit myself down and take a breath, but the next second, somebody's hollering again.

"Fall in! Line up!" We march right back outside. We stomp back to the metal house, and they give me a coat! A coat—heavy sheep wool, double-breasted, better than any coat I ever had. Soon as I get me some time and make my wages, I can send Mama hers back so she won't have no reason to complain.

I look around and see some girls turning up their noses. "It's too big," I hear somebody say. Mine looks to be too big, too, but I am gonna *take* this coat. Ain't nobody got to ask *me* twice.

Then they give me some wool underwear, some leather gloves, and a knit cap to pull down over my head. It must get some cold around here. All I can think about is my coat. It is mine, and I ain't got to share it with anybody.

They make us sign up for three towels, a toothbrush, and a comb. That little comb make me think of Feen, who is tender-headed and always had her mouth poked out when I combed her hair. That makes my eyes sting, and before I can stop it, I got some water in my eyes.

Poor Feen. I have been gone two days. She has probably wrote to me, but I am not there to get her letter, nor her address. No way to let her know where I am, nor why I don't write. But it is best that I left. It is best for everyone, especially me.

By the time we stomp back to the barracks, I got my eyes dry, and they tell us to go to bed.

"Lights-out in fifteen minutes!"

I hurry myself to get undressed and under the scratchy wool blanket. There is ten or twelve girls and me, but I don't know what to say to nobody. Ain't nobody said nothin' to me, so I lay out my bed and fall in it. I think I ain't never going to sleep with all these girls up in here, but it has been too long since I saw a bed. I fall into sleep hard.

Next thing I know, somebody shakin' my arm, talking about, "They said get up!"

"What?" I rub the sleep out of my eyes.

"They're playin' that horn," this girl say real loud. "It's reveille. It's time to get up!"

"What time is it?" somebody moan. Six-thirty. I'm wide-awake, and my hands is shaking. This is it. I am in the army.

"Reveille!" somebody hollering. "Ladies, get moving!"

We dress, make up our beds, and stumble outside. This place is laid out like the Israelites in their tents—we in little bitty houses, far as the eye can see. There is some brick buildings a ways off, and a little chapel, and more buildings, but I can't look too long. They say we got to keep our eyes straight.

The lady—she a lieutenant in the Women's Army Corps, she say—points out that we got three barracks, and then headquarters, and the supply room, and a mess hall. The colored girls line up and, across the way, the white girls line up, but the lieutenant say we need to "fall in." Lieutenant Hundley make us do that two or three times. Little colored woman march up and look us over; she our captain, Captain Ferguson. She reads our names from a list, tells us to answer her "ma'am." 'Cross the way, the white girls doing the same thing.

"Baines!"

"Ma'am!"

"Barnes!"

"Yes, ma'am!" A tall, light-skinned girl to my right straightens up.

The woman looks up, frowning. She writes something on her list.

"Borland!"

"Ma'am!"

This girl who answers is shorter than I am, with real long hair all pinned up. The army woman squint at her and frown some. She don't say nothing for a long, long time.

"Ma'am?"

The army woman scowls. "Twenty gets younger all the time," she say.

My heart climbs up into my throat. She don't believe *that girl is twenty*, but she look older than me. *Lord, don't let that army lady look at me too close*. What happen if somebody told them my name, say folks in Bay Slough missing a girl who up and stole her mama's coat and lied like a heathen to get here. Maybe they going to call out my name and take me away.

"Bowie!"

"Ma'am!" By the swing in her voice, I know that girl's from Texas. I heard her tell she done already caught the eye of one of the enlisted men back home.

"Boylen!"

"Ma'am," I croak, my throat all dry. I have to clear my throat and say it again. "Ma'am!"

"In the army, you'll have to learn to speak up, Boylen." Captain Ferguson look at me close. "You'll learn. Brant!"

"Ma'am!"

"Brown!"

"Ma'am!"

"Carter!"

I look around. Nobody looks to be coming to take me back. Don't no one seem to be paying me any mind at all. *Thank you, Jesus*. The sweat dries on my face as my heart settles down.

After they call the roll, Lieutenant Hundley march us to the little house they say is for "mess." We look around, and the food ain't nothin' like we get at home. Here they got eggs and bacon and sausage all at the same meal. I hope Feen getting food this good in Philadelphia.

My heart hurts a little when I think that. Feen getting
fed up good at Aunt Shirley's. Feen going to be just fine, I tell
myself, but my throat swells up so I can't hardly swallow.

The girls sit about six to every table, and everyone gets
my name: Peaches Carter, Ruby Bowie, Phillipa Barnes,
Dovey Borland. There's a girl all the way from New London,
Connecticut, at my table, Annie Brown. I like to hear her
talk.

"You from around here?" she ask me first thing.

"Nah. From down Bay Slough way, Alabama. You been
to Iowa before?"

"Nope. I've barely even been out of New London."
Annie grins. Her big brown eyes remind me of Feen's. Even
though my throat is tight, I grin back at her. I hear her tell
she got *three* brothers, all in the service, and she the youngest
one in her family. She is a ball of fire, looking around and
grinning like she own the place. I like her.

They line us up, march us to another little metal house
for "inoculations." We get shots for diphtheria, the typhoid,
and such and learn to say, "Yes, ma'am," to all Women's
Army Corps, or WAC, personnel and, "No, sir," to the regular army men. Some girls squall when they see them nee-
dles, but I don't. It don't hurt worse than black mud-dauber
wasps at home in the summer.

I don't waste time thinkin' about *home*, though.

All day long, seems like we march back and forth. We
stand around and wait while some white man holler at us,
"This ain't no beauty college! What made you such-and-such
women think you could be in this man's army?" We march so

much my legs hurt, till Captain say, "You girls don't need to stomp *that* hard." When we do march right, it sounds good. They make the tall ones line up first. We short ones in the back got to march quick to keep up.

After lunch, they give us tests for typing, using tools, and some math. Then Captain makes us march to our barracks. She take apart our beds, tell us how to make them again, and then leave us be. All of us just want to get clean and pass out.

Peaches Carter in my barracks. I know why they call her Peaches, even though her mama named her Pamela Jane— she's got those pretty round cheeks always pushed up in a big old smile. She got her hair all pinned up in braids round her head, say she heard that's how all of us have to wear it. Ooh, that girl's crazy! She makes us laugh with her imitations of the army folk. "This ain't no beauty college!" she say, high-stepping around like she crazy. I like Peaches. She just turned twenty-one, and she went to secretarial college in Atlanta last year. She say she'll teach me how to type.

We still giggling and laughin' when they blow that horn at night, all sad and low, and someone hollers, "Lights-out!" I feel funny not catchin' the bus to Young's, but I am too tired to think of that for long. Then somebody start to sing.

> Day is done. Gone the sun
> From the hills, from the lake, from the sky.
> All is well, safely rest;
> God is nigh.

My heart squeeze so hard it chokes me. I put my face in my pillow so nobody don't hear me cry. It makes me so lonely for Feen and even for Mama that I can't stand it. I was too tired last night to say my prayers, but tonight I whisper, "God bless Feen. God bless Sister Dials. God bless Miss Ida. God bless Beatrice . . . and God bless Mama."

Even though she won't never forgive me for this.

8.

∩ O W

Tali is sleeping, but I'm watching the rain. I miss Mom. After Mare told us about the day she left home to join the army, I got homesick. If I wasn't ever going to see Mom and Dad again, I couldn't just leave without saying goodbye. I really don't know how Mare did.

I guess it's too quiet, because Mare clicks on the radio to NPR. While on I-8 through San Diego, we hear soft-voiced commentators play us upbeat world music, gently murmur about the weather, and calmly give us endless news commentary in a serious monotone. The radio is making me sleepy, but I can't go to sleep. Mom and Dad said we're supposed to keep an eye on Mare, and since Tali's passed out in the backseat, I guess it's on me now.

Earlier, when Mare pulled over to let Tali drive, those big rigs weren't the only things going slow. Tali is scared of trucks, and every time one of them came up beside her, she panicked. Twice she made Mare and me screech, letting the car drift in the lane, rattling over the lines. She could speed up and pass them, but she got all tense every time one came anywhere near her.

"Just relax," Mare kept saying, and Tali started yelling.

"I am relaxed! You guys just have to stop talking. I can't drive while you're talking."

She wanted to pull over pretty badly by the time she'd been driving for an hour, but Mare said no.

"The only way to get past fear is to get through it," Mare told her. "You stick to it, Tali."

And she did it—she drove for almost three hours, in between RVs and eighteen-wheelers and big trucks pulling trailers. When we stopped for gas, her back was all sweaty, and I could see her legs were shaking, but she was happy. She was even happier when Mare said she'd take over from there.

I'm actually kind of proud of my evil sister.

The sky is dark, and there are no stars. Every once in a while, I click on the little flashlight on my house key to check our route on the map. I wish Mare would stop. There are no buildings on the road this far away from town, and I thought I saw lightning in front of us. If it starts storming out here in the middle of nowhere, I don't know what we're going to do.

"Mare? Are we stopping pretty soon?"

"In a while now," Mare says unconcernedly. "You don't need to use it again already, do you?"

I roll my eyes. "No. Just wondered if you were going to drive all night."

Mare turns her head, and her teeth are white blobs in the dark as she smiles. "No, Octavia, I am not going to drive all night. I just want to get across the desert while it's cool, that's all."

"Oh."

Mare checks the rearview mirror. "It's only nine-forty-five. I know you girls stay up later than this."

"Well, yeah . . ." I shrug. "I thought you said you weren't going to drive at night."

"I did." Mare glances at me again. "You want to drive?"

I look out over the two-lane road into the blackness beyond and back at my grandmother, goose bumps prickling my arms. Is she serious? "Can I drive in the morning?"

"Nope." Mare laughs. "Now or never."

I look back over the empty, dark road. I *really* want to. Mare's car is an automatic, there's no one else out here, and it's a flat, straight road. Sure, I don't have my license, but what could it hurt?

I open my mouth to say Yes when a low white streak shoots into the headlights, freezes, then bounds off in a blur.

"Whoa!"

"Jackrabbit," Mare says calmly. "Little suckers are all over the place."

She didn't even swerve.

I relax my grip on my seat belt, wide-awake and blinking.

If we pull over for me to take the wheel, Tali will wake up. She'll want to know what we're doing, and Mare will tell her that I'm going to drive. And then Tali will freak. She'll be all, "You don't even have your permit. You just want to drive because I did." Even if she isn't a jerk about me copying her, I don't want my sister watching me make mistakes.

"What's it gonna be, Octavia?"

It's so dark outside it feels like no one exists anywhere else in the whole world except inside this car. If it were only Mare, I wouldn't mind, but if I go over the line or run off the road, I know Tali will never let me forget it.

And then there are the jackrabbits.

If I hit one, I think I would die.

What if I swerved and flipped over the car? What if—

My grandmother clears her throat.

"Mare, I don't want to drive right now," I say finally, reluctant to admit it. "Will you ask me again tomorrow?"

Mare laughs. Thunder booms distantly above us, and I smell the strange ozone scent that is rain on hot ground. "We might be on busy roads tomorrow," Mare says, turning on the wipers as the first few drops begin to fall.

"So, you won't ask me again?"

Mare reaches across the seat and pats my leg. "Sometimes you only get one chance to do a thing," she says, and I feel my shoulders droop.

"You know, Octavia," Mare says as I swallow hard, "when I was your age, I took all kinds of chances. Didn't think I could ever join the army, but I did. You're going to have to learn to take your chance. Live a little, girl."

My disappointment is so sharp and heavy it feels like a rock in my throat. I don't answer.

"When your father was little, he was just like you," Mare muses. "I took him to the boardwalk, and I had to force him to ride the carousel. All the other little boys were having a great time, but your father—he screamed the whole ride long."

I stare out into the dark. "Maybe he was scared of the horses," I mutter, humiliation making my voice low. I remind her of a little kid?

"Could be," Mare agrees. "And since he was only three back then, I don't hold it against him. It'd be a shame, though, to be afraid to try new things like that for the rest of your life."

"I'm not afraid!" I insist hotly. "I'm not scared at all. It's just—it's raining," I say lamely.

Mare tsks and drives on silently.

"Live a little." I hate that phrase. People always say it when they want you to taste something gross or try something that might hurt. "Live a little," is what people say when they want you to risk total and complete humiliation. Mom said it last summer when she signed me up for tap lessons at the community center. "Live a little," she said. "You'll never know if you'll like it till you try."

And when I tripped over my own feet during the recital, the world didn't end, but I still looked like an idiot. People like Tali never look stupid. Nobody ever tells them to "live a little," because they're already living a lot. Tali never makes plans or worries how things will turn out. She just does stuff. And she would have said yes if Mare had asked her to drive.

The rain's really coming down by the time Mare pulls off the highway. We drive along slowly on a two-lane road, past gas stations and fast-food restaurants, until we find a brightly lit hotel a few miles off the interstate. We splash through a huge puddle under the carport, and Mare puts the car in park with a sigh.

"I'm going to get two rooms tonight," she tells me, sliding out of the driver's seat. "Wake up your sister and grab your bags."

In a few minutes Tali sleepwalks into our room and into the bathroom. Mare sets her luggage down and turns around to go outside to move the car.

Yawning, I dig through my bag for my umbrella and trail after my grandmother. Tali should really be doing this. Dad said for *both* of us to keep an eye on Mare, not just me. My legs are stiff, and I just want to go to sleep.

"Where are you going, child?" Mare looks amused. "Go on to bed. I'll get you girls up in the morning."

"I was just going to walk you out to the car," I tell her. I hold up my umbrella. "See?"

"I don't need you to come with me." Mare smiles. "I know your daddy said to keep an eye on the old lady, but I'm not sugar, and a little rain won't melt me. Go to bed."

"Mare . . ."

"Unless you want to park the car?" Mare holds out the keys to me with a quizzical expression.

My hand twitches at my side. I step back in the doorway, too annoyed to take her teasing me again. If I said yes, would she really let me park? Can I park, in darkness, in the rain, without hitting another car?

"Good night," I mutter, and close my door. I put my umbrella back inside my bag and hope the Wicked Witch melts into an evil puddle when she's walking back.

Suzanne Labruchérie
16 Sandpiper Circle
Walnut Creek, CA 94549

Hey Suze,
So my grandmother ran away to join the army when
they first let African American women join back in
WWII. It totally explains a bunch of things about her,
including her habit of GIVING ORDERS like I'm going
to jump up and salute.

I'm so bored I'm beginning to like Mare's music. You've
got to do something. Have an accident, and then have
your parents tell mine I have to come home and sit at your
deathbed. Either that or I'm going to find some way to
make your parents send you here.
Fact: I will **not** survive this.
Help.

 Tali

P.S. Yesterday I drove for three hours. (!!!) I asked Mare if
she doesn't think Dad should give me a car if she would
give me hers—when she dies. She gave me the DIRTIEST
look. I SAID when she DIED. I mean, hello? Once she's
dead, why should she care?

9.

then

Oh-five-hundred, that's what the army says is five in the morning, and Lieutenant Hundley is hollerin' at us *already*. My feet hit the floor first note that horn sounds. I have been here a week, but don't nobody got to tell *me* to get up twice.

Last week we got on with our processing at classification. My stomach gets tight when I think what all they were asking. "What do you like to do, Miss Boylen? What kind of work?" Now, I don't know what I *like* to do, but I know what I can do. Nobody asked me what I like to do before. I don't know what I like to do, and that's what I told them. I don't know, but I sure mean to find out. All I want to do is answer those questions right so they let me stay.

Today, Hundley say we moving on from receiving to training center. Today, we get squad assignments and start five weeks of basic training.

Annie, Ruby, and Dovey are in my squad, with four other girls I don't know too well yet. Phillipa and Peaches are in another squad. I don't mind too much; it is just for school.

Before I get time to be happy about starting my training, Hundley does inspection and gets on us about our hair, about our clothes, even about our shoes. She tell us we don't wear nothing from home anymore, not even our drawers or shoes, unless our uniform shoes don't fit right.

"You women are not civilians anymore," Hundley says. She tells us how to iron our uniforms and how to shine our shoes, tells us to wear our hair up, in a roll, and how to wear our hats. I am glad I don't have as much hair as some girls. A girl in our barracks has two fat plaits down her back she brushes out every night and pins up every morning. Some girls leave their hair pinned and wear wigs.

Now, doing Miss Ida's got me ironing real good, and no child of Edna Mae Boylen does not know how to at least do up her plaits, but back in Bay Slough, didn't nobody I know razor-shave her legs. I cut up my legs something awful borrowing Phillipa's shaver, and I was too 'shamed to say nothing about it. Ruby say next time she will teach me how so I don't bleed all over my stockings. Sometimes I don't feel like I know nothing about nothing away from Bay Slough.

The U.S. Army is just not ready for all of these women up in here. They want us to have dress uniform, work uniform, winter uniform, and summer uniform as well as stockings and three kinds of shoes. Most of us got only a piece or two of each uniform and no decent shoes at all, so far. Peaches, whose mama is a seamstress, took in my jacket. When I see myself in the mirror, I swell up proud.

When we wear our uniforms all together, we look sharp.

Even Lieutenant Hundley say so. The skirts are all the same length, even though they don't hit nobody's legs in the same place. We halfway look like we are in the army now.

Today, Lieutenant makes us work before we eat. All of us, coloreds and whites, march around and pick up cigarette butts and march off to breakfast. They call it "policing."

We got three platoons, the First and Second for the white girls, the Third for the coloreds, and the First and Second has to trade off with us, the Third, and police the grounds three times a day. I am working hard when I pass this light-skinned girl named Gloria Madden, and she looks me over, up and down, like I did something wrong.

"It's not fair some people got better uniforms," Gloria says so I can hear her. She's supposed to be working, picking up butts like the rest of us, but she's standing around running her mouth. She's got those real long nails, like she never did nothing in her life. Her hands are probably soft, too.

When I don't say nothing, Gloria keep talking. "You think you're cute, don't you?"

What? I look up. "Peaches Carter did up my clothes," I say. "Somebody will do yours." I don't know who will do hers, since Peaches only did mine 'cause we're friends. Gloria Madden is not no kind of friendly type of girl, but she's in Peaches's squad. I look at her jacket pinned up crooked and her skirt all rolled up on her waist. No wonder she looks mad.

"What kind of a name is Peaches? You girls are too country." Gloria flounces off before I can answer, and I see Lieutenant Hundley coming, so I keep my mouth shut. It is just as well.

We march to mess, and Hundley start a song. We can't hardly march for laughing.

> *You can tell a WAC from Fort Des Moines*
> *You can tell her by her walk*
> *You can tell a WAC from Fort Des Moines*
> *You can tell her by her talk*
> *You can tell a WAC from Fort Des Moines*
> *By her appetite and such*
> *You can tell a WAC from Fort Des Moines*
> *But you cannot tell her much.*

Hundley calls a halt, and the captain stands at the door of the mess, looking over each of us. Hundley stand next to her and look at us march. But it 'bout stops my heart when Captain looks me over and says, "Boylen, you're a really little gal, aren't you?"

"Ma'am?" I am so scared I can't swallow. Behind me, I hear Annie suck in breath.

"You're little, Boylen. Too skinny to look like you're more than twelve. You sure you're one hundred pounds?"

"Ma'am." My voice cracks. I can feel the sweat starting at my hairline. First few days here, they teach us "military discipline." They say you can't say nothin' to no commanding officer 'cept "yes" and "no," and only that when they ask you something directly. I don't know what else to say.

Cap stares at me awhile, then shakes her head. "Better feed up—eat your three squares, Private."

"Yes, ma'am," I say, and just about choke on my tongue. I march into mess with my platoon and know I better dig in and eat seconds today. Can't have nobody looking at me too closely. What would I do if they sent me home?

"You all right, Mare?" Annie askin' me.

"I'm all right."

"You aren't twenty yet, are you?" Phillipa asks. "But you can't complain since your mama gave you permission."

I just smile. Don't nobody know my secrets, and don't nobody need to. I hold my head up and go to my seat, and I eat till I'm fit to bust.

After breakfast, we march off to school. School ain't like what I thought—we learn what they call "the GI way" of doing things. They call it "customs and courtesies." We learn the organization of the army: division, battalion, company, platoon, and squad. We learn how to care for our uniforms— the pieces of them we got anyway—and how to salute. They tell us how to hold our arm, our hand, our fingers.

There are just too many rules about saluting. We got to do it fast, too; anybody salutes us, we got to salute them back. Everybody's been here longer than us, so we got to salute them first. And here, a man don't open a door for us girls, 'cause *we* got to open the door for anyone with more stripes than us—more rank. I know what the sleeve stripes mean and the difference between a captain and a lieutenant, 'cause we got those with Captain Ferguson and Lieutenant Hundley. A major's got some oak leaves on his arm, but I don't know too much about the rest. What I do know is nobody is nothing around here without stripes. I am on the bottom of the heap, an "enlisted man" they call it, with no stripes at all.

We learn the army likes letters for words. Nobody talks without using some of them letters. They leave up notes on the board that say *QTRS*, and we know that's the bunks, or our "quarters." Then the important one—*CO* for our commanding officer. Then there's *APO* for army post office, *CQ* for charge of quarters, *HQ* for headquarters, *AWOL* for absent without leave, *PX* for post exchange, *KP* for kitchen patrol, *PT* for physical training, *NCO* for non-commissioned officer, and more letters than I can keep count of. And don't *talk* to me about the time. It's oh-five-hundred hours this and seventeen-forty hours that. There is no one o'clock p.m. in this man's army, no sir. The hour after noon is thirteen hundred hours, and you best be well in your bed and fast asleep before zero hour, or midnight.

Lieutenant Hundley has to say most things twice, but Annie say don't worry. A body has to be here awhile for anything to make sense.

Des Moines is cold and dry, but I am getting used to it. What I can't get used to is how folks talk round here. It isn't just Annie Brown from New London or Ruby Bowie with her Texas swing who talk funny. Lieutenant Hundley got her ways of saying things, and Captain Ferguson talk like she went to finishing school. This morning, at mess hall, she asked about my uniform. I got my salute up right, and I told her I ain't got boots yet. She give me a funny look.

"Boylen. Say 'don't.'"

"Don't?" I wonder if I should say "ma'am," too. I chew my lip.

She gives a sharp sigh. "Yes, Private. Say 'I don't have boots.'"

"I don't got . . ." My voice chokes off as her eyebrows rise. "I don't have boots. Yet. Ma'am." I look at her nervous-like, and she give me a short nod.

"That's better. Ain't no 'ain't' in the dictionary, Private," she says.

Captain Ferguson is short and she don't hardly raise her voice, but she is the boss lady for sure. She tells Lieutenant Hundley what she wants us to do, and she tells the other two companies what to do, too. I am scared to open my mouth after Cap said ain't no "ain't," but Company Twelve has got to make Captain Ferguson proud, so before I speak, I listen to the girls from the city. Peaches started to look at me funny after a while, because I wasn't hardly talking no more; I was scared to try.

"I don't know when I've been so sore," Peach moans one night after marching.

"I . . . ," I begin, then stop and smile self-consciously. "Tired. Me too."

"Marey Lee." Peaches sits up, unlacing her boots. "You know you've hardly said a word since Captain Ferguson told you there's no 'ain't' in the dictionary?"

I look at her warily. "Yeah?"

"Now look," Peach says quickly. "You can't stop talking just because you might say the wrong thing! We can all help you with that, you know."

The skin on my face feels tight and warm. "Now listen here! I don't need nobody's charity, Miss Peaches Carter—"

"Anybody's," Peaches says. "You don't need anybody's charity. It's a good thing, 'cause I'm not offering charity. I'm offering a deal. Boylen, you show me how you crease your uniform so I don't keep getting marked down like I always do, and I'll tell you when you get words wrong and help you say things right. Deal?"

I give Peaches a hard look. "I don't need anybody's charity," I tell her clearly. "You wouldn't never get marked off if you didn't do such a slapdash job with the iron."

"Then show me how," Peaches insists. "I wouldn't *ever* learn by myself." She pushes up her round cheeks in a smile and puts out her hand. "Deal?"

I hesitate for one last second, then stick out my hand decisively. "Deal."

❉ ❉ ❉

Yesterday, we got more uniforms. They call 'em "fatigues." We got a little light seersucker dress and our gym uniforms to wear for "physical training." After all that marching, Lieutenant Hundley say we got to run around and be "physically fit."

Lieutenant Hundley put up a bulletin board so we know what uniform to put on and can find out our duty for the day on the duty roster. Today, we got on our Class A uniform, and I have to police the area before my class. We also have to go to the dentist, have him check our teeth.

I have never been to a dentist. Where I come from, only rich folks see the dentist. Mama's been seein' to me and Feen's teeth since we were small. She pulls 'em out when they gets loose and makes us rub them with baking soda. Feen had a toothache once, and Mama gave her a bit of clove to chew on. Here they give us tooth powder, and we all have to brush.

Peaches says it doesn't hurt none, they give you gas and you don't feel a thing, but first thing I see is a needle in there, and I come over sick. They tell me they give me gas if I need it, but I tell them no. They poke at my teeth, and I try not to bite down. Dentist say I got a jaw like a bear trap.

"No cavities," the man says, and he says he don't have to drill.

Peaches doesn't have no drilling, either, but poor Dovey Borland came back with her head all wrapped up in a scarf and lay down in her bed. I wish I had some clove oil. That's what Mama put on Feen's teeth when hers got sore. Course, I'm not thinking about Mama or anything.

I wrote a letter to Mama care of Sister Dials, but nobody answered me yet.

Today, some new white girls came in, and I looked at 'em real hard, see if I can see Miss Beatrice Payne anywhere. I wonder if she ever got on to Daytona and away from her mama and her ladies' college. I wonder if Saphira Watkins's boy is *really* in the navy, if the colored boys have their own barracks and their own mess and their own company, too. Don't nobody— nobody—sees no colored boys around here nor any boys, but there are all kinds of men. Some old army men are coming down to see us march next week, I hear. That's what Annie says, and she finds out all kinds of "latrine gossip."

Tomorrow, Sunday, is my birthday. Back home, Reverend Morgan at the AME is gonna ask Mama where I am. I wonder what she will say. Maybe she will stay home so Sister Dials can tell the gossip without her. Maybe Mama won't go to service anymore at all. Maybe she *and* Toby will stay home.

Tonight, the sad "taps" song, as Peaches calls it, doesn't make me cry, but it still makes me miss Feen. I did right to come here, I know it. If I can just hide out without anybody sending me home, I will make a little money and put it by till Feen is done with school. They say we going to go to school here, and I will learn something to help me keep body and soul together later on. Maybe I will learn to type and be a secretary and get a good job in a city.

In my mind, I talk to Feen and tell her all about it. I lay in my bunk with my eyes open, listening to the crickets outside. I pretend that this is my room, in my house, and Feen's tucked up in her bed. I pretend I am twenty-one and we are going to services in the morning, where we will wear our good hats, and I will wear red lipstick from Woolworth's, and Feen will wear a gold circle pin.

Feen will wear my green coat and borrow my gloves. I will wear pearls.

Someday.

10.

then

Lieutenant give us inspection in the morning. Peaches gets full marks, but Annie has her cap tilted on her head, and Hundley tells her to fix it, like she does almost every morning. Annie say that hat is too ugly to go straight on her head. She likes to have a little style. Hundley says if Annie doesn't cut out that mess, we'll never win our inspection. Whichever company wins inspection gets to march with the flags and be the color guard. We have not won yet.

The first time I see *KP* by my name on the duty roster Sunday, I know I am in for it. Annie says kitchen policing is the hardest job on the post. They are always tryin' to tell us to "police" something around here. Those of us who have KP fall in and march toward the mess hall. It smells like dirt in the mess hall kitchen, dirt and grease, and there is steam hissing from big old kettles. It is hot, and something is burning over on the range.

"You gals get an apron on," the cook hollers, "and lend a hand here!" She looks like Betty from Young's, and her arms are as big as a man's.

The Army must think all girls know how to cook and such, but they have another surprise coming. I know for sure Miss Ruby Bowie hasn't hardly ever turned her hand to a spoon, and she keeps trying to duck out the back door and have herself a break. She picks up a chicken like it's gonna bite her, and Cook has to tell her two or three times how to pluck it. That girl probably can't boil water to save her life.

The second time Ruby jumps back from steam in a pot, Annie laughs out loud.

"Ruby, what do you *do* at home when your mama tells you to get in the kitchen?" Annie teases her.

"I make sure I've got a good place to hide!" Ruby says, and we laugh.

"Have a heart, Annie," Ina White says from where she is rolling out biscuits. "You're the only girl in your family, so you got all your mama's time to teach you. Not every girl has three brothers!"

"*They* all can cook, too," Annie laughs. "Come on, girls, excuses aren't the GI way!"

There are potatoes in the mess, and we got to fix potato salad for Sunday dinner. Potatoes is something I know— Mama made me peel potatoes, snap beans, and mix up biscuits for Sunday dinner back home since I was eight or nine. I peel potatoes like I was born doing it.

"Marey Lee," Annie say, "now, how do you do that, make the peel all come out in one curl?"

I just grin. I might not know nothing about nothing in this man's army, but I sure can handle myself in a kitchen. Miss Ida should see me now. "Just hold your knife like this,"

I say, and all my squad turns toward me. Sure feels good to teach *them* something for a change.

Later, we go to the post chapel for service. It is a tall brick building with nothing but high windows and a slant roof, but we know where we is when we get inside. The pews is all lined up straight just like at home.

The chapel is blessed quiet, with nobody hollering about nothing to anybody. Some girls from the squad—Doris Smith, Maryanne Oliver, and Dovey Borland—all sit with me in the front pews, right where our mamas taught us to be. Doris and Maryanne are both from little farms and little old towns like me. Doris homesick for a boy she was sweet on, but he got the draft, and she hasn't got nowhere else to be but here, waiting on him. She tell us she joined up to make the war go shorter. Dovey joined up for the same reason as me— to get away from home.

"I had a look at things, and I can tell you what—I wasn't going nowhere in that town," Dovey says, shaking her head. "I could go to secretarial school, but what would that do for me? They weren't gonna hire a colored woman to work in an office, not where I come from. I was gonna go to the city, but I read about the Women's Army in the colored paper, and Mama said I couldn't do better than working for Uncle Sam."

Peaches comes in almost late and sits with Phillipa and that stuck-up Gloria Madden on the row behind us. Peaches pokes me in my back and smiles, and I smile back, but I don't have nothing nice to say to Gloria Madden, even in God's house, so I turn around quick.

Dovey sings real sweet, and we all get quiet to hear her singing the hymn. Then Gloria sing, too, only louder, so we can all hear *her*, and even though Miss Gloria Madden works my nerves, I sure wish I could sing like that. How can a girl with such a sweet voice have such an evil way about her? Mama always say the good Lord don't make no mistakes, but sometimes I am just not sure.

After hymns, we say our prayers and sit down. We don't have a reverend, but one of the officers says she is chaplain for the day, and she speaks the Word as good as any man preacher. Captain says we can go to church in town sometime. I might just do that.

Even though she makes full marks on her uniform now, Peaches is still helping me. Sunday night she show me over and over how to make the bed the GI way. We got to have that top sheet folded down six inches, long as our tooth-brushes, and they got a measuring stick to tell for sure. I hate them tight sheets, but when we have inspection, Lieutenant Hundley tears it up if it is not "right and tight." First time I actually saw a quarter dollar bounce on just some sheets, I knew I had to learn that trick.

"Tuck it tighter than that," Peaches say. "You make it loose, and nothing's gonna bounce off it but the covers when Hundley pulls it apart. Do it again."

"Don't know why anybody wants to make a bed like that anyway," I mutter. "Can't breathe in there."

"You'll be glad you can't breathe later on. It'll be down-right cold in here come winter."

I learn how to make that bed just right, but it does not

stop me from tryin' to get into it without messing it up and slide out in the morning to pull it straight. Peaches just looks at me like I'm pitiful and shakes her head.

***

Monday we get back to the everyday work—rising at 0530, making beds, washing up, and picking up cigarette butts the folk drop down, then sweepin' the walks the officers walk on. We march to breakfast, stand cleaned and starched and shined and ironed for inspection; we march to classes by 0800; we march to a meal break at lunch, 1200. We eat, and study till 1600, and march some more. We march to the parade grounds and practice raising and lowering "the colors," which we call the flag.

Every day, we study worse than we ever did in school. We learn sanitation and first aid, military customs and who to salute; we read maps; we study German chemicals and gas and how to watch out from the air and defend from Japanese planes. We do supply runs and keep tabs on all the food, all the weapons, and all the uniforms and gear. We learn how to run a clean camp 'cause they say tiny little germs will kill us all if we let them.

I learn my keyboard and type drills every day. We learn signal corps duty, about how they look for patterns in words and numbers to make or break a code. We learn our telegraph keys and listen to the little *dit-dah-dit* for the messages they be sending. After the first day, we can all tap out an emergency signal—three short, three long, and three short: SOS. I got to teach that one to Feen.

When they call out my name at roll call, my legs start
shaking, and I know it is a letter. I am not too disappointed
that it is from Miss Ida. Bet she never wrote a colored girl a
letter before that didn't have nothing to do with cleaning
her house!

May 1944

Miss Marey Lee Boylen,

*Though she won't say, your mama is upset
something awful about you going away, and I
told her you thought you were grown, just like
my Beatrice. Young girls today don't have the
good sense the Lord God gave you, leaving
your homes to work with all of those men. You
ought to be ashamed of yourself, Marey Lee
Boylen. I have half a mind to tell those officers
that you are not as old as you have said and
haul you back home for your own good.*

*Marey Lee, make sure you're still a clean
Christian girl when you get back. We hear how
some of those girls are over there, sliding down
to the sins of Sodom and Gomorrah.*

*Your mama comes to help me now, and I
am glad. They marched Italian prisoners of
war into this town, Marey Lee, and I can't
sleep at night, just knowing that something
terrible is going to happen.*

Gasoline is scarce as hen's teeth, and we

haven't had butter in weeks. We make do on
fish, and we save our meat rations for special
occasions. I will be so glad when this terrible
war is over.

I remain,
Mrs. Ida Barrows Payne

Ooh, Miss Ida makes me mad. What is she talking about, hauling me back for my own good, and about the sins of Sodom and Gomorrah? She had better *not* tell nobody how old I am, and if I hear somebody is coming for me, I'll run. Ain't nobody going to make me go home before I am *good* and ready.

I got a good mind to write Miss Ida and tell her a thing or two. She don't—doesn't—think I know how to act, but I will show her.

I will show *everybody*.

11.

ΠΟW

The morning is so new the horizon still has bits of pink at the far edges of the sky. It's just after five and too early to be hungry, but Mare makes us visit the hotel's breakfast bar anyway, and we pack pastries, fruit, and small bottles of juice into our bags for later on. I don't know how Mare got up at "oh-five-thirty" every morning and had an appetite to eat breakfast when she was in the army, but I guess they were on the move so much they ate as much as they could when they had a chance, even if they weren't hungry.

Most of the people we see on the road are alone in their cars, sipping coffee or applying makeup. I slump in the corner of the seat farthest away from my grandmother and look out over the flat yellowish landscape, thinking about putting my feet up on the dashboard. The map shows nothing exciting on the way for miles and miles and miles. Inside the car, we reflect the same featureless boredom—three people staring out at the morning with nothing to say.

The traffic slows to a crawl as we reach a business district.

Mare looks distracted, slips on her sunglasses, scowling. She turns on the radio, tapping her long nails against the steering wheel as we move through the slowdown.

"In more news, the president has announced sanctions against—" Mare clicks her tongue and changes the station.

". . . stop-and-go traffic on the expressway, as police are still clearing the site of this morning's big rig—"

"Should players who fail steroid testing get into the Hall of Fame? Fans argue that—"

". . . amid rumors that the group will feature the recovering rocker in a reunion tour—"

"Students at a German university rioted last night over proposed—"

Mare shakes her head and pushes in a CD.

From the backseat, Tali lets out a loud sigh as the gravelly vocals and twanging guitar of Muddy Waters fill the air.

"Mare," she moans. "It's too early for blues. Can we at least listen to someone who doesn't play guitar?"

"Oh, *Lord,*" Mare groans. "You put in what you want, girl. God knows it's too early to listen to you whine about my music again."

Tali rummages around in her bag and thrusts a CD case in my face.

"This one," she says. As usual, Tali doesn't bother to say thank you or ask me if I had something else I wanted to listen to. She never thinks of me at all, and I'm right here in the front seat. Mare and Tali are completely alike—they both expect people to do exactly what they want exactly when they want. I slide down in the seat and cross my arms as the music fills the car.

"Well, she's got a nice voice at least," Mare says grudgingly as the smoky-voiced musician begins to sing.

"I thought you'd like her," Tali says smugly. "You should try a little music from this century every once in a while."

Mare laughs, a surprised-sounding bark that leaves her coughing. "From this century?" she sputters. "What for? There's no good music to listen to these days. Now, back in the day . . ."

Mare and Tali are debating the relative merits of Erykah Badu versus Sarah Vaughn when out of nowhere, it seems, a raised pickup truck, red-crossed flag flying from the antenna, zips out of the stream of traffic. Swerving up from the right lane and into ours, only half a foot ahead of us, he barely fits himself between us and the next car. Mare slams on the brakes and, on a reflex, throws her arm across my body. The tires squeal and she swears as we lurch to a stop.

"Jerk!" Tali yells, reaching around me to lower my window. The car behind us also screeches to a stop, the driver leaning on his horn.

"Tali, *don't*," I warn her as she unclips her seat belt. "You're not even driving."

"I don't care," Tali fumes. "That freak cut us off!"

"Look at the flag on his car," I say. "Isn't that a Confederate flag? What if he's a skinhead or something?" I can feel the hair on my arms prickling as my stomach tightens with dread.

"Don't go screaming at him, Tali. You don't know what those people can do."

Mare sighs. "Miss Talitha, put on your seat belt, will you please," she says calmly. "A lady does not *shout* at strangers, no matter how piss-poor their driving skills."

Tali says something particularly unladylike and slouches sullenly.

"And, Octavia," my grandmother adds after a moment, "for your information, the red Saint Andrew's cross on a field of white is the state flag of *Alabama*, not the Confederate flag."

I shrug. *Your point?*

"Folks mistake the state flag for the Confederate flag since we had a narrow-minded governor of Alabama who ran the Confederate up the pole at the capitol for years, but the Confederate flag is actually a blue Saint Andrew's cross with white stars on a red field."

"Okay, so it was the wrong flag. Whatever," I say, bumping my foot against the door. We're not even in Alabama, and the truck is long gone. I'm embarrassed to have been so scared, and I wish Mare hadn't decided I need a history lesson right now.

"So, tell me," Mare goes on, "if this fool driving *was* flying a Confederate flag, how would that make a difference with Tali hollering out the window at him?"

"Well, duh," I say before I can stop and think it through. "People who fly that flag are skinhead neo-Nazis and white supremacists."

Mare's penciled-in brows are high, thin arcs. "*All* of them? Really?"

I know what Mare is objecting to, and I scowl. "Fine. Some of them," I say. "A *lot* of them."

"And?" Mare continues to peer at me from over her sunglasses.

"And what?"

"How does that make a difference to your sister?"

"It doesn't," Tali interrupts angrily. "Anybody who drives like that—"

"Well, it should." I bite my bottom lip. "People have to be . . . careful."

Mare looks at me and nods slowly. "I see."

For a while, we drive in silence, just letting the music from Tali's CD slide between us and allowing our heartbeats to slow. I have slouched back and have just leaned my foot against the glove compartment when Mare speaks again.

"Octavia . . ."

I quickly straighten. "Huh?"

Mare sighs, and I change my response. "Yes?"

"Do you know anything about Claudette Colvin?"

"Who?" I ask, thinking she's another character from Mare's history.

"Oh, I've heard of Claudette Colvin," Tali volunteers. "She's the girl who wouldn't give up her bus seat in Alabama—before Rosa Parks."

Mare glances at me, and I shrug. "Well, I've heard of her now. What about her?"

My grandmother looks at me over the frame of her sunglasses. "She was fifteen, the same as you are, but she wasn't about to let anyone push her around."

I thump my foot against the door, wishing that Mare would come to the point.

"The people who dragged her kicking and screaming off of that bus certainly were what you could call white supremacists," Mare continues. "She had to have known that something was going to happen if she kept sitting where she wasn't wanted. But she stayed seated," Mare goes on, flicking a glance over her left shoulder and smoothly changing lanes. "Sometimes you just have to act on the strength of your convictions, no matter what someone else might think."

I curl my toes in my sandals. "What's that supposed to mean?"

"Skinheads, neo-Nazis, white supremacists—they believe what they please, but don't let that change *you.*"

I open my mouth, but Mare keeps going. "Granted, I'd better not catch you *ever* rolling down your window and shouting like you don't have some kind of common sense, but you can't let people control how you act. Don't let them make you afraid."

"I'm not afraid," I insist. "I just don't want to get killed because stupid Tali gets all road-rage-y and yells at some skinhead."

"Shut up, Octavia. For your information—"

"*Hush.*" Mare's voice is flint.

I sit, seething, while Tali leans back and looks out the window.

"So, whatever happened to Claudette Colvin?" I blurt. "If she was so great, why hasn't everybody heard of her?"

Mare sighs. "Well . . . the civil rights movement had a minister as one of its foremost leaders. Claudette got pregnant by a married man just about the time her case came to trial, and they decided she wasn't such a good poster child for equal rights."

Tali clicks her tongue in disgust. "That is *so* completely wrong."

Mare sighs again. "Well, things were different back then."

The sun continues to climb in a cloudless blue sky. The CD ends, and Mare turns on the radio again to NPR and is listening to an author interview. Tali is staring out the window, looking glazed.

Just before Mare says it's time for a bathroom stop, we pass an old truck with Tennessee license plates, a gun rack, and a Confederate flag in the rear window. The truck is dusty and brown; the driver, old and leather-skinned. Unable to stop myself, I risk a look into his face, feeling my stomach clench as our gazes meet.

He gives me a brief, impersonal glance, then his eyes return to the road.

In a moment, he's a receding speck in the mirror, just one brown truck out of many on an endless road.

Ms. Crase, English Dept.
c/o Vallejo Canyon High School
1500 W. Johnson Street
Pleasant Hill, CA 94523

Dear Ms. Crase,

You said I should practice writing like a journalist so I can join the paper next year. I am finding a lot to observe this summer already. I'm on a road trip with my grandmother and my sister across the country, where we'll attend a family reunion somewhere in Alabama.

My grandmother was in the Women's Army at Fort Des Moines in World War II. Remember that movie we watched about the Navajo code talkers? My grandmother was actually learning Morse code about the time they were getting started. It's a little hard to believe.

Hope you're having a nice summer.
Sincerely,
Octavia Boylen, third-period journalism

12.

then

All week long, the lieutenant has us marching our close drills. It is hot on that parade ground, and we stand and sweat till our clothes stick to us, but we do the best we can. When it is too hot, some people faint. First time that happened, folks start to break ranks and carry on, and Lieutenant says we can't be doing that—we have got to keep our eyes *forward*, no matter what. She calls it "military discipline." I call it crazy. If I drop dead out there, somebody better be coming to pick me up!

Sometimes I don't know what Uncle Sam needs with women in this man's army. They tell us we here to "free a man to fight," but I don't see no men being freed up by all this marching back and forth in this hot sun. They got a song they sing, the WAC song, which is all about duty and defending our country's honor. Well, I don't know about *that*. All I can say is, "Better the devil we know." And I know we sure don't need no Japs coming all the way from across the water trying to boss folks around.

Some of these girls would like to have died when we had to clean the latrine—but Lieutenant said, "Ladies, make us proud," and we did. That commode at Miss Ida's gave me all kinds of practice, and I make sure everyone sees I don't mind getting *my* hands dirty. We clean it once, then we study at class, then we polish it again—on our knees. Lieutenant said she wanted to eat off that latrine floor, and she could. I can't wait to write Feen and tell her we *all* get to use the flush commodes here. Won't hardly know how to act when I get home.

Not that I'm putting home in the front of my mind.

For inspection, we need to lay open our footlockers and have our gear on display. We have to hide things we ain't supposed to have or we get on the hot seat. Can't nobody stop Annie from bringing in fruit from the kitchen, so we eat it quick before the captain comes. Then we drill and march and drill. The lieutenant says she's gonna put rocks in Phillipa's shoe so she can tell her left from her right, but I have got the hang of it now; I have a corn on my left toe, so I know my left from my right. We got more shots, and they make me sick, but the army don't let nobody die unless they get on sick call first. We all of us have got stiff arms the next day, but we still have got to salute.

Lieutenant Hundley posts a paper on the duty roster that shows us how to lay out our bunks, our shelves, and our clothes rack. Gloria Madden come into our barracks to see Phillipa about some trifle or another, but then she stays, leaning against our bunks like she ain't got nowhere to be. Ever since she got her uniform together, that Gloria thinks she's cute, trying to pass inspection wearing her red nail polish and flipped-up hair.

Gloria leans down to where I am working on my footlocker and points into my box. "What's this?" she say, reaching for a little bit of paper sticking out under my cosmetic box.

"Nothing," I say quick, and poke it back in.

"Oh, nothing is nothing." Gloria tries to make her voice like she's the commanding officer. "What you got in there, Boylen? Love letters? That wouldn't be GI, now would it?"

"Cut that out," Peaches says. "Gloria, can't you find your own footlocker?"

Gloria smiles, but I know she's feeling mean. "It's probably letters from her mama, trying to tell her to get her behind home," she says. I can't help it; I flinch. Everybody knows I haven't got but one letter all the time we've been here.

"Gloria Madden. Don't be like that," Phillipa says, looking ashamed of her friend.

Gloria stretches out her eyes all big, like she's sorry. "Oh, Marey Lee, I *forgot*," she says, her voice all honey sweet. "Now, how come you don't get any letters like everybody else? Didn't you tell anybody where you were stationed? Or don't your people know how to write?"

I hear Peaches suck in a big, loud breath. My neck heats up, and I slam my footlocker hard.

"Calm down, Marey Lee," Peaches says, but I don't need that. I know better than to get into it with Miss High and

Mighty. She's out looking for trouble, and Lieutenant Hundley say there'd better not be none around here unless we want to be get "gigged," what they call being on punishment detail, peeling spuds and scrubbing latrines with toothbrushes the rest of the month.

"My people knows how to read and write just fine, Miss Gloria Madden! My sister, Feen, was top of her class last year. Don't you talk mess about my family, Gloria Madden. There ain't no call for that."

"I was just asking, Marey Lee," Gloria says. She raises up her hands and backs up all sweet, like butter wouldn't melt in her mouth. "I didn't mean any harm. I swear."

I throw open my footlocker again. Lieutenant Hundley won't be happy if that letter from Miss Ida pokes out from my things. I have got to get ready, and I don't have time to pay any mind to Miss Gloria Madden.

But like a low-down snake, Gloria flicks her forked tongue out to say one last poison word.

"Don't worry, Marey. You'll hear from your folks soon. Unless you ran away and didn't tell your mama where you went . . . You know I hear some girls do that? They aren't even twenty and go off without anybody's say-so."

I keep moving my hands in my footlocker, making my uniforms and equipment all nice and straight, but I can feel my face freeze. I can hardly hear over the roaring in my ears. Peaches say something, and then Gloria says, "Goodbye, girls," as sweet as birdsong.

"Marey Lee. Are you all right? Marey?" Peaches looks worried.

I ain't gonna let a little piece of nothing like Gloria Madden rattle me. She does not know a thing about me, nothing. I force my hands not to jitter while my heart slams hard.

"I'm fine," I say, and my voice sounds loud.

I'm scared deep down, in my gut, but inspection is coming. I dust off my knees, straighten my hat, and get on with it.

❈ ❈ ❈

The battalion captain is a big white man with white gloves. He rubs the walls. He looks under the beds. He looks under the mattresses. He hollers that our shoes aren't in a straight line, but I swear he kicks one. For once, Annie's got her hat on straight. Nobody finds no fault with me, except my necktie ain't—isn't—straight. Shoot. Well, you can't win 'em all. When it is over, we draw a deep, deep breath and fall out. It is time for the Saturday parade.

We march out to the field and stand at attention while the brass talks. We stand till our feet are numb, but I can take it, 'cause I hear tell we draw our pay today, after lunch.

I haven't had wages since I spent all I had to get out here. The first time the paymaster doles out my pay, my knees go weak. A private draws twenty-one dollars a month wage, men and women alike. From that they deduct my gear: my uniform skirts, blouses, jackets, and caps—winter-weight wool and summer-weight cotton khaki; my gloves, vest, hat, anklet socks; my winter all-weather utility coat; my neckties, scarves, stockings, exercise togs, tags, comb, towels. Even my slips come out of that. Even my drawers—winter-weight wool, summer-weight cotton khaki—are part of the uniform, and if Lieutenant wants to see 'em, they'd best be on me during inspection. Still, by the time they equip me and I send some money to Mama, I still got more change than I know what to do with. We hear the white girls are buyin' bonds, and some of us buy bonds, too, to support Uncle Sam while puttin' a little by for later on. Me, I'm aimin' to save my money in my own purse. I want a house. A brick house, with a big kitchen and white curtains.

But first, I'm gonna get me some lipstick, and Annie says she dying for a cherry milk shake from the lunch counter in the PX. She says we should request to go to a dance off base, but I don't know about that. I ain't seen many colored boys yet around here, and I know we won't be dancing with no white U.S. Army officers. Peaches say girls dance with girls sometimes. Makes no difference to me, since I can't dance nohow, but Annie Brown is crazy. We got to go somewhere— soon. Annie's been sneaking out to officers' clubs to spy, and she is going to get her behind kicked straight out of here before long. She says cleaning grease traps on punishment detail won't bother her, but I say that girl is out of her cotton-picking mind.

Last thing I buy at the PX is a box of stationery. I sent a letter to Aunt Shirley, care of the Philadelphia post office, and I been waiting three weeks so far, but there is no word. No telling how long it will take for them to find one Shirley Wright in all that big old city, so I been saving up and writing a little to Feen every day on the back of my letter from Miss Ida, till Peach give me some notepaper. Now I got pretty cards of my own, and all I need is a place to send 'em.

I think about Feen so hard it seems to me that she ought to feel it all the way in Pennsylvania.

When Lieutenant Hundley tell us one morning to fall out in our physical-training uniform, I know we've got a long march coming. Sure enough, we march at double-time a mile away to a little house, where we form up lines and wait for our orders.

We have equipment to train with, and we know it from class. At school they train us how to use the gas, and they say it don't make a noise. They say death comes at you like swamp fog if you're not careful. We've already been drilling and drilling to open our packs, put on our masks, and take 'em off quick. When Lieutenant pulls out masks again, somebody gets to groaning about another drill. But then Hundley point us up the hill, says it's time to go to the little house.

It's real quiet in that little brick house way up there on the hill, away from everything else. If Lieutenant Hundley let us stand around and look long enough, we would've seen the whole camp laid out—mess hall, chapel, reviewing stand, barracks, supply. Lieutenant Hundley marches us way up there, then lines us up to instruct us. She looks at us hard.

"Ladies," she shouts, "listen up! You'll go in. You'll put your mask on and pull it tightly against your face. We will open a tear gas canister in the chamber and you will note that it has no effect on your breathing—and you'll know the mask is working. Then, when I give the signal, you will take a deep breath of air and pull the mask off. You will hold that breath of air! The gas will fill your mask. Now listen up! You will put the contaminated mask back on and blow hard into it. This will clear the mask of gas and let you continue breathing. You will not mess up! If you mess up, you will not soon forget it. Fall out."

"You will not soon forget it," she says. I square up my shoulders and find out my breath is coming hard. Hundley gives the order to move, and we march in and do what we are told. I know my drill. I put my mask on quick, and I stand there, looking out those bug eyes. The mask is musty, and my stomach is jumping. Annie Brown behind me says, "Keep me, Jesus," and pulls on hers. The way the lieutenant talked, she's got us all scared.

They say that gas kills you slowly.

We all march up and hang back when we get to the entrance of that little house.

The lieutenant shouts, "Move! Move!" and we pick up the pace and stop dragging our feet. The door clangs shut behind us like eternity.

Once we're inside, I can hear my breathin' in the mask, loud in my ears. My heart is drummin' and bumpin' up in my chest. The gas is as silent as breath. It gets foggy, but I can breathe, and my chest eases up some. We look around at each other, blinking behind our masks, and we are all right. Then Hundley hollers something, and I see folks wrestling off their masks. I take a big old gasp of air, pull off mine, and hold it . . . hold it . . . hold it. . . . My eyes start to burn, and my skin starts to sting. I got to cough. I lose my breath. I try to say something to Lieutenant Hundley, and that gas catch me by the throat with fangs like fire.

I try to hold my breath again, but I can't hold it, and I got to cough 'cause the gas got me choked and is burning my eyes. I can't see, my eyes is pasted closed 'cause they burn like fire, and I burst out coughing, trying to breathe in, and it burns like lye—in my eyes, in my nose, in my mouth. I can't breathe—it's in my eyes. I can't breathe. I can't breathe.

I can't breathe!

Lord Jesus, we gonna die in here.

I can hear somebody hollerin', but I can't scream 'cause I can't breathe and I can't suck up no breath. I remember my mask and try to pull it on, but there ain't no air, and I can't clear it out. My eyes burning up in my head, and I got snot choking me. Somebody hit me, chokin' and coughin', and I go down, hard, on one knee, then stumble up again. Some folks start spitting up like drunks. I can't see nothing, but folks is shoving, trying to find the doors. I slip to my knees, and someone kicks me, and I know I'm gonna die in here. I can't get my breath, and that burning is on my skin, and my ears are ringing. Next thing I know, somebody is dragging me outside.

I pull off that mask and cough and cough and cough, rolling around in the dirt, snot smearing all over my face. Girls is cryin' and folks is vomiting up all over the place. Lieutenant Hundley is hollerin' at us, "Face the wind! Don't touch your eyes. It is just tear gas. It is just tear gas, you big babies! I said *take a breath and blow it out!*"

I cry worse than Feen cried in the dark. For the first time since I left home, I cry like my heart is broke for Mama, for Feen, for Bay Slough. I ain't going back in that little house and can't nothing make me, not Captain Ferguson, not nobody. Lieutenant Hundley is trying to kill us. Somebody vomits on my shoes, and I don't got nothing to wipe them clean with, but I don't care. I am sick and shaking and howling with my mouth wide open.

I cry till my eyes can open. My throat is all swollen up, and I can't hardly talk. When we can finally see, we got to wipe out our masks. Everybody use the same rag and scrub hard, but we can't see what we are wiping away. Gas has no color.

Hundley comes around to see if we are all drinking water, but I don't care. I don't want nothing but to go home.

"Get up, Marey," Dovey croaks at me. Her voice sounds like her throat pipe's been scrubbed with steel wool. "Hundley says we got to do the drill again."

I can't. I can't. *I can't.*

"Come on, Boylen," Dovey croaks again. "Get up, girl."

Before I can say nothing, I hear Gloria Madden squalling like a baby. "I can't! I can't do it! I'm not going back in there." I wipe my eyes, looking around. High and Mighty Madden bawls just like a motherless calf. Now, I am not no braver, but won't nobody catch me hollering about it like that. This can't be no worse than the time Mama packed my arm with salt that one time I tore myself against a barbed wire fence. This can't be worse than the time Mama popped my shoulder back. I been hurt before. I been scared before.

"You can't make me!" I hear Gloria scream and cry some more.

That is enough to get me right up on my feet. I might be so scared I can't even run, but I put my hand to the plow, and I don't aim to look back. My swollen, watery eyes find Dovey's.

"Let's go," I say. She puts her arm around me and leads the way.

Gas. Gas! Looks like fog, but it kills you dead. For the first time, I wonder 'bout those soldiers we studied back in school. They must have been scared to death out there in France.

"Fall in!" Lieutenant Hundley holler, and our platoon get into place. Then Lieutenant say, "All right, ladies. Let's do it again!" and we do. We march in there with our legs shaking, and I can hear Annie praying behind me. Underneath my mask my lips move as I do the same.

The Lord is my shepherd; I shall not want.

"Gas!" Hundley holler, and we see that fog coming till we can't hardly see.

"Masks!" Hundley holler louder, and I fight myself and make myself take it off. I stop my sobbing and drag in a breath and hold it . . . hold it . . . hold it. . . . My head is getting light. I can feel my heart beating.

Yea, though I walk through the valley of the shadow of death, I will fear no evil. . . .

"Masks on!"

My fingers are fumbling. I get that mask sealed, but I blow too soon. I got no more air, but I keep that mask on my face and blow even though I got no air. Then I take in a big breath and start coughing. It is not so bad this time. The air is still stinging my eyes and nose, and I can't see, but it is not as bad as last time. Pretty soon somebody will open the door.

Surely goodness and mercy shall follow me all the days of my life. . . .

"Fall out! Wipe your masks and fall in! We are going to do it again!" Lieutenant Hundley hollers out as she open the door. With our legs shaking, we march out.

Much later, we march half-time back to camp. My eyes are swollen, my nose is snotting, my throat is sore, and I still got vomit on my shoes, but I went through my gas drill over and over and over, and I made it. When I pass her on my way to barracks, Hundley say, "Well done, Private," and gives me a nod. I can barely open my eyes, but I know she means it.

We got to do it again tomorrow.

But I am not scared. I am not scared of nothin' now. I got blisters on my heels, my hands is cut up, my shoulders are sore from marching with a pack, and I can't never get enough sleep, but I wouldn't trade nothin' for this. Not a thing.

Didn't nobody ever tell me I was this tough. Didn't nobody ever tell me no girl could work this hard, and nobody never said that work this hard could give you pride. My nails might not be nice enough for polite folk, and my face might not be clean, but I earned my place in this man's army. I earned it.

And ain't *nobody* gonna make Marey Lee Boylen go home.

13.

then

We finished up with basic and were awarded our first leave. Annie hears the news and grabs me and screams.

"Third Platoon is steppin' out on the town," she sings. I put on my garrison cap with a tilt, and I step out with the others in our off-duty summer uniform, holding my clutch purse and wearing my white gloves.

After a bumpy, jumpy ride on the trolley, we find a colored soda fountain, and Annie finally has herself a milk shake. When we find a dance joint, it's just colored Women's Army Corps there, and we're all from Third Platoon. Do we dance anyway? Do we ever! Somebody puts on some Cab Calloway, and everybody get to actin' crazy then. Annie say it ain't—isn't—so much fun without some handsome boys to walk us home. Still, it is nice to watch Peaches and them cut loose out there on the dance floor.

"Marey Lee, get out here!" Peaches hollers to me, holding up her arms and doing some fast steps to the music.

"I can't dance," I say, crossing my arms. "You look real good, though."

"Oh, go on." Annie plants her hands on my back and gives me a shove. "Girl, if this music doesn't make you want to move, I don't know what's wrong with you!"

"But I don't know how!" I whine, and try to sit back down.

"Come here." Peaches drags me by the hand. "Look. Just hold my hands and do the opposite of what I do, all right? Listen to the music. That beat goes one-two-three-four, right? So just step from one side to the other, left-right-left, one." As she says "one," she pauses on her right foot. "Now right-left-right, one," she says, and pauses on the left.

I try to copy her.

"No, just little steps, Marey Lee. Now try again."

Clumsy and ashamed of it, I follow her movements, but it's hard to be embarrassed for too long with everyone else stepping and shimmying around me and the music on nice and loud. Next to me, Annie does the same thing I'm doing, but she throws her hips into it and gets a real shuffle going on. I imagine what this dance might look like if we weren't in our uniform skirts. Boy, we could really twirl!

I get so good at my simple step I try to throw in a twist, too, but I do it too hard and almost land on my behind. Peaches just about falls on hers, laughing.

"Not so hard," she giggles. "Take it easy, hepcat!"

We have so much fun that Annie says she almost didn't miss walking home with some boy. I can hardly stop boogying all the way home, but Peach says I'd better stop.

"Girl, you're going to be beat in the morning!"

I am, but I just don't care.

❊ ❊ ❊

The paymaster has been helping me send money home, but I still ain't heard nothing from Mama. Sometimes, after lights out at 2100, I lay down still and think about that.

I wish I knew what lies Toby done told Mama about me. I got a feeling that once Feen left for Philadelphia, Mama didn't want to be nobody's mother anymore. Maybe the next man that comes along she'll tell she don't have kids, and if she don't let Feen come home, it will seem like it's true.

I wish Daddy hadn't died and left us. I am afraid Mama wishes she hadn't had Feen and me at all. She could be happy with her man Mr. Toby if it weren't for Feen and me.

I can't think about that too long. If I start cryin' about home, I might not stop.

❊ ❊ ❊

We still don't have all of our uniforms yet, but finally, they send Third Platoon down to the warehouse for a clothing fit. Don't nothing fit nobody—anybody—quite right. Skirts that fit across Peaches's broad behind are too big for her tiny waist. I don't have hips to speak of, so most things fit my hips just cut into my waist. Poor Dovey's got such long arms that her jackets have to be taken out, and it's getting too hot to wear her winter jacket anymore. Girdles are regulation, but mine bunches up when I sit. We all are a sorry sight and have a lot of work to do with the seam-stress to get things right.

At least our summer fatigues fit. There just isn't too much wrong you can do with seersucker, and the little hats we wear with them are not too bad. As usual, Annie has to wear hers tipped back on her head so she can be cute.

All we hear about for weeks is Play Day. They say maybe Mrs. Roosevelt's gonna come out to see all of us WACs, but I doubt it. Mrs. Roosevelt's busy with them poor kids with polio, and anyway, colored girls in the mid-dle of nowhere know better than to think the wife of the president of the United States is gonna come see them. Somebody's always startin' some kind of rumor around here. These army folks gossip worse than Sister Dials!

Every Saturday, we got inspection, and every week, some new brass comes in on the train. We got folks from D.C. tryin' to look at the Women's Army, and everybody, coloreds and whites, got to march, drill, and post the col-ors for 'em. Some of them generals stare at us like they've never seen colored girls before. Some of them don't look at us at all. Sometimes they got whole families at the re-viewing stand—old generals and their wives, grandkids, the works—and the USO, the United Service Organization, which brings recreation for troop morale, gives dinner dances for the brass. They get up to some big doings, too, and there ain't nothing like doing KP for a fancy dinner.

It takes hours. We got to chop vegetables, peel eggs, and make ninety-nine platters of this and that. (Only the fancy dinners get real eggs—we got powdered ones for our breakfast most of the time.) Somebody got a song about it, too:

> Over sinks, over pails
> With the sergeant on our tails
> All the KPs are scrubbing away.
> Shining pots, shining pans,
> Cleaning out the garbage cans
> All the KPs are scrubbing away.

We end up with greasy skillets, pots, and pans that look worse than Young's on a Saturday night. The army don't waste a thing, either, so we got to be draining grease, cutting up fat, and chopping up those vegetables mighty fine. We'll be on our feet all day with it, a full eight *hours*, and after all that, we don't want to do nothing but fall and fall down out when we get some "rest and recreation" time.

Saturday afternoon, just after we get off, Lieutenant Hundley come by, her face lookin' hard. She holler out, like we doing drill, "Peaches Carter!"

"Ma'am!" Peaches says. Peach has been workin' in one of the offices 'cause she went to commercial high school and took up shorthand typing. She says she doesn't want to be no army grunt, but Lieutenant Hundley has always got another job for her.

"Carter, front and center," she say. "We had a request for you."

"A request, ma'am?" Peaches put her hands on her hips.

Our company just got showered, and Peach is in her WAC-issue maroon bathrobe, getting ready to paint her toenails. "I'm off duty, ma'am."

"I am aware of that, Carter," Lieutenant says, and she act like her face got frozen. Peaches straighten up fast. "Yes, ma'am," she say. Hundley does not play around when she's got that look.

"Captain Jennings is in need of a sitter for General Craig's twins tonight. Their regular housekeeper is ill. He knows your work and considers you conscientious and feels you would like to earn the pocket money."

Peaches looks like her jaw just broke. Her mouth hangs open, and every girl in our company looks like she's just been slapped. Now we know why Hundley looks like she's about to spit. Nobody in their right mind is gonna ask any of the white girls to watch after some general's babies after eight hours on their feet, but they're after the colored girls all the time to fetch and carry and "help out."

"Get a load of that," Annie Brown mutters under her breath. I shake my head. Peaches works hard in that kitchen, harder than anybody, and since she doesn't like to cook nohow, she's got to try twice as hard. She says Cook hollered at her all day and she about cut her fingers off, with all the chopping she did. She's tired like we all are.

Peaches lets out her breath like a popped tire. She looks like someone kicked her in the stomach. Her shoulders slump, and she puts down her polish and picks up her shoes.

"I'll go, Lieutenant Hundley," I say. I can't stand Peaches's broken-down look.

Peaches cuts her eyes at me, and I ignore her. "Peaches hurt herself doing KP. I'll go see to those twins."

Hundley looks at me like she's trying to drill nails in my head. "They are babies, Boylen. Children. Do you know anything about children?"

"Yes, ma'am. I helped to raise my sister. I will take good care of them. Ma'am."

"Boylen . . ."

"I like children, Lieutenant Hundley," I say, standing tall, daring her to shut my mouth for speaking up. "Peach is whipped; we all see that. I'll go."

Peaches mutters, "They asked for me, Boylen," but we both know it don't make no never mind who goes to see to those twins. The brass aren't be too picky when they're asking for a colored girl to work in the house.

"I got it, Peaches," is all I say.

Hundley stares at me for a moment, then looks around the barracks. We all stand there in complete silence. There is something in her face that says she's got a lot to say, but she doesn't say it to us. I roll my stockings up over my knees and lace up my shoes while she watches me. Annie hands me my jacket.

"This isn't right," Lieutenant Hundley says finally, and her voice is quiet. "You girls . . . You women are in the army. Someone will hear about this. . . ." Hundley looks at the floor, clears her throat. She straightens her shoulders and nods to me. "Let's go, Boylen."

Peaches is about to say something. She grab on to my

hand before I go out the door, but she doesn't say it. Instead, she looks at me; looks at me, then lets me go. I think about the look on her face all the way out the door, to the jeep that takes me to town.

✳ ✳ ✳

They've got trees in this town, tall, tall trees like they've been there forever. The yards have got those nice white fences, and they've got flowers behind those fences, fat pink roses and big white daisies that the colored boy keep weeded and nice after he cuts the grass. Some of these houses have got those gold stars in the windows on that red, white, and blue background. They've got someone in the service at these houses.

These houses look like my house. Mine and Feen's. That redbrick house we're gonna have, someday, looks just like this.

There's colored folk everywhere, walking home now that day's done, walking home from the big houses where they work all day while the white ladies work in the USO, making sure the white officers got someone to give them parties. I go in the back door of one of those houses, a big brick house with white trim, a wide sitting porch wrapped around it, and long white drapes in the window.

I think of the look on Peaches's face when I walk into that place, past the kitchen with that fine electric icebox, down the hall with the fine paper on the walls and those fine paintings. I think of that look when I see the nursery with the big rocking horse, and the electric lights above the diaper table, and those big jars of pins and cotton balls, and stacks of pure bleached cotton diapers, all as sanitary and neat as a Woolworth's counter. I think of that look as I see the little babies lying there, like little pink puppies all curled up. They are just babies, and they sure don't owe the world no explanation. But I look down at them for a long, long time.

"Keep prices down," they tell us. "Use it up, wear it out, make it do, or do without," is what all those war posters say, but when I look at the newness all over this house, I know that only some of us have to make do. Our soldiers are fighting to make the world better for these babies. WACs are workin' to free a man to fight for freedom. But sometimes it seems like these babies, helpless as they are, is more free than I am. When are Peaches and me gonna be as free as them?

14.

∩ O W

It's only an hour after our last break, but when Mare pulls off
the interstate in search of a gas station, I'm just as glad for another stop and a break from the story. I get out of the car and
stretch, yawning as Mare heads briskly for the restroom.

"You girls, go and look around in the store. See if you can
find a keepsake," my grandmother calls over her shoulder.

"You don't need your lighter to go to the restroom," Tali
calls after her pointedly. I shrug and yawn again as Tali
quickly digs into her bag for her headset.

Mare decided that we should buy something from every
single place we stop, so we have one of those little bobbing
birds from the hotel where we stayed last night, a cornhusk
doll from Bartlett's Fruit Stand, where we stopped an hour
ago and bought plums, and this gas station has a little gift
shop, too. I can't see why we need to look at another piece
of junk just because we need to use the bathrooms, but Mare
seems to have an insatiable need to shop.

Before I can pry my reluctant body away from the car, my
phone rings.

"Hi, honey! Haven't heard from you girls for a while, so I wanted to check in. I got your postcard." Mom's voice on my cell sounds tinny and too cheerful. "Where are you?"

"We're at a gas station. Everything's fine." I know better than to say anything different. "I tried calling you this morning, but I couldn't get reception." It's kind of a lie—I did open my phone and think about calling my mother, but it was too early to make that kind of effort.

"So, are you having fun?" my mother presses. "And is Mare . . . Is everything going all right?"

"Mare's fine," I repeat, raising my voice over the crackle of static. "We're just stopping at a gas station for a little, um . . . to get some snacks."

I don't want to worry my mother, but Mare's stomach hasn't been right since last night. She says it's nothing, and she took the keys from Tali this morning as usual, but she's been really quiet. I'm afraid she doesn't feel well enough to finish her story.

"Tell your mama you're at a gas station because her mother-in-law ate a bag of plums for breakfast and nothing else," Mare says loudly, emerging from the bathroom in a cloud of perfume and breath spray. "Tell the truth and shame the devil, Octavia."

Tali quickly pulls out her earphones. "Nobody wants to know *that* kind of truth," she objects. "'Tavia, ask Mom if I got a catalog in the mail from Cal-Berkeley yet. And tell her not to throw away my magazines!"

I hold out the phone. "Did you want to maybe talk to her instead of screaming in my ear?"

Tali complains about her a lot, but she and Mom are just alike. They even laugh alike, and listening to Tali while she tells our mother about our day so far makes me miss her a little. Not that I'm homesick or anything like that; it's just that I wish Mom were here. If nothing else, she'd at least be kind of an ally . . . someone on my side. Now that Mare and Tali aren't spending as much time on each other's nerves, they're ganging up and getting on mine. I feel kind of outnumbered.

The more time we spend with Mare, the more ways I see how Tali and Mare are alike, too. They both get into their little moods, they both like confrontation, and they both like to have the last word. Dad's like that, too, and I always thought Tali got her attitude from him.

Now I find that Tali's like Mom, Dad, *and* Mare.

I can't figure out how I got born into this family.

I think Mare likes Tali better than me, and it's not fair. It's not my fault I'm not like anyone else in this family. And shouldn't Mare understand? She wasn't like her mother or her sister.

Sometimes I feel so different from Tali it feels like I was adopted.

And sometimes I wish I really were.

"Okay, Mom," Tali says. "Right. Bye."

"Wait!" I shriek as she hangs up. "Tali! I wasn't done."

"Sorry." Tali hands me the phone, unconcerned. "Mom's at work, you know."

"Well, she called on *my* phone," I snap, furious.

"You're the one who gave it to me!" Tali exclaims. "What's your problem?"

"Nothing. Never mind." I slam the door and stalk across the parking lot toward the shop.

"Find a keepsake," Mare says. Keepsake, nothing. I don't want to remember any of this.

Last night while Tali was driving, Mare mentioned to her that she would have let me drive last night.

Tali said, "Why? She doesn't even have her permit yet. She doesn't even *want* her permit."

My sister thinks she knows everything, but as usual, she's wrong.

I want my permit. I want to stand in line, fill out the papers, walk up to that high counter, and take the test, filling in the squares with the right letter of the multiple choice.

What Tali doesn't know is that I already took my permit test. And flunked. Big-time.

I looked at the paper and those lines of answers. Which one was right? Which one was half right? There were too many ways to choose, and I just . . . froze. I couldn't mark anything. Mom waited and waited for me, and when the DMV was ready to close, I crumpled up my paper and walked away.

The lady was really nice. She said I could come back and try again. I was crying too hard to answer.

I made Mom promise not to tell Tali. Or Dad. Or *anyone*.

Everyone knows that only freshmen ride the bus. It's bad enough that Tali might get a car. If I can't even get my permit, she'll think I'm an even bigger loser than she already does.

The bell jingling in the doorway of the gift shop isn't the only thing ringing. There are something like seven different kinds of wind chimes for sale, all cheap aluminum and clattering pottery. The lady behind the counter looks up as I walk in and frowns as Tali comes in behind me.

"What can I do for you girls?" she asks suspiciously.

Tali, hands in her pockets, gives the saleslady a bored look behind her sunglasses. "Do you have visors?"

"That's your keepsake?"

Tali rolls her eyes. "Might as well be," she answers me. "It's not like I want anything else from here."

The woman frowns, obviously offended. "I've got caps, not visors. Top shelf in the back on the left."

Tali shrugs and moves away from the counter. I wander along behind her.

I'd say this gas station in Yuma, Arizona, was a tourist trap, except there's nothing here any tourist in her right mind would want. I mean, fake turquoise on leather key chains, little kachina dolls, and all that stuff would be fine, except most of it even *says* it's made in China.

I hear the little bell on the door jingle again, and the air sets all the wind chimes clattering.

"Tali. Can I have the keys?" Mare's voice is too loud for the tiny air-conditioned trailer where we're browsing.

"Yeah, all right." Tali slouches from around a corner and hands them over, then sniffs. "Did you have a nice smoke?"

"Girl, don't you start with me," Mare warns her.

"Actually, you're doing pretty good." Tali grins. "I'll bet

I can get you to quit by the time we get back home. You'll live longer, Mare. You'll thank me."

Mare huffs and turns to riffle through the postcards at the front of the store while Tali twirls the sunglasses display next to her.

"Have you girls sent your mama another postcard?"

"We've only been gone for three days!"

"Folks should write more letters. Pick out something anyway," Mare insists.

"Octavia," Tali bleats. "Come help."

I put down an orange Somebody in Yuma, AZ, Loves Me T-shirt and shuffle up to the front of the store.

"Oh, look at that one. That's cute," Tali says, waving a postcard with a smiling sun under Mare's nose. "I'm sending this to Suzanne."

"Your girls look so much alike," the saleslady says, beaming at Mare. "Are these your daughters?"

I roll my eyes. Tali is tall, and I am short. Tali's hair is wild and dyed and cool. Mine is, at the moment, shoved into a frizzy ponytail. This saleslady really wants us to buy something.

"Mare, I'm bored," I interrupt. "I'm going back to the car."

"Give me your keepsake first," Mare says.

I point to a random postcard. "That one."

"Yuma's Tiny Church?" Tali gives me a look. "Okay, that's random even for you."

I look at the postcard I pointed to and see a picture of, as she said, a tiny church. Flipping over the stiff rectangle, I read that the church is only seven feet by twelve feet and is built "just north of the Swinging Bridge to Nowhere."

I don't want anything to be funny right now, but this is. My smile stretches across my face and eases the tightness I've been feeling around my chest. The Swinging Bridge to Nowhere. It totally sounds like our trip.

"I want two of these," I tell Mare, grinning.

"That's a nice church," she says absently. "Did you want to drive out that direction?"

"No, thanks. I think we're close enough to the Bridge to Nowhere already." Smirking, I head back toward the car.

Greetings from the Swinging Bridge to Nowhere!

We're barely out of Cali, and you'll be really happy to know
that Mare and Tali are getting along like a house on fire.
Without any water. Kidding! The two of them are A LOT alike.
Tali's even starting to drive like Mare!!! If I make it home
alive, I'm never getting in a car with either of them ever again.
EVER!!! 😦

We got plums from a fruit stand today. Mare said one time in
the army she ate about five pounds of raspberries she and her
friends got from a farm. Mare hadn't had them before. You
don't want to know how that story ends. . . . I love that back
then Mare did even dumber things than Tali and me!!!

♥ Octavia

Mom
7529 Poppy Way
Pleasant Hill, CA 94523

15.

then

It is nothing but time passing, but I can't hardly remember what Bay Slough looks like. I have been here at the training center in Fort Des Moines for eight months, and it's up at the reveille horn, then listen for the whistle, fall in, march, fall out, work, mess hall, lights-out, taps. My feet get tired of these boots, which we got to wear all day now that we marching in the mud, but I am used to them. We have got physical training every day, even if the weather is bad, and I don't get worn out running no more. "We are making soldiers out of you civilians!" Hundley hollers at us like she is possessed. She runs us in close order drill, and rumor is going around about something big they are making us train so hard for, but nobody knows what for sure.

There's a snap in the air now that it's November, and we wake up in the dark, and we shower in the dark; it is dark at breakfast and dark at dinner. The army keeps us running all day long! No day with Miss Ida ever wore me out like this.

Before lights-out, most of us head for the shower 'cause

it's never enough time to get all ready in the morning. It tickles me to remember the first time we got to the showers. We all about had a fit 'cause there isn't nothing but showerheads, all six in a row, and no curtains, no walls for privacy. There ain't—I mean, isn't—no privacy in the army, they tell us, so we go in and shower and keep our eyes on the floor. Now we all so tired don't nobody—nobody cares anymore. You should hear the songs we sing in there, too!

The uniforms they give us
They say are mighty fine
But I need Lana Turner
To fill the front of mine.
Oh, I don't want no more of army life.
Gee, Mom, I wanna go home.

I don't want to go home, though, not me. Last thing before I go to sleep, I close my eyes and think hard of Feen. I still say my prayers, but Mama always say the Lord doesn't have no use for girls who can't act right. Maybe I am one of those girls. Maybe I am uppity to have left Mama and Bay Slough. Maybe I won't ever have no home. Sometimes I still don't know if I did right.

It has been raining for ten days straight, and we spend most times wet and cold. The army issues us all long raincoats, but when we have to stand out till they call roll, all those things do is leak. Captain say wear a bath towel up under the collar so at least we don't get wet all down our backs. That helps some. We march double-time to get to class and to mess, but we can't run too hard. We still have to stop and salute. Isn't that some kind of crazy? We are going to catch our death standing around like fools in the rain, but officers stand there until they get their "courtesies," and God help you and your demerits if they don't get them fast enough. Annie broke down and cried this morning 'cause she can't stand to get up out of bed and get rained on and have to salute and salute all over again. We have all been gigged pretty regularly since the rain began.

It is so cold I can hardly stand it. It didn't ever get cold like this in Bay Slough, and after lunch we stand in formation doing mail call, shivering so hard we can hardly hear.

"Boylen!"

"Ma'am!" My ears suddenly get clear.

"Letter, Boylen!"

All around me, everybody is looking. I see Gloria Madden rear back like somebody just slapped her, she is so surprised. I turn and give her a *look*.

Ruby grabs my hand and squeezes it. She's been feeling awful sorry since she gets something from her sisters, her cousins, her mama, *and* her Sunday school class almost every week.

"Thank you, ma'am," I say when Lieutenant Hundley hands me a letter from . . . Feen!

I can't keep my teeth from chattering, even though I have what feels like fire in my stomach.

When we are dismissed, I run back to my bunk. My hands are shaking as I open the envelope.

November 12, 1944

My dear sister, Marey Lee,

I found out from Sister Dials where the Women's Army Corps is stationed. I hope you get this letter.

Marey Lee, I sorely miss you, though I like it just fine in Philadelphia. I am at the top of my class and best friends with a girl named Francine Simpson. She calls me Josey.

We are collecting for the March of Dimes to end polio and to buy a P-38 named for our school. The school is selling war bonds and collecting scrap for nickels and dimes.

Everything is lively up here in the city. There are big buildings, and to get our stamps, we line up on the walk downtown. There is a butcher shop and a candy store right down our block, and it's just a street over to get milk. Aunt Shirley makes a fuss over who I walk with 'cause some of the girls don't have manners like I do. Aunt Shirley fusses a lot.

Have you seen Miss Beatrice Payne in the army? Aunt Shirley says it isn't decent for a girl to be working with all those men. She says to watch out for certain kinds of mannish girls up there 'cause they've got unnatural desires.

Aunt Shirley says the army has you girls there to keep the men happy. I know you are

not up to THAT, Marey Lee. Anyway,
Mama won't let you come home if you get
pregnant. And I know you're coming home to
get me! If you did get pregnant, you know I'd
help you. We could live in a house by
ourselves, just us.

Sister Dials wrote to say that Mama is
keeping company with a man again. I am glad
you aren't there.

Your loving sister,
Josephine Louise Boylen

I can't hardly stop laughing to start crying or start crying 'cause I'm smiling so hard. I can't hardly wait to run to mess after that. Peaches and Annie and Ruby look at me with sharp eyes when I sit down, stare at my red eyes and my swollen-up nose. My hands are still shaking when I pick up my fork, but that can't stop my smile.

Since I was small, Mama always said, "Watch out for your sister," and I put myself between Feen and the rest of the world to keep her safe. I put my plans on hold to watch over her. I got lost when Mama sent Feen to Philadelphia, but now everything feels all right.

I feel like Sister Dials always says she feels at church, like the glory has come down on my soul. My shoulders feel like something has just slipped down, and off, and fallen on the ground. I want to stand up and shout. It feels like forgiveness. It feels good.

I stop my foolishness, though, when I think about that girl talking about me and a *baby*. The only men around here I see are the ones hollering at us to hurry up and march, and Staff Sergeant Hill's surely not a man. And I have a thing or two to say to Auntie Shirley about filling Feen's head with talk about mannish girls. Aunt Shirley had best look to her own business and leave mine and the U.S. Army's alone.

I'm relieved, the next day, that I *got* Feen's letter 'cause next morning we fall in and Lieutenant Hundley gives us the order to pack up to move out! All the gossip about going to move somewhere is true—Captain Ferguson's got our orders. Suddenly all those hush-hush rumors get downright loud. We pack up our gear, and they tell us we better take everything and ship the rest home. I don't have much civilian stuff, so I send on Mama's coat, write Feen a quick note that I got her letter and I'll tell her more when we get where we're going, and then get on with it.

I've got fifty pounds of gear on my back when we climb up into the troop carrier. We bump and jounce over the roads to town, then get on the train.

Peaches marches by with her head up high, but she got her a look on her face.

"What have you heard?" I ask Peaches when we get on the colored car. The lieutenant makes us sit in groups, by squadron. Miss Communications Department Carter has to pass me and sit in the back.

"We're going to Paris, France," she hisses at me, and keeps stepping.

"What'd she say?" Annie wants to know. "St. Louis?"

I don't know nothing about no Paris, France. Annie say they talk English there, but I got a ball of nerves in my gut. We're going over where them Germans be shooting their gas. We're supposed to "free a man" to go to the front. What happens if he doesn't want to go, neither?

What happens if I forget how to use my mask? If I get that gas in my lungs, it will kill me dead. I hear about folk who didn't duck fast enough when those grenades came in and got their hands and arms and legs blown clean off. I can't go to France. I can't go where they're throwing them grenades. I can't go and leave Feen. I can't. I can't.

"Marey Lee? You feeling all right?" Annie looks my way.

I sit down in my seat and breathe real deep, trying not to let her see me sweat.

"I'm all right," I say. Isn't anything a body can do now but wait.

❋ ❋ ❋

After all them nerves and my stomach twisting like I ate some bad shrimp, I shoulda known Peaches Carter didn't know no kind of nothing. We shipped out as far as Fort Oglethorpe, Georgia!

Things are different at Fort Oglethorpe's Extended Field Service Training Center. For one thing, we know a little something when we get here—that we are in for some "training," for "extended field service." We going overseas for sure now.

Some folks are not happy about that. Miss Gloria Madden, for one. She was all set up to do specialist training back at Fort Des Moines. She thinks she wants to be some kind of officer. As for me, I am glad there is no chance of that just yet!

We march off that passenger car in Chattanooga, and they load us up onto more trucks—but this time, we got seats and a tarp over our heads. When we finally get out to the post, they march us over to supply and give us *more* gear. Now we've got helmets—like green metal slop buckets with straps—and wool helmet liners. They tell us to sign for snow jackets and liners Annie says folks use when they ski. We sign out wool and twill trousers, wool gloves, high-top lace-up brown shoes, and shoulder bags. We have to wear some of that just to march it back to our new barracks, and it is heavy and warm. We are going someplace pure cold, as I see it.

The barracks here look like somebody just threw them up with a few nails, just little shanties with no niceties. The walls are raw timber, and there's no paint anywhere. Everything smells like pine, and little beads of pitch leak out of the walls, making everything tacky. There are gaps under the doors.

"How are we supposed to keep our uniforms looking good?" Dovey rants, pointing to the gap. "How're we supposed to keep that pine tar off of everything, and the *dust?*"

We complain and mutter, but barracks aren't the worst thing we see as we fall back in and march through our new digs. As we take in Fort Oglethorpe, we are shocked that it is right-out, loud-and-clear *segregated.*

In little old no-'count Bay Slough, we don't bother with

segregation. We don't have Whites Only signs; Bay Slough barely is big enough for one stoplight and a drinking fountain outside the courthouse, not to mention two. Nobody needs signs to say who can be where or do what. We all just know, and what we don't know, we get told right quick by our mamas, our aunties, the church folk, or just someone passing on the side of the road.

At Fort Des Moines, we were segregated, sure, but not like this. At Fort Oglethorpe, there are signs—Colored Drinking Fountain and White Drinking Fountain; Colored Latrine and White Latrine. Annie and Phillipa march ahead of me in the line, and I see them stiffen right up. Those signs make me feel unwelcome, but we don't have much time to think about it.

Other than the signs, there ain't—isn't—much difference between Fort Des Moines and Fort Oglethorpe except size. We still have classes just like at Fort Des Moines, and our training continues with Staff Sergeant Hill and a man this time, a Staff Sergeant Bothwell, who run us all over the place. In school, they give us pictures to look at so we can identify types of ships and types of enemy aircraft we might see in the sky. We look at guns of all kinds and have to memorize what kinds they are by sight. They show us maps of the whole world, and we look and see where Europe is, just a little bitty bit of land way over there across the Atlantic Ocean.

The first time I looked on the map, I couldn't hardly tell what it was way out there. Europe didn't look like much, but that evil Hitler wants to take it anyway. Hitler also wants Russia, and that's a big old country, bigger than the States, for sure. Staff Sergeant Bothwell says if we don't stop him now, Hitler might just bring those Nazis this way.

Not if the Women's Army Corps has anything to say about it!

Our second week, they teach us the "protocol" in case we get captured. That is a terrifying thought, but they tell us that the Germans know about the Geneva Convention, and they won't kill us. They tell us what we can say—our name, rank, and serial number—and what we can't say—nothing else. We won't tell those Nazis nothing, but mostly 'cause we don't know nothing *to* tell them.

As the days go on, we run through obstacle courses, climb over huge logs and up walls, and even wriggle around on our stomachs in the dirt under barbed wire. Our drills have something new: guns. The first time we ran our drills with our packs on our backs and I heard those guns go off above my head, I would like to have died. Me and just about every girl in our platoon started hollering and screaming as loud as she could. Ruby screamed, but she kept moving. She says her mama taught her to shoot back home. I screamed, but for a while, couldn't nobody make me do nothing but put my hands over my head.

Toby. Mama. That night. It is all I could think of.

I didn't do it anymore after the first time, but it makes me want to die every single time they pop those guns off over our heads. There is smoke and bright flashes, and it's like we are out running in the fires of hell. It works my nerves to hear all that noise, but Staff Sergeant Hill says a battle would be much, much worse, so we carry on, and we don't let her hear us complain. I get used to filth and dust and dirt, sweat and grime and splinters, and I do myself proud, keeping my mouth closed when one of them smoke bombs goes off next to me. Can't nothing scare me. I got muscles in my arms and legs now something fierce.

When Staff Sergeant Bothwell takes us out on long marches, he gives the order, "Cover!" and we got to fall in ditches, then hop out again quick when he give the signal and form up again at a run. Gloria Madden was in the same ditch as me and Dovey one morning, and she ducked her head down, whispering, "You girls can't hide here. We're too full." Dovey and me didn't pay her no mind. There were five of us in there, and we fit just fine. Miss Gloria Madden with her little airs and graces doesn't bother me none at all. Only thing that set me back one time was there was a rat in one of those ditches. Dovey and me both jumped up screaming that time. Lord Jesus, don't make me lie down in the dirt with no rats on me.

One morning out to the training field, they say we're going to learn to climb ropes.

"Ropes?" Ruby looks at the tangled-up snarl, all confused. "This isn't rope like at school, Sarge. I could climb ropes at school. What kind of ropes are these?"

"Actually"—Staff Sergeant Hill pushes the edge nearest her with her foot—"this is a cargo net. If ever you are required to get aboard ship where there is no dock, you must be able to board a ship by way of the cargo net. Now climb, ladies. Go!"

It is a hard drill. First we climb the rope net, then we climb a rope with knots in it. I can hardly stand the burning pain in my arms. We hang there until we either fall or make it to the top. Lieutenant Hundley says we have *lots* of time to practice this one because some of us will be doing it every day.

She smiles when she say that.

We come away from ropes drill every day so tired that it is all we can do to keep up doing the double-time Lieutenant Hundley has us marching back to barracks. When she dismisses us, we break and run for the drinking fountains. We line up behind each other, hot and tired and ready to head to the mess hall for supper.

"I hear we got surprise drill," Charline Spencer say, leaning against the girl in front of her. "Ina White heard it from Doris, who heard it from the supply sergeant. They're gearing up to take us on a night run."

We all groan. I'm so beat I can't see how I'm going to make it. Gloria Madden is in front of me, taking her time drinking from the fountain. "Leave some for the rest of us," somebody say, and everybody laughs.

I'm so tired I want to lie down. And then I realize we are lined up behind Gloria, and the whites-only fountain is free. Didn't anybody even think to use it.

Would it really change something if I stepped over to

take a drink? Does it taste better? I chew my lip and look over my shoulder at the girls behind me. I take a breath. . . .

I move fast, before anyone can say a word. I bend and suck down sweet water, splashing cool wetness across my cheeks and over my teeth and tongue. I am hot and thirsty, and water when I'm thirsty is *good*. I don't care what the sign above it says. As soon as I have my drink, I stand up and move aside, looking at the others.

A few girls behind me cluster over to the fountain. Some of them are still skittish and take a look behind them before they bend to drink. Others wait, all nerves, for Gloria to finish, staying safely in the colored line. One of those girls is Ruby, and I wave to her as I pass.

"Make sure to get to bed early for the night drill, huh?"

Ruby looks away from me.

"Hey, girl." I pause my steps and look at her closely. "What's the matter?"

"I can't do it, Marey," Ruby says, her voice low. "When I was home, I saw a girl get beat down bloody for less than using the wrong fountain. I just *can't*."

"I only did it 'cause I was thirsty," I tell her. "Can't anybody call me an anti-segregationist or anything like that. You don't have to do it, Ruby."

Ruby looks down at her boots. "I'm just not brave like y'all are," she mumbles.

"You are brave *just* fine," I tell her, and stand with her in the colored line until she gets her drink.

We walk to mess together in gut-tight silence. Ruby

Bowie is in my team, in my squad. I am downright ashamed that Ruby feels like she is less than me. I hate that these folks put up signs to remind us to keep our place. Whites *only*. Like they the only ones in the U.S. of A.

Lieutenant Hundley told us that we are to be sure not to do anything to cause comment, and already I am breaking the rules because they are wrong. And they are wrong, I know that. But Ruby being scared is wrong, too.

It's a shame a body's got to be brave these days just to get a drink of water.

16.

then

It is hard to believe, but while everybody is gossiping about where we're going and where we're shipping out to, December comes, and Christmas is on top of us before we know it. Our company gets together and puts on a show for the whole base. There is singing and dancing and skits. We all dress our parts, and Phillipa recites a Christmas poem, while I read the story from the book of Luke. Peaches says I have come a long way with my elocution.

Dovey sings "Sweet Little Jesus Boy," and, of course, that Gloria Madden has to do her one better by singing something new we heard on the radio, "Have Yourself a Merry Little Christmas." She sure has a pretty voice for being such a low-down snake. Our whole show gets written up nicely in the base newspaper, *Special Delivery*, and I am proud as a peacock that my reading voice is complimented. I clip out the story and think about sending it home to Mama, but I send it to Sister Dials instead, since sending it to her is as good as telling all the colored folks in Bay Slough.

Suddenly Christmas is on everybody's mind. Of course, it means nothing to Lieutenant Hundley. She doesn't play around about holiday decorations and says the Third Platoon had better not try to "deck the halls" with anything, or else we all have policing details for the rest of the month. Still, even Hundley can't stay grouchy. When we sound off, she makes up marching songs about Santa Claus that get most of us laughing, even at 0530.

Though my heart is aching to, I don't dare go see Feen. On base, I am safe from the likes of Mama, Aunt Shirley, and Miss Ida Payne and anyone else who might think to drag me off and send me home. Like everyone else with no place else to be, I go to the Christmas Eve service the chaplain gives, and there I see Lieutenant Hundley, singing the hymn. She wishes me a merry Christmas same as everyone, and she looks really nice in her dress uniform. I think she even wears a little rouge on her cheeks—which is almost against her precious regulations!

Most of us have a little bit of money set by, so for Christmas we treat each other to a few gifts from the PX and some things from town like a lipstick, a handkerchief, or some scent. Mostly, though, we trade movie magazines and get into the kitchen and do a little KP, hoping to talk the cook into letting us make more cookies or pies to share. It is a quiet Christmas, but it is just fine.

In quiet moments, I think of Feen and where we were last Christmas. I hope that she is happy. Doris got a camera, and my gift to Feen is a photograph of myself in uniform. Doris took it the day we came to Fort Oglethorpe.

I look a sight different than I did back home. I think I grew another inch or so, and I am wearing stockings, but the picture still shows the muscles in my legs. My arms are full of muscles, and with my hat on, I don't hardly look like myself.

I look like Mama.

Soon as I realize that, the shakes hit me. Why won't she write? How can Mama be like this to her own blood? Would she treat Feen like this? Would I ever be like this to a child of my own?

I have no answers. I put the picture in its paper frame, seal up my Christmas card, and take it to the post.

✳ ✳ ✳

After a few days, folk start coming back from leave, and Dovey brings me back some "tipsy cake" from her auntie Bess. She tell me we'd better eat it while the liquor is still good. That cake smell like a still; they doused it with that sour mash whiskey and sugar. Ooh, Mama would've had a fit if she could have seen me! We did not dare let Lieutenant Hundley find us with food in our quarters. We ate it all at once, and boy, that cake was good, good, good.

New Year's Day, we came back to the freezing cold barracks to hear Annie in her bunk crying like her heart had broken. She called home, and they told her one of the boys she grew up with is missing in action. His unit got shot down somewhere in Belgium, and they can't find him. Annie was so torn up she couldn't hardly breathe, and we all sat with her until Captain Ferguson came. Ferguson told her "missing" doesn't mean "dead" and that Annie's got to pull herself together and decide what she gonna do now.

Annie might go on home, and no shame to her, Cap says, but I sure hope she doesn't go. I am used to all my girls, and I don't want to think of doing without them. I pray Annie's friend gets found so nothing has to change, but Annie's tears are a reminder that this is serious all over again. The U.S. Army is fighting a war, and I am part of the U.S. Army.

Annie says she's got to do her part and her place is here, but for a while, the Third Platoon is serious and quiet. For Annie's sake, we work hard to get ready for whatever is coming.

Once again, we get gas masks and do gas drill every morning, only this time, we got to smell and say what kind of gas it is. By now, I know I can do it right, but my knees want to give out every time. Staff Sergeant Hill runs us through our paces most every day, and by now, even the rope climbing comes easier, although I sure hope nobody ever is after me to get somewhere quick trying to climb up a straight rope.

"Brown, can you do this?" I hear Lieutenant Hundley ask one morning when we come back from drill.

"Yes, ma'am," Annie says, and she stands up straight, even though she cries in her pillow at night. She doesn't think we hear her, but all of us know.

"You can go home," Captain tells her. "You don't have to go overseas. You have served your country."

"This is where I need to be," Annie tells Hundley, and that's what she tells me every night when I hand her a cold cloth to wash her face. She says her prayers have to be prayed by her getting up and walking on her feet. She's got plenty of praying getting done, as often as we're on our feet here at Fort Oglethorpe.

The news is that the Soviets got back Warsaw. The Polish folks have been on the run from the Nazis for almost longer than anybody, and folks around here give a cheer when they hear it. With the Russians hitting 'em from the east and the Allies hitting 'em from the west by way of France, it can't be no time at all before we run that Hitler and those Nazis out of town.

As I wait for Dovey to finish shining her shoes, I write some more to Feen:

> January 17, 1945
>
> Dear city sister, Miss Josey,
>
> It is nice to get so many letters from you! I got two today!
>
> Here at Fort Oglethorpe, there are no men at ALL, colored or white, not even officers, so you can tell Aunt Shirley AGAIN that she's got her story wrong.
>
> I told you before about my buddy Miss Ruby Bowie. Ruby is from Dallas, and she is so citified she can't boil water! Don't you forget what you know now, Philadelphia girl. I'd hate to have to come back for you and find out you are too citified to slop hogs!
>
> After New Year's, the girls in my squad

decided to roast some chestnuts Ruby brought. Well, we put 'em on the heater, then forgot about them. Feen, you should have heard us hootin' and hollerin' like Sister Dials on Sunday when those things popped off of that heater! The chestnuts were good, though. Not like our pecans, but sweet—starchy like sweet potatoes and tasty. They left our fingers black from the ash, though. Someday I will buy you some.

I can't tell you where I am going, but we are getting on a ship to go a ways away to free up more men to fight. I am not sure whether to be excited or scared, but I am in this man's army, and I am prepared to do what I can. I will write more when I can tell you more.

Tell Sister Dials that I am still faithful and go to services every week. Don't pay Auntie Shirley too much mind, but don't give her any sass, either. If you hear from Mama again, tell her I am thinking of her. I know she is still put out with me, but don't let that worry you.

Till we meet again, I am,
Your loving army sister,
Marey Lee Boylen

✳ ✳ ✳

In the dead of night, we fall in at the signal, our coats pulled on over our pajamas. They give us orders, tell us to pack up to ship out. They been doing this to us too many nights, so it is like habit by now to roll out of bed, pack my footlocker and duffle up tight, and fall in. We don't leave a thing in our barracks, not one toothbrush nor one tube of hand cream. We lock our footlockers, shoulder our packs, and then we march, fast.

But this time, it is not too long before we realize this is not no drill.

"Double-time!" Staff Sergeant Hill say, and we all but flat out run, our packs jouncing up and down on our backs. Down the road, through the big gates, in six lines of six across, an arm-long space apart. The sound of our feet is like rifle shots in the ice-cold air. We might be half asleep, but at least when we're marching, we get warm.

I wake up hours later when the train stops. We are in Virginia and heading further north. There is not much time to rest or stretch out; the train only stops for a minute, and after this, they say it won't stop anymore. Lieutenant Hundley passes out box kits, and we eat where we sit. It is long hours until we reach Camp Shanks, New York, and by then it is almost morning. The train is full of our smells from hours of riding, but it is still a shock to get off into the cold wind again.

We fall into formation and march in our wrinkled field uniforms to a ferry and onto a loading pier. The icy air off of that water cuts us sharp, and I stomp my feet down real good in that cold till my breath billows out like white clouds. I'm moving by habit, but I'm scared out my mind. I could be still in my bunk back at Oglethorpe, working in the kitchen or doing specialist training at motor transport school to drive around the commanders, generals, and all the other folks wearing brass medals. Why didn't I stay?

My teeth chatter. I am cold and scared, but isn't nothing I can do about it now. I take a deep breath, square up my shoulders, pray a little prayer that God bless Feen and Mama. Then I get on the boat. After all this time, I don't aim to be left behind.

17.

NOW

The best blackberry pie I have ever had can be found at a truck stop somewhere in the back of beyond in southern Arizona off of Interstate 10. What's even better than blackberry pie is having it for breakfast.

Mare is nursing black coffee and buttered toast, as if her stomach is still bothering her. She is buried in the newspaper, catching up on world news and probably reading "Dear Abby" like she's done every morning of the trip so far.

"So, where were they sending you?" I ask when she emerges from her reading for a moment.

Mare sighs. "Girl, let me read my paper and eat your . . . pie," she says, shaking her head and giving my breakfast an amused look.

I shrug and fork up another mouthful.

Mare doesn't bother to make us eat anything in particular, and especially after the incident with the plums, she really has no room at all to complain about what we eat, which is why for breakfast this morning I opted for pie and ice cream. Tali is eating hash browns and slurping down a milk shake. If Mom were here, she'd say that someday eating like this is going to catch up to us, but today, I don't care.

"More coffee?" The waitress hovers.

"Thank you." Mare glances up as she turns the page. Her glasses make her eyes look huge and watery.

"Another milk shake for you, hon?" The waitress looks dubiously at my sister.

"No. I think I'd like a biscuit now. With honey butter."

"All righty. And for you, miss? More pie?"

"Yes, please," I say, blissfully licking my spoon. This is the best breakfast ever.

Last night, we got to the hotel early enough to have time for a nice shower and a decent meal. We drove away from the interstate to eat at a place with tablecloths and then walked through the town for a while as the cooling desert encouraged us to stretch our legs.

Ms. Crase would have loved observing someone else's town. We saw flyers for the June Jamboree Play Day Tractor Pull and Car Show and a school with a big marquee in front that said Congratulations, Graduates and had Seniors! singed into the front lawn. We saw little kids trying to roller-skate on the sidewalk and whole families lined up at a hamburger joint, getting soft-serve ice cream, the little ones whining when their cones dripped. On a lawn in the middle of a sprinkler spray, a terrier lunged and barked at the bubbles in his wading pool.

It was kind of a surprise, but people looked the same to me as they do back home on a warm summer night—glad to be out and about, ready to say hello to their neighbors and enjoy a cool breeze. Most of the people we saw were even friendly enough to smile and nod at us as we walked by.

When we reached the town square, Mare was the first one to notice the tiny theater.

"Look at this," she said, and dragged us toward a small building with a lit marquee. "A movie house."

"That can't have more than two screens," Tali said, wiping her forehead. "Do you think they have AC?"

"Let's go see." Mare sounded like a little kid, and Tali looked at me and sighed.

"Mare, do we have to?" she groaned, but Mare bustled off ahead of us and peered through the tinted glass.

"On Tuesday it's showing *Spellbound* and *The Postman Always Rings Twice*," Mare called back. "I think I saw both of those right when they came out."

"I've never even heard of them." Tali shrugged.

"*Spellbound* had Salvador Dalí and Alfred Hitchcock in it," I said smugly, glad to know something Tali didn't. "I saw that on *Jeopardy!*"

"Dork alert," Tali said snidely.

"Boy, oh, boy," Mare had sighed, looking nostalgic. "They just don't make them like this anymore."

When we got back to the hotel, Mare and I watched movies by ourselves. We found *Stormy Weather* on a cable station, and it was pretty funny to hear Mare going on and on about how she'd just loved Lena Horne when she was young and wished she could sing and how her friend Dovey Borland had had a set of pipes just like Lena's. Sometimes Mare sounds so much like me and my friends I forget that she's old. Sometimes I think even she forgets she's old.

I love hearing what Mare did in the military and all the stuff she learned. It's hard to believe that she just essentially walked off a farm and learned Morse code. It's amazing.

Tali scrapes down into the bottom of her milk shake with a long metal spoon, dragging up the last of the cookie chunks and melted ice cream. Mare reaches into her bag and sneakily puts her hand on her lighter but stops and rolls her eyes at Tali's huge fake coughing spasm.

"One of these days . . . ," Mare mutters, and puts her lighter away. "Octavia, get me some gum, will you, baby?"

I can't believe they've both still kept their agreement: Mare doesn't smoke where Tali can see her, and she's not too good at sneaking out when Tali doesn't notice. Tali doesn't listen to her music where Mare can see her, but I know what she's doing every time she puts on a hat or pulls up her hood. So does Mare. To help herself out, Mare has been chewing nicotine gum, and Tali's been enduring the silence in the car by asking questions.

"So, Mare. Weren't there any other African Americans overseas?"

Mare pops a square of grayish white gum out of its plastic compartment. "Sure there were—but they were male soldiers. Something like one point two million African Americans fought in World War II. They sent a lot of us overseas. I'd say almost fifty thousand."

"That many African Americans?" Tali asks. "Too bad there aren't that many pictures."

"Pictures?" I ask.

"You know." Tali gestures vaguely. "In history books and stuff."

I don't remember ever hearing about African American women in World War II before. Everyone knows about Rosie the Riveter, and probably most people know that there were Red Cross nurses sent everywhere. At school we heard a little about the Tuskegee Airmen, but I didn't know anything about this. I never even heard of the Red Ball Express till Mare mentioned them. And I wonder why I didn't know that there were so many African American truck drivers in Europe during the war.

I can't believe our teachers never mentioned this and that my parents never said anything. I know Mare embarrasses Dad, so he doesn't talk about her a lot, but shouldn't other people, or at least history books, have had something to say about the African American women who went overseas? I expect there to be some kind of plaque somewhere or some kind of statue commemorating them. But when I mention it, Mare says there's not—at least not one that she knows of anyway.

"But it's history," I insist. "Shouldn't people tell you about history?"

"It's there if you know where to look, but the colored WACs are also part of segregation history," Mare reminds me. "Talking about segregation isn't as nice and neat as talking about being the 'greatest generation' that won the war. For some folks, it's just stirring up bad memories."

Tali licks her spoon. "The Women's Army sounds like bad memories anyway. I could never see enlisting. Can you see me putting up with drill sergeants hollering in my face all day?"

"It wasn't all hollering," Mare says, "and you could take it if you had to, Tali, but you don't. Your parents are doing better for you than my mama did for me, and I thank God for it."

Tali sounds subdued. "Yeah, things would have to be pretty bad to make the army look good." We're quiet for a moment, then Tali puts down her spoon.

"Mare?"

"Mm-hmm?"

"Did they ever put Toby in jail? Did anyone ever . . . do anything to him?"

Mare looks away, her expression closed. "That's not how things were back then."

"Then I'm glad we don't live 'back then,'" I blurt. "He could have killed you, and nobody did anything? How is that 'the good old days'?"

Mare shrugs away the topic. "Nothing else we could do. We lived with it. Folks did what they had to, and we all got by." She sighs and glances toward the door. "You girls about done with that mess you call breakfast? We'd all better use it before we get on the road again."

"Mare," Tali groans. "Telling me to 'go potty' before we leave? Hello? *Seventeen*. I'm. Seven. Teen."

"And you still have to pee at seventeen same as seventy," Mare says complacently. "Get a move on, girl. I want to get to Las Cruces before it gets dark."

"Ooh, so we're going to New Mexico!" I exclaim, imagining keepsake stops for turquoise jewelry and incense.

"For tonight," Mare replies, flicking my nose with one of her long fingers. "With as much iced tea as you had, you'd better get on to the bathroom, too."

I drag myself toward the line for the single small bathroom and wait almost forever. Inside, Tali is singing in that off-key way she does when she has her earbuds in and can't hear herself. And when we finally get outside, Mare has put on perfume and ducks around us into the bathroom to brush her teeth.

Tali and Mare both decide not to notice that each of them has broken their promise. I ignore them both and gallop out to the car, remembering the dancer, Katherine Dunham, from the movie Mare and I watched. I slide into the front seat, and Tali looks at me like I'm crazy.

"You'd better not have so much sugar at lunch," she says, and puts on her seat belt.

"I'm in a good mood," I snarl, immediately offended. "What's wrong with that?"

Mare takes the car out of park and lets out one of her

rattling machine-gun laughs. "You girls," she chuckles, then glances in the rearview mirror. "All belted in?"

"Yes, ma'am."

"Then let's hit the road, Jack."

It's morning on I-10, and we're headed for the horizon.

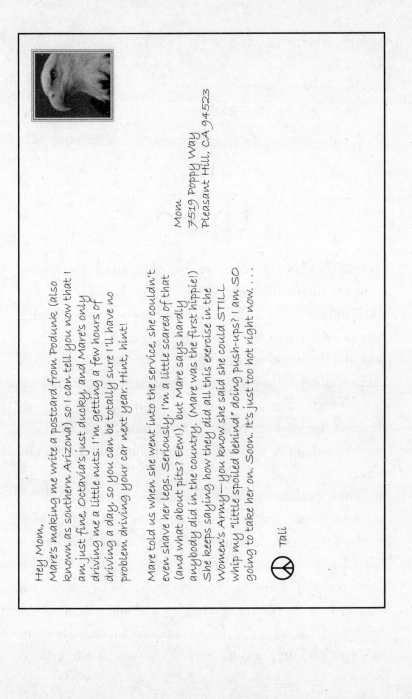

Hey Mom,

Mare's making me write a postcard from Podunk (also known as southern Arizona) so I can tell you now that I am just fine, Octavia's just ducky, and Mare's only driving me a little nuts. I'm getting a few hours of driving a day, so you can be totally sure I'll have no problem driving your car next year. Hint, hint!

Mare told us when she went into the service, she couldn't even shave her legs. Seriously, I'm a little scared of that (and what about pits? Eew!), but Mare says hardly anybody did in the country. (Mare was the first hippie!) She keeps saying how they did all this exercise in the Women's Army—you know she said she could STILL whip my "little spoiled behind" doing push-ups? I am SO going to take her on. Soon. It's just too hot right now. . . .

☮ Tali

Mom
7519 Poppy Way
Pleasant Hill, CA 94523

18.

then

At first, all I know is that I feel boxed in, and I can feel the engines thrum right up under my feet. Once we get used to the boat moving, it is better. We are bunched up tight, with twenty-four of us to a room—three triple-deck bunks on each side, and the bunks are hung with chains. Ruby say the men pack up closer in these things than we do, though I don't see how. She says they go down underneath the deep water in those submarines, where they stay for months, and they get less space than we do. Once again, I thank God I am not a man!

These bunks are tight and the latrines—or the "heads"—are tight as well, because we're all jammed in there, trying to clean up in the morning. We do almost everything in shifts, and there are more women on this ship than it's probably ever seen. Captain Ferguson and Staff Sergeant Hill keep us busy, marching up and down, doing lifeboat drills twice a day, KP, marching, inspection, and all, but sometimes we've got nothing but time—time to be sick, time to kick off our boots and crawl over other folks' bunks to get to ours, and time to miss the fresh air, since they only let us topside about an hour a day. Mostly we stay confined to bunks, and the ship feels like a swing you lay down in that goes up— then right down.

Outside, it's foggy—isn't anything much out there but cold, cold water—but most of us look out any porthole we can. We have never been on a ship and might never be again.

Being that squashed up next to so many people doesn't always set well, though. Sometimes I walk out of my bunk just to be walking. We are supposed to be in quarters after lights-out, but can't nobody stop me from visiting the "head," or the "necessary," as Staff Sergeant Hill calls it. I'm not surprised to see Peaches one night standing at a sink, patting on cold cream.

"What's cooking, Peaches Carter?"

"Marey Lee, you ever wonder if this is where you're supposed to be?"

Peaches sounds riled up and worried. "Well, I don't usually wonder if *this* is where I'm supposed to be," I tell her, motioning to the toilet, and she lets out her big old laugh.

"Be serious, Mare. You ever wonder if we're doing right being in this army?"

I splash some water on my face. "I don't know." No wonder Peach can't sleep. I straighten up. "I don't wonder if this is where I'm supposed to be 'cause I have no place else to be. Everywhere I am, I've got to do the best I can do right while I'm there, you know?"

Peaches nods slowly. "I guess so."

I perch on the sink next to her. "What are you worrying about anyway, all serious in the middle of the night?"

Peaches shrugs. "Just . . . things." She sighs and smooths the surface of the pink cold cream with her fingertip. "I got a letter from home, and it got me thinking."

"Aw, Peach, you homesick already?"

"No." Peaches shakes her head. "It's not that. Almost all my girlfriends from school are engaged, my friend Adelaide just got married . . . Cousin Julia's about to have her first baby, and . . . well, here I am."

"Well, you won't always be here. Soon as this war's over—" I begin, but Peaches interrupts, her eyes wide.

"No. Marey, I'm here . . . and I'm glad. This is where I *want* to be. I can't imagine me having anybody's baby nor wearing anybody's ring. This army thing, this is the best thing I've ever done, Marey Lee. I'm good at this stuff—at working for the communications officer. I'm good at Morse code, cryptography is fun, I can do the teletype and switchboard in my sleep—I'm good at everything. I don't miss home much anymore, and I don't ever think about getting hitched. I'm . . . starting to think something is wrong with me." Peaches glances at me, then looks down.

"Wrong with you? 'Cause you're happy?"

"No . . . well, not exactly. There might be something wrong, Mare. Something serious."

"Like what?"

Peaches flicks a glance at my face. "You *know*."

I open my mouth to say, "No, I don't know," but then I do. I know exactly what Peach is telling me, and my tongue just freezes up. I can't think of a word to say.

"Skip it." Peaches puts the lid back on her cold cream, keeping her eyes down. "I think I'm sleepy after all."

I can't force myself to move as Peaches cleans up and tightens the belt on her robe. She's halfway into the hall when I close my mouth and grab her sleeve.

"That's not right," I blurt, yanking her back into the bathroom.

Peaches looks at me, wary, but I am sure of what to say. "You've been on this boat too long, Peaches Carter, 'cause, girl, you have *lost* your mind. Now you *know* that just because you are *good* at something a man might do, that doesn't make you a *man*. Girl, my mama butchered hogs and picked cotton and kept a roof over me and Feen's head, and she is definitely not a man. I chopped wood and about near killed myself hauling grease and scrubbing floors out at Young's Diner, but I'd sure rather do that than have a baby, thank you all the same. You tell your cousin Julia she'd best leave you be." I tap Peaches's arm emphatically, then hurry out the rest of the thought before I lose my nerve. "But even if you are like *that*," I add softly, "even if you are one of those girls, you are still my friend, Peaches Carter."

Peaches look up at me, her dark eyes intent. "You sure?"

"Didn't I just say so?"

Peaches lowers her voice to a thread. "You be real sure, Marey Lee. Mama's friend Lydia is . . . a woman like that, and Lydia won't see us anymore. She's afraid we'll get her reputation."

"Peaches, just about all of us on this boat are gonna have a reputation. Folks back home in Bay Slough have already been telling me about how some girls around here ain't no better than they should be, telling me to watch myself. But you know what? We don't have time to worry about all of that. For one thing, we know what is and isn't true. For another thing? Cap Ferguson has us do too much work to worry with carrying on about that."

"You know, *that's* right," Peaches sighs, slumping against the sink again. "Sometimes I think Staff Sergeant Hill thinks of stuff for us to do just because she can."

"It will all be different when we get to Paris, though, huh?" I grin, knowing I will set Peaches off.

"We are going to Paris," she says, frowning at me. "I know you don't believe me. . . ."

"Last time you said Paris, France, we went to Fort Oglethorpe, Georgia, is all I'm sayin'."

"Girl, don't you start. We are on a boat, crossing the ocean. . . ."

"Ina White say she hear we going to Scotland."

"*Scotland?!*" Peaches forgets to whisper. "Scotland's not—"

The door opens, and Lieutenant Hundley pokes her head inside. We both snap to attention, arms at stiff angles while we salute in our bathrobes.

"You ladies were just leaving?" Lieutenant Hundley looks sleepy, but her eyes are sharp.

"Yes, ma'am," Peaches and I say in unison.

"Good night, then." Lieutenant Hundley returns our salutes crisply.

"Good night, ma'am," we say, and march meekly back to bed.

Lying in my bunk, I think about what Peaches said. Peaches Carter is close like kin, and I could no more not be her friend than I could make Feen not be my baby sister. All of the girls—Ruby, Annie, Dovey, and Phillipa—are like kin, too. No matter what Peach is or what she says—nobody and nothing nobody could say about her would ever turn me against her or any of them.

I make up my mind to keep an eye on Peaches. Kin takes care of each other; that's what Mama always taught me. The Third Platoon takes care of its own, even the likes of that mealymouthed Gloria Madden. Nobody deserves to feel sad and low out here on the ocean. We are too far from home to not lean on each other.

✳ ✳ ✳

Those of us who don't have the heaves the next morning have a good time playing cards and talking about what we think we going to do. Dovey Borland's mama is a hairdresser, and she puts up our hair, even though the sea air makes it crimp up again in no time. Every time we go outside for drill, our hair gets sticky and stiff from the salt, but it doesn't mat- ter 'cause we got our helmets on and we sweat under them, while the fog drips off their tops. When we have free time, we go to each other's bunks, paint our nails, and read each other's mail and *Life* magazines. We have to lie in the bunks to read and then lean out 'cause there isn't ever enough light. Most girls write letters all day long, they are so bored. Dorothy Rogers is going to write herself a book one of these days.

"Your deal, Phil," Ruby say, and Phillipa grabs the cards and deals out ten to each of us.

"Which one's the knock pile again?" I ask. Mama always said that cards are the devil's business, but Phillipa's granddaddy is a preacher, and she plays gin rummy all the time. Phillipa's teaching me, and what Mama doesn't know can hardly make her mad, can it?

"This one." Peaches points and leans forward. Since I'm sitting on the edge of the top bunk, I sneak a look at her hand.

"Girl, don't you try to—"

And just like that, the whole room rolls over.

Probably just about everybody on the whole ship sucks in a breath, and then the screaming starts.

I fly off the bed, screaming in pain as my knee slams against the iron frame of the bunk across from me. I fall hard, and Peaches lands on top of my head and raps her elbow on a footlocker. My teeth come down on my tongue, and I can taste the metal in my blood. We hear crashes and screams from all over the ship as perfume bottles, duffles, shoes, books, pillows, and soldiers go sliding across the decks. Playing cards fall all around us like rain.

"What's happening? Oh, my ribs, my ribs!" Dorothy, who was in her bunk, is on the floor, wailing.

"Ruby!" Peaches is screaming, and I can't turn my head. "Get Ruby!"

Fear chokes me up, and I got a pain in my head and a pain in my neck, and my shoulder that Mama popped back is killing me. I finally get my head turned. Ruby's got blood all down her face, and Phillipa is trying to crawl across the floor to get to her.

The ship groans, sounding like a cow about to calf. Outside, men are hollering orders and we can hear folks running. Peaches look at me with her eyes bugged out, and Phillipa starts to cry. I look at all that blood on Ruby's face. She don't look like she's breathing.

"Lord Jesus," Peach whispers as the ship lurches again, and I know right then and there I might not get back to Feen like I promised. I might not ever be anywhere but on this old ship ever again. Sorrow knots up my chest, and my heart pounds so loud I can feel it in my head. What if I die? What if I didn't do right and Mama can't never forgive me? Who's gonna take care of Feen without me?

"P-Peaches, come h-help me," Phillipa stutters, finally up on her knees, trying to mop the river of blood from Ruby's face. Peaches gets a blanket and starts tucking it around Ruby using only one of her hands, which is shaking. She keeps the other one tucked up against her body. Her elbow is all swollen up and turning purple. Phillipa's teeth are chattering, she's so scared, but she and Peach, they're trying to treat Ruby for shock like they taught us.

We are all shocked. Peach has got a shiner already started from where something smacked her in the eye. Phillipa can't talk straight without stuttering. Dorothy is spitting up, but I can't get to her; there are too many trunks, and the ship keeps on rolling. Peach is just crying and holding on to me and crying some more till I can't sit still. I have got to get out and see what happened.

My knee is swollen from hitting the bunk, but it takes my weight when I get up slow. I wipe blood off my chin. My ears is ringing.

"Marey Lee, what are you doing?" Peaches ask, but I open the door anyway. Girls are talking loud and shouting. Some are just crying. "What happened?" somebody hollers. The white girls down the way don't know any more than we do, and for a while, everybody just cries and looks around, trying to find out what we hit. One of the girls say she sure we hit an iceberg, and everybody starts crying then. Finally, we see some officer or other coming down the hall to make an announcement, and we snap to attention.

"As you were," the sergeant calls, and we wait, trying to hear.

"It's Germans," somebody hiss, and we all shut up for real then. The sergeant says we are being followed by a German U-boat. They issue a "general quarters," which mean all hands have to stay belowdecks, in our bunks, and strap our stuff down. But Ruby can't wait for any all clear. Medics come and wheel her out while we try and pick up. Dorothy limps to sick bay to tape up her ribs, and Peaches gets a sling for her arm. Annie comes in crying and balls up with her Bible. I hunch up over my sore legs and listen to her pray.

Mama used to say the devil would catch us up short when we forgot ourselves. Today, I see that's the plain truth. We forgot ourselves. This wasn't ever a pleasure cruise. This company is on a ship to go to war. We got to painting nails and we forgot what we were doing.

✳ ✳ ✳

From now on, we keep our life vests out where we can see them. We march to mess twice a day and stand and eat from trays on them counters, bracing ourselves with one hand and trying to keep our mess kits and our forks and our food in front of us with the other. We march right back to our bunks, wearin' our helmets strapped to our heads. Staying in quarters, Peaches gets seasick, and then Annie, lyin' in her bunk, moans like she is dying. Once Annie starts to retch, we are *all* sick.

Then, in the dead of night, a storm blows up. All we can hear is the wind howling and the chains of our bunks rattling as we go up and down. Pretty soon the air gets foul as more folks start vomiting, and there is no way the few of us who are well enough can keep up. In the latrine, the floors are slick with more than just water.

Annie cries in her sleep, and I don't hear nothing from Peaches. I sniff some, but I got to be strong. If I start up, then we are all gonna start hollering in here and ain't nobody's mama coming to hush us up and say it's all right.

I tell God if He let me get back to Feen, I will get back to church a little more often. I promise Him if it's not right, I will put down my cards for good. I promise Him I might be sweet to Gloria Madden and her uppity self. I promise everything except that I will go home and work for Miss Ida again. I can't do that. It strikes me that I would rather die than go back to Bay Slough, Alabama, especially now that Feen's not there.

I promise God I will be better and make things right with everybody . . . if He just doesn't let this storm or the U-boats kill us now.

19.

then

God must have turned it over in His mind for a while to see if I was serious. We rolled and ran from those Germans for forty-five long minutes, and then we dodged winter squalls and furious seas for five days more.

Eleven days we are on that ship, tied down to our bunks, strapped into helmets, and carrying our life jackets. Eleven days of holding on to railings, sliding on our behinds, wading to the latrine in smelly boots, and bringing up what little we eat. The evening of the eleventh day, the brass says we are coming to land. I am too sick of that tub to care where we are, but when we muster out, march down that gangplank into the dark, the captain says we are in Glasgow, Scotland.

Tired as I am, I have got to smile. I know Peaches must be some furious. She was so sure we were going to Paris!

The Third Platoon stands there looking like we forgot how to stand up straight, leaning on each other like a herd of drunks. The word "Scotland" has no kind of effect on me. Don't know where it is, and I don't care. All I can do is stand

there feeling the sick rise up out of my gut. The ground seems
like it's still moving.

Lieutenant Hundley look at us like she worried, then she
start hollering about get our helmets on, and *atten*-shun!
Some Red Cross ladies come by with carts of coffee and
doughnuts for us, and the coffee at least makes my head stop
spinning. In time, Hundley calls out orders, and we hike up
our packs, do a slow march out from the shipyard on to a
train station.

It's a good thing we got a train. Peaches says she won't be
going on a boat never again. Guess they've got to bridge over
the great Atlantic to get that girl home.

As we get on board, we can hardly march in step, but it
feels good to be moving. Hundley says the train is taking us
on to England. Annie nudges me and gives me a nod. She's
still too sick to grin, but she sure likes to let me know she
knew something I didn't. Hmph. I know she just guessed we
were going to England. She doesn't know nothing more than
I do.

When we get to quarters, they say we are in Birmingham,
where we will stay. We barely got time to set down our packs
when we get our assignments. We, the 6888th Battalion, are
now Company C, under First Lieutenant Scott. Lieutenant
Scott explains to us that our job is to process the mail from
home for the soldiers. But first, they tell us we have three
days to get our uniforms in order, our laundry done, our shoes
polished, and ourselves healthy. During those three days,
we'll march and drill every spare minute we can, 'cause they
tell us after that, we've got to march in a parade.

A parade! And we'll hardly have had our gear unpacked, and some of us are still sick and banged up from rolling around on that ship! Still, we'll do our best to do the company proud. Since three days is what we have, three days is what we'll take.

This place doesn't look like any kind of barracks I have ever seen. There are none of those nice brick buildings like we had at Fort Des Moines. There are not even the WAC shacks oozing pine tar like we had at Oglethorpe. These are just tall old buildings with little windows at the top and a sign that says King Edward School. Can't see a reviewing stand nor parade yard, but no playground, either. This is where they tell us to set up, though, so we do. A GI will make do with what she's got.

The day of the parade comes too soon. I pin up Dovey's hair in a twist, and she does mine. We get into our gear— dress uniform, double-breasted wool coats, wool stockings, and leather gloves. Our ears are cold, but that is too bad. We put on socks over our stockings, then sturdy brown loafers, and fall in, stomping to stay warm.

Our company has about two hundred girls lined up from here to there, and we form up in turn, by squadron. Finally, the call comes.

"Forwaaaard, march!"

The echoes of our footsteps bounce off the buildings up and down the street. We march through Birmingham to the field where we will parade. It tickles me that we are marching down the street in Birmingham, *England*, not Birmingham, Alabama. I can't wait to write Feen and tell her *that* one.

It is a strange parade. We are dog-tired, but we are as crisp and perfect as we know how to be, trying to do the U.S. Women's Army proud. The English folk look at us with their mouths wide open, as if they'd like to catch flies, as if they ain't—haven't—never seen no girls marching before. Or maybe it is that they don't see many colored. They gawk and look, and then they start talking. One little missy with her hair scraped back into plaits sticking out from under her hat say right out, loud as you please, "Mum! Lookit all the *black* gels."

Black! The word comes out her mouth like something she spit. Black! What she talking about *black?!* My skin is as brown as pecan shells; it isn't black. They don't even know to say "Negro" round here, and the little ones got no better sense than to stare. The girl point her fingers till her mama swats down her hands. She say, "But, *Mum* . . . !"

Least *that* much is the same between here and home. Mama would smack me one good, pointing like that.

We stare past their heads, eyes straight, fingers lined up with our seams, till we strut by the reviewing stand and snap our eyes to the right and salute. Lieutenant Scott say we have to observe military courtesy, so we don't stare at those English folks just now, but I plan to get a good look so I can write to Feen. "Black," she says, when we are standing here as brown as we can be! Feen will get some laughs out of that.

When they call the company to halt, we stand at attention with the crowd standing all around us. The band plays, and the flags flap in the wind, and then they come and inspect us. We stand only blinking, trying to keep from freezing to death and falling over in the wind.

The English people respect the military police, and the MPs make some effort to keep folks back, but nobody tries to stop them once we're dismissed. We fall out, and Lieutenant Scott says to make it back to base in one hour. We've got time to look around town, but most of us head straight back, stumbling over the rocky street.

Annie is walking with me and Ina White. Ina is talking about the "cobblestones" on the ground that would mess up her good shoes. Annie says they have real nice paving stones in the big cities, stones that are more even than this. We don't know we've got company till Annie chances to look behind us.

"What?" Ina says, looking around.

"Nothing but some kids," Annie says, and she rolls her eyes.

It is more than just a few. Most of them are trying to hide behind each other, all staring at us with big, wide eyes. One of them, about eight, don't even have the shame to blush once I turn around and stare her in the face.

"Military courtesy," Lieutenant Scott say; we got to be courteous, so I don't ask that little twig where her mama is and didn't anybody gave her any home training. I just nod and say, "Good afternoon, miss."

Then she turns around and runs.

Ha. Guess she didn't know no "black gels" could talk.

✳ ✳ ✳

Ruby, Dovey, me, and some of the others go to the post office warehouse to report for duty the first day, dressed in our field jackets and wool slacks under our utilities. The room they have the mail in used to be the gymnasium for the school, and it is cold, cold, cold under that big, high ceiling. That is not the worst. The mail is stacked up over our heads, almost touching the ceiling. Must be a hundred million letters just sitting there, and the troops moving somewhere new almost every day. The group of us just stare.

Before we get started, our CO give us a speech. She say that stealing the mail is a federal crime. I have to shake my head. Much as I like getting mail, I can't see trying to read up on everyone else's! And there is so much! Too much. They say we have got six airplane hangars full of what didn't get sent out at Christmas. We have got *work* to do, and nobody has any idea how.

But once we get our orders, we set to it. Lieutenant Scott says we need to get in and make it right in a hurry. Everybody is worrying about the soldiers' morale.

We hear that word "morale" all the time and how we have got to keep it up in the soldiers. They got to hear from home, or they get to feeling low. I know all about feeling low. It is raining and foggy all the time and cold so deep it settles into the bones. I haven't ever been so cold in all my life. We get on shift wearing our coats and our hats and drinking coffee to stay warm. Seem to me somebody should see about our morale, too. Folks from the Third Platoon all look run-down and terrible. Peaches got a cold as soon as she got here, and

she's been snottin' and sniffling all day. Ruby's still got a scar
on account of being popped upside the head that day on the
ship, and Dovey doesn't hardly want to even be inside without her hat since her hair looks so bad. Even Gloria Madden,
with her high-and-mighty ways, is looking downright sor-
rowful now that she's wrapped up in wool all the time. I expect things will get better, but right now we're working like
dogs to get through the mail. Lieutenant Scott says we've got
to work round the clock, three eight-hour shifts, seven days
a week, till we get a handle on things. They say, "No mail,
low morale," and we've got to fix that or the Nazis might
take advantage.

At the army post office, we get mail that gets sent back
and try and find where the soldier is now. We've got index
cards all typed up with each soldier's orders, and we try for
thirty days to get a soldier his mail. Peaches works the type-
writer, makin' up changes, 'cause even though every soldier
is supposed to fill in a change-of-address form, sometimes
they don't. The army has got forms for everything, but we
can't help folks if they don't fill 'em out. There are six hundred of us in the Six-triple-eight, and we have got seven million folks to get mail to. Lieutenant Scott is right—we have
our job cut out for us.

Now that we are here in Birmingham, there are new
army letters to learn. Lieutenant Scott says we are in the
ETO, which is the European theater of operations. We are
also in the *UK*, which is the United Kingdom. They've got
a King George here, and he's got a palace like a kingdom in

one of them fairy tales. I know Feen will get a kick out of that. These UK folks have got fancy words for everything, including the latrine. Here the door says WC for "water closet." Even the smallest house has got the tub and the commode in separate rooms. I bet they never even heard of an outhouse!

After a while, we get a little more used to the cold and the wet and working our shifts. We get to laughing and singing while we work sometimes, and the Red Cross folks have always got coffee, and some days we drink tea like the English folks. At the end of my shift, my head feels likely to split. It is too dark in that mail warehouse, but it is good to keep busy. When we got too much free time, I get to thinking about home and about what is going on in the States.

I didn't ever take myself to be someone patriotic—but I haven't ever been away from home, neither. When I see that old red, white, and blue flag of ours, I just stand up straight and remember being at school, where they had us lay hands on our hearts. When I see it, I think, There's a little something from home.

I guess it is strange to these Birmingham folk to see so many strangers and colored girls all in one place. They don't exactly *say* nothing, but they get quiet, and they watch us. We sure enough watch them back, and Lieutenant Scott tell us to look folks in the eye and say, "Good morning," but it gets us nervous, especially Ruby, to have them following us around when we march. Nobody goes anywhere alone, not even Gloria Madden, who thinks she know something about foreigners and "the British."

Now and then, some folk get a bit too curious, and once or twice, we have had men try to come into our base at the school. We have guards at the gate, just like at Oglethorpe and Fort Des Moines—two WAC MPs on shift at all times—but a couple of males tried to sneak in here to see what we were doing. At home, the white folks don't pay nobody colored any mind. But here—!

***

We have been working for two weeks when Dovey comes busting in one night with a scarf over her head like some of us wear when we are off duty and it's cold out at night. She stands in the middle of the room, and she waits until we all look at her.

"Dovey Borland, what are you up to?"

She just grins and pulls off her scarf. Her hair is marceled in perfect, pretty waves on her head, and she struts through barracks like she a movie star. We all jump up and Phillipa start screaming.

"We got a beauty shop!"

Our battalion commander, who is in charge of all the women, got together with our own brass in special services and requisitioned a beauty shop, including marcel irons and straightening combs. Since Dovey knew folks who had been beauticians when they were civilians, she got wind of it first thing and made herself an appointment. I can't help smiling when I see her looking so happy. Dovey hasn't hardly smiled twice since we got here.

"Where is it?"

"Can anybody go?"

"They got some hair tint over there?"

Dovey laughs as we just about fall over our feet trying to put on our coats and grab our handbags and gloves and be out the door first. This is what we need for *our* morale. It maybe don't make much sense to those five-star generals, the commanders, and the rest of the brass, but those English looking at us all the time don't seem so bad now. When we look this fine? They can stare all they want to.

20.

NOW

Mare promises to teach me how to put up my hair in pin curls, but she says it's too humid, and it would be too much work and way too much hair spray to flat-iron it, then pin it up with hundreds of tiny pins.

"Maybe when we get home," she tells me. "Right now I need a nap."

Mare goes in through the bathroom we share to her hotel room, and I point the remote at the TV and flip around for a few channels. Laugh tracks rattle by as I pass stale eighties sitcoms, so I press Mute, then linger for a moment on a channel showing a big sea animal. It's a killer whale. I flip the channel before the hapless seal it is tracking is caught. We read a poem about this in English last year, something about nature being red teeth and claws. It's true.

"Octavia."

"Huh?" I've found a documentary on surfing. It always looks so easy in all those old pictures. Just standing up on a board in water. Running on sand in big, loose shorts. Even wiping out looks graceful and fun. I've always wished I could surf.

"Do you think you can tell if someone has a new best friend?"

"Huh?" I roll over on my bed and look at my sister. For once, she isn't plugged in to her music or reading a magazine.

"Suzanne's been blowing me off for the past two days. She was kind of ticked that I had to go on this trip." Tali shrugs. "I think maybe either she's got a new best friend or she's got a boyfriend."

"Oh." I chew the corner of my mouth. "Well, if it's a guy, do you think it's anybody you know?" I ask finally.

"Probably," Tali says, sitting up and staring at the TV screen. "Before I left, I told her this boy, Brent Moore, wanted to know what I was doing this summer, so . . ." Tali slides down on the pillows and sighs.

"So?"

"So I said she should find out if Brent had a girlfriend. I mean, she knows I like him, and she said she'd find out, but Julie Guiao just texted me and said Suzanne went to WaveWorld with Brent today."

"Maybe she was asking him if he had a girlfriend," I say cautiously.

"She wasn't supposed to *ask*," Tali mutters. "And anyway, she wouldn't need to hang out with him all day."

Oh. "Well, did you ask her?" I ask.

"She's not answering her phone."

"Harsh."

"Yeah."

I sit up on the bed, tucking my legs underneath me. I find I am almost holding my breath, waiting for Tali to say something else.

That feels kind of lame, that I'm so desperate, but the truth is, my sister and I haven't really *talk* talked to each other in a while. Even though at home she lives in the room across the hall, it's not like we're connected. She's always on her way somewhere else, somewhere I'm not. And she gets mad if anyone asks her where she's going.

Tali is rubbing her bottom lip against her top teeth, a nervous habit from back when she had braces. Now that she's only wearing her retainer, it isn't shredding her lip, but it still looks painful.

I try to find something intelligent to say. "Couldn't you just call Brent?"

My sister's eyes focus on me. "And say . . . what? 'Did you hang out all day today with Suzanne Labrucherie, and what did you talk about?'"

"Okay, maybe not . . . but, I don't know, if Brent called *you*, why couldn't you call him? Ask him what he's doing. I mean, you're on a road trip. You could tell him about it."

Tali shrugs. "I'm sure Suzanne already told him everything. 'Oh, you know Tali Boylen, yeah, she had to babysit her little sister and her geriatric grandmother, so she's busy, but I've got time to be with you.'"

"*Baby*sit?" I look at my sister disbelievingly. "Mare buying you whatever you want and taking you on a trip is babysitting? You're not babysitting me, Tali."

"You know what I mean," Tali says, waving a hand. "Anyway, I can't call him."

"So don't." I turn away.

Why do I bother? She's completely mean without even trying.

I flip some more channels, scowling. I hope Suzanne really is trying to move in on Tali's crush. I hope they totally get together and go to prom next year and rent a limo and a Jet Ski and a helicopter and everything. It would so serve her right.

"Do any of your friends have boyfriends?" Tali asks after a pause. "Your little friend Rye is really cute, and Eremasi could be the next Alek Wek—you know, that African supermodel?"

"Rye's playing soccer, and Eremasi's working at the vet's this summer, cleaning out cages. None of us have boyfriends."

Tali nods knowingly. "Well, you guys are sophomores next year. Life will get better."

"Life is fine now." The channels race by in a blur.

Tali slides off her bed and sighs. "You know, Tave, have you ever thought of doing something with your hair? Maybe something kind of forties, like parting it on the side and wearing it waved like Mare did back in the day? You know, if you tried a little, you could be kind of pretty."

I keep flipping channels, holding on to the remote control so hard my nails are white. "Kind of pretty." Tali is the queen of half insults. And Mare already said she'd help with my hair.

"You haven't done anything new with your hair since

sixth grade, when you stopped wearing barrettes and pigtails. And you should let me do your makeup and cut you some bangs," Tali adds, standing in front of the TV. "Even Mom says you need to get your hair out of your face."

"Move," I complain, leaning around her to see the picture. "I'm watching this."

"C'mon, Octavia," my sister wheedles, reaching out to tug on a handful of my hair. "You can keep this mess on your head if you want to, but at least let me cover up your zits—"

"Cut it OUT!" I yell, turning off the TV.

"What?" Tali says hotly. "I just offered to do your face!"

"Well, I don't want you to do anything to me or my face. I'm fine."

"Octavia, how could you not want to look any better? You don't even try!"

"Tali, you stand there saying, 'You look craptastic—let me fix you up,' and I'm supposed to be all happy?"

"Well, I'm just saying if you don't care what your hair looks like—"

"YOU don't care what my hair looks like, either. Leave me alone, Tali. I'm serious."

"Ever since we came on this trip, you've been totally sitting around pouting like you hate everything, and I'm trying to hang out with you, and you're throwing it back in my face."

"You're only even talking to me because Brent and your best friend Suzanne are too, um, busy." I use the nastiest voice I can.

I can tell she knows it's true, even as her eyes get hard

and sharp. "Whatever. I'm trying to help you pull yourself together, but if you want to keep your loser look and your loser life—"

"At least my friends answer their phones when I call them!"

"Shut up, Octavia. Just—" Tali shoves me, hard, then marches into the bathroom and slams the door.

I turn on the TV and crank up the volume, but part of me still wants to throw the remote at the bathroom door. There are some hours of some days when I hate my sister. She just looks at me, and immediately everything's wrong about me. I swear the only time she notices me is when she can mention a zit I have, or if my hair is a mess, or if I have a spot on my shirt. The rest of the time, she doesn't even see me.

And when I do let her make me up, I feel like a poodle in a dog show. Tali trowels on way too much, and I look like some runway wannabe with tarantula eyelashes and not like myself. When we go to the mall afterward, I get lots of looks, sure, but probably from people thinking, What did she run into face-first? When I won't wear makeup, Tali doesn't want to be seen with me. It's like she can't understand that nobody wants to be her project all the time.

Tali throws open the bathroom door and points her hairbrush at me. "Octavia, just let me fix your eyebrows, okay? I won't even put any makeup on you. Just let me fix your eyebrows and trim your hair, and I'll leave you alone. You'll look a lot better. Octavia, people *pay* to get stuff like this done, all right? Think about that!"

"Just call Brent, okay? That's what you really want to do anyway. Just call him and leave me alone."

"I don't want to!" Tali repeats. "I told you that. I *don't* want to call him. He's going to think I'm stupid, some lame girl who's not even at home calling him to find out what he's doing."

"Who cares if you're not at home?"

"He'll think I'm thinking about him on vacation!" Tali shakes her head. "You don't get it, Tave. I'm not calling him, so drop it." She vanishes back into the bathroom.

"You ARE thinking about him on vacation." I pick up my sister's phone from her bed. "I'm sure you've even got his number in here. Just call him."

"Forget it, Octavia. We're doing your hair now."

"I'm going to call him."

"No, you're not," Tali says disgustedly.

I turn on her phone, scrolling through the record of incoming calls.

"Octavia?"

I double-check the number, then close my eyes, cross my fingers, and push the button.

"OCTAVIA!" My sister hurtles out of the bathroom. "Don't touch my phone!"

I leap up, balance on the edge of the bed, and hold the phone out of reach. "Too late," I say. "It's ringing."

"I hate you! Hang up! Hang up!"

"Shhh!" I put the phone to my ear and wave my hand, but Tali leaps toward me. I jump back, banging my arm against the wall. "Shut up! If I hang up, he'll see your number. Shut up!"

"I will kill you," Tali hisses. "Give me my phone."

"What's up?" A friendly male voice comes over the line.

Tali lunges and I relinquish the phone. "Octavia, you idiot," she says in dull fury, putting the phone to her ear, and then stops, her mouth dropping in shock.

"Brent? Oh, hi, sorry, I was talking to my sister. Yeah, it's me, Tali. I'm good. I'm just, um, doing this road trip with my sister. Yeah? Well, I'm at a hotel in New Mexico."

Tali drops onto her bed, rubbing her teeth against her top lip and glowering at me.

"Tell him we're going to Roswell," I whisper.

"Really? Well, we're thinking of going to Roswell tomorrow just for fun," Tali goes on, looking like she's going to choke. "Oh, you did? Was Suzanne there?"

I edge slowly toward the door, on the far side of the room. I know as soon as my sister gets off the telephone, she's going to come looking for me, so I make plans to hide in the safest place I can find. I tiptoe into the bathroom and knock gently on the adjoining door.

"Hey, Mare? Can I come in?"

Hey Brent,

Was really good talking to you! Roswell is kind of a freak show, but I like it.

So far, vacation isn't that bad. My grandmother lets me drive, so at least there's that. I'm actually not looking forward to the family reunion—maybe I'll just keep driving!

Don't get too attached to Suzanne. I'm coming back, you know! Just kidding. I'm glad she has someone to hang with.

Later,

☮ Tali Boylen

Brent Moore
17 Newbridge Heights
Pleasant Hill, CA 94523

21.

then

"Good morning."

I look up from waiting for Annie and smile. That little English girl, with her long socks and big old sweater and all that hair scraped back into two brown plaits, is always standing out in front of our barracks, watching us. Today, she is toting a piece of biscuit with a little smear of jam. Somebody had some sugar ration saved up for sure.

The girl has got those skinny, knobby knees like Feen used to. She is like all the kids around here—she stares at us from across the street, stares at our uniforms, our shoes, and I don't know what all else. This the first time she says anything to me.

I give her a nod. "Good morning."

"Do you luck gem?"

I frown. What kind of nonsense she talking? "Do I luck *what*, missy?"

"Do you like gem," she say again, all impatient.

Jim? I just look at her, full of confusion, till I notice what she got on her bread. "Oh. You mean, do I like jam? Well, sure," I tell her. "Your mama make you that biscuit?"

"It's not a biscuit. It's a scone."

"It's not, huh? Looks like a biscuit to me," I tell her, and the little girl stares at me like I'm crazy. From up the street, I hear a window scrape, and then the little miss is running like somebody already calling for her.

I laugh at her and look for Annie again. Annie's just got word from her folks that her friend is alive and well, a prisoner of war somewhere behind enemy lines. She's got the iron in her now. Annie Brown is like a leopard that changed its spots. She is up first thing in our barracks and she works hard—writing letters to her newspaper at home, volunteering for extra guard duty as an MP, working as a clerk—and she's got me working with her, too. When we're not on duty at the post office, we're in the Red Cross building—writing letters to the boys in the field, making up packages, and donating blood. Annie doesn't have time to clown and spy on officers anymore, and she can't be bothered about going dancing and such. It takes all I've got just to drag her out to the beauty shop.

Annie is mad clear through at the Nazis. She call them "Krauts," and she got nothing good to say about them nor the "dagos" in Italy or the "Japs," neither. I don't hate none of them. I don't know as I have even ever seen any of the dagos before, or even any Germans back in Bay Slough; they all just look white to me. Annie hasn't seen none of them, neither, but she says she would beat the tar out of 'em if she met any.

Most of the time, it seems the *Post Gazette* says we are winning the war. The Allied troops are winning, they say, and they tell us the bombs we hear mean the German army's on the run, but it doesn't always feel like winning. Not when someone personal gets on the casualty list; then it doesn't feel like winning at all.

When a bomb hits in Birmingham, you can't tell too much by the next day. The English folks sweep up the glass and the rocks and smooth out the road. Broken windows are boarded up, scorched paint is painted over, and as soon as possible, it is all like nothing has happened. First time I heard one of those V-1 bombs, I was scared spitless. And every time, I still get scared; we all of us do. But we don't show it. There are WAC girls all over England—and some in London—who have got to live with this every single day and night. The lieutenant say if the folks who live in Birmingham, the English, can take it, then the U.S. Women's Army Corps can take it, too.

❊ ❊ ❊

Annie finally comes out from the barracks, tying up her scarf, and we walk across the square to the beauty shop, trying to enjoy that little bit of weak sun coming down on us. The jam-eating girl is standing across the road in her yard now. I just nod to her and keep on going, like I used to do to Feen. Little kids will talk to you *all* day if you let them.

Some of the girls want to go home and eat dinner with the English folks they've met and gotten friendly with, and Lieutenant Scott says that's okay with her as long as we make

curfew. Now, I don't know about eating with these folks—
they can't make no kind of coffee, and I don't know about
that tea, either. And Peaches says they eat kidneys for breakfast, and she doesn't mean beans. I have got enough problems with Spam and soybean sausages for just about every
meal. I can't believe that Ina White says she likes 'em.

The bell rings as we go in the door of the shop. Peaches,
Annie, and me have been getting our hair done regularly on
our mornings off. Nobody but Sister Dials and Mama ever
did my hair back home, so to sit in a beauty parlor, even one
like this one with electric cords and chairs all jammed together in a little room, makes me feel like I'm grown.

WACs don't wear those fancy pin curls and updos, not in
this wet and fog. Every time I go to the beauty shop, I remember Lieutenant Hundley way back in basic hollering at
us girls for having our hair past our collars and wearing too
much jewelry. When my turn comes, I choose a side part and
roll the rest on my neck nice and neat. One of these days, I
am going to go out on the town and get myself one of those
pompadours I saw Lena Horne wearing in *Life* magazine. I
am going to put flowers in my hair. I am going to step out!

When I catch myself thinkin' that, I know I have been in
this cold and fog too long. Where would I be going all dolled
up like that? And with who?

I shake my head at myself, then Peaches comes in, smiling. "Hey, girls, guess what? I'm going to be in a magazine,"
she says, and sits down next to me.

"What? Why?" I ask.

"I just talked to a lady reporter from *Life* magazine," she tell me.

I roll my eyes, and Annie just clicks her tongue and sighs. "Peaches," she says, "you've got to find something better to do with your time."

That starts them off arguing, as usual. Me, I'm not trying to talk to no reporters. For one thing, Peaches is still helping me talk like a city girl, and I don't need to forget and say "ain't" with any newspaperman listening. For another thing, those reporters sure don't tell the truth. Phillipa's been down at the mouth since one of her aunties sent her the colored paper from Cleveland. Seems like they're telling the folks back home that we don't know what we are doing out here. Even worse, Lieutenant Scott says now we have got to watch what we say and how we carry ourselves 'cause the reporters have been reporting that most of us are out here whoring and the rest have found a soldier somewhere to get us pregnant. You could've knocked me down when I saw it. They wrote that in the paper, in bold black and white like it's the gospel truth!

Peaches thinks she can change folks' minds about what goes on here, but I know better. Folks always do believe what they want to believe about everything. You can tell them the truth, then tell 'em again, but they just don't always want to hear. Anyway, our CO says that we'd best not pay the papers no mind and get on with our business.

Later, we walk on to the base post office for work. It is fine out, so we take our time. Hardly anybody has cars around here, and there's not much gasoline—or "petrol," like they call it—and only a few buses anymore, so we are walking smack in the middle of the road, arms linked, feeling fine with our sharp uniforms and our fancy hair. Peaches has got fancy hair anyway.

We hear planes growling far off in the blue sky. Then the bus comes and moves away wheezing and sighing, letting off a cloud of black smoke. Folks are all heading home to pick up rations to fix their dinner—or "tea," which is how they call it. I still don't know how "tea" could be two things, but they don't make no kind of sense to me anyway.

I am not surprised to see that little girl tagging round after us again; this time, she's got herself a doll, and she is marching, her little skinny legs going up one-two-one-two, her arms down at her sides, straight. Two or three other little girls are hanging around, watching her clowning while she walks along behind us. The grown folks act like they don't see her, trying to hide their smiles.

"Hey, little miss," I say to her over my shoulder. "What you doing back—" Then I notice the quiet. I stop my mouth and listen.

I hear a crack, and then it sounds like thunder over Bay Slough. We hear that every day, five and six times a day, but this time, it is so close the ground shakes. Everything is still while that growling carries on louder and louder. Even the wind don't make a sound as it pushes past my face, real soft.

"Helmet." Annie only says the one word, and Peaches groans. "Why is it always just after I get my hair done?"

"My heart bleeds for you, Peaches Carter. Don't be a fool." Annie looks at me.

Miss Annie Brown doesn't have to say a thing to me. I already got my helmet off my arm and buckled down under my chin. I look around for the little girl. She is backed up to the side of the road, flattened up against a house. She is looking up. The other girls have run indoors.

The grown folks have stopped where they are. Some of them are looking up. Some of them are looking for a place to hide. One lady takes off her scarf, which is a faded red, and stuffs it into the pocket of her old wool coat, like she scared them Nazis gonna see a little bit of color from way up high. A man squats on his heels, shading his eyes with his hand, watching.

"You get along home, too, miss," I tell the little girl, but she acts like she can't hear me.

I click my tongue. If that were Feen, I'd give her a piece of my mind and a swat on her behind. "Scram, girl!" I say again, and her eyes roll toward me, then back up at the sky. Poor thing's so scared she can't move.

Annie, Peaches, and I crouch in front of a house, craning our necks to see if we can see something. As long as you can hear that little motor on that buzz bomb whine, you know you're all right—it's still flying. Everybody ducks when the motor stops, though. Those bombs glide down in perfect silence—you don't know where they will land. Sometimes we don't hear any explosion at all. Those times, the bomb may not have gone off; it maybe just fell somewhere and is lying in a field.

We wait.

Somebody's baby start to crying, and they hush it.

We wait.

A door opens and we hear a voice shout, "Victoria!" The little girl starts sidling along the houses till we can't see her no more.

The door slams.

We wait.

We wait, we wait, we wait.

The times when we hear nothing, we go on, just thankful it didn't hit here. Today, we don't hear a thing, and after a while, the squatting man clears his throat and stands up.

"Not today, hmm?" he says in his funny, fast way, and then it's like everybody thaws. We all straighten up, move, stretch. The lady puts her scarf back on. The world gets started again.

It doesn't take much time for us to get to talking again, it happens so often. Peaches unstraps her helmet and swings it over her arm, fluffing up her hair. By the time we walk on to the post office, we hear engines growling again. I rub my eyes. "It's going to be dark tonight," I say, and Annie nods.

"Hate those blackout shades." She sighs. We strain our eyes trying to read the names on the packages, but there's nothing we can do about it. After dark, everybody in Birmingham has on blackout shades so we don't give off light to the enemy flying overhead.

When a siren goes off later on that night, we just put on our helmets and keep working. I stand to pick up a package, and I almost fall as the ground shakes. Dust sifts from the walls as the bricks shift. I grab a table to keep my balance, and everybody looks around, smiling kind of nervous.

We have had a hit.

When the chips are down, we do our duty. I pick up my package and listen to the girl next to me muttering. She is saying the rosary, still working, reading off serial numbers and slotting her packages in the right piles. I remember to say my prayers, too.

22.

then

April 5, 1945

Dear Miss Josey,

Hope you had a good Easter. Thank you kindly for the card you sent. We got real eggs for Easter breakfast, not powdered. Nothing to do but go to church and listen to the radio. The Duffle Bag program take requests, and Dovey plays "I'll Walk Alone" till I am sick of it. Poor girl, she misses her man, but that song really works my nerves.

We had payday the 31st but no base passes until today. Time moved up one hour at 0200 hours last Sunday. Didn't think that "daylight saving time" kept up all the way over here, but it does. Feels like we'll get no extra sleep now!

Do you know, somebody told these English folk that coloreds have tails that come out at night!

They say you don't ever see the men's 'cause they
wear slacks, but if they look real close after
midnight, they can see a tail on a colored girl.
Lieutenant Scott let us out of curfew just so we
could be seen on the street after midnight to prove
we don't have tails that come out after dark. You
can be sure some white soldier told them that mess
and they believed it. It shook me up a little to hear
it—I thought folks were different here than they
are back home. I guess folks are the same here as
anywhere. Some are good, and some are not.

You might read in the paper that there are
bombs falling here. We don't get too many—they
going mostly to London or sometimes out in the
country. Nobody here even worries about getting
bombed, so don't you worry about us, either, you
hear? Some of the English folk started calling these
V-1 bombs "Bob Hope" bombs. You bob down
when they call the alert, and you hope it won't get
you!

Every day I work at the post office on my
eight-hour shift, I think I want to tell everybody in
the world how to send their mail. If you write
Sister Dials, tell her when she sends a package to
her boy in the navy to wrap it tight. I don't know
about the navy, but people will send the army

*some of the most raggedy packages! Sometimes it's
impossible to put them back together.*

*Every morning after shift, we have exercise in
our auditorium or march back to our quarters (we
are still at the school) and have "tea" because only
the Red Cross makes coffee that taste like
anything. We have a few hours free, and then we
hit the sack. I don't have time to get into trouble,
Feen. You keep telling Aunt Shirley that. You-all
don't have to worry about me.*

*It is still raining. We have nothing but clouds
on clouds out here. Lord, this weather is about to
wear me out.*

*Looking for spring, I am,
Marey Lee Boylen, Private, Second Class*

Our third weekend pass, Ruby, Annie, Peaches, and me
sign out to go to London. We have been here almost three
months now, and Annie say it is *past* time for me to see it.
Other folks have taken the train to Paris already and spent
time on R & R all over the place, but I like Birmingham just
fine. Still, Peaches says I have got to see London once before
I die.

It is not really a weekend pass since we leave on Thursday
and our orders are to report back for duty Saturday at 0800
hours, but we will take what we can get. It is the first time we
have all managed to get away together, and Ruby won the

drawing for a forty-eight-hour pass to London. The four of us are looking forward to taking in the sights.

It is easy to see London, Ruby and Peaches tell me, 'cause the train takes you all the way there, and in uniform, a WAC rides for free. It will be fun, Annie says, because we will see London Bridge and Big Ben.

Now, I don't know that I care about London, but Annie says that's because I am a "country rube" who hasn't seen anything yet. She and Peaches talk so much they talk me into it. "A trip to London is just what the doctor ordered. They've got a WAC hotel for enlisted girls there. They've got noncommissioned officers' clubs!"

"They've got men," Peaches says, like that should settle my mind.

What settles my mind is this: today is my birthday. I am eighteen years old.

I have already heard from Feen. She has sent me a card she made with scraps of lace, paper, buttons, and paste, and she even sent me a paper flower for my hair from Woolworth's. Letters home are postage-free for all WACs, but Feen still has to pay for postage. No matter what, she still writes me faithfully.

Mama still hasn't written me a word. At all.

I think *probably* she doesn't even know where to write me. Last time I wrote, we had just gotten here. Probably she's sent something by now, and it is making its way to me. Probably . . .

But when I talk straight to myself, late at night, I know there's no "probably" to it. Even though I am her firstborn child, seems like my own mama could not care less about me.

And then that feeling a bit low gets lower about some other things. Three weeks ago, our CO called a full base meeting that shut down even the two "eight shifts" at the base post office. Gossip ran that HQ was about to cancel all leaves without a base commander's say-so. Folks had it that something real bad had happened, and when we crowded into the auditorium—all thousand of us, enlisted and officers—there wasn't room enough to sit, and we were packed in like sardines.

Then our CO tells us some Red Cross ladies went and found us a hotel in London—a hotel of our own, just for the Six-triple-eight. Seems the Red Cross doesn't think we colored girls are "happy" mixing with the white girls at the enlisted WAC hotel in London. Our CO asked us not to go to the colored hotel, just to make a point that we are as good as everyone else in the Women's Army Corps, and we won't be pushed out from where the rest of the enlisted WACs stay. Our CO says she'll hold out curfew in time for us to get back to base and sleep in our own beds since the trains run all night. We can go back and forth to London all weekend long that way. Or we can stay in a hotel and pay on our own or we can stay with a family.

Most folks didn't take to that really well, and it has just brought me lower than before. It is crazy to be here fighting for freedom and democracy when we are not free. It tears me up to wonder why we are here, why our colored men go down fighting, when things will stay the same at home. I just don't know if I did right to join the Women's Army.

I guess I forgot that other folks just see "colored" wherever we go, even though all we see is worsted khaki uniforms and folks fighting on the same side around here. All of us planning to see London are fit to be tied.

"Are you kidding me?" Phillipa says as we head back to barracks. "How are we supposed to take a pass to London if we've got to come back in time for bed?"

"Well," says Dovey, "if you can't beat 'em, guess you gotta join 'em. As long as they're stretching out curfew to match the train schedule, I'd rather sleep snug in my own bed anyway. You know you've got to put a sixpence in those little heaters all night long anyway, and some of those hotels are bound to have bedbugs."

"I don't know why those Red Cross ladies want to put us all by ourselves out there. Don't they know we want to go to London to meet new people?" Annie shakes her head. "It's just segregation all over again, plain and simple. I sure thought over here it would be different."

Ruby shrugs. "It's not the end of the world. London's still a real good time."

Peaches say she got friends of folks in the city where we could stay, but I think I'll take a rain check on that. Today, I am no kind of good company. I was sure I'd hear from Mama before now. It hurts me that she would let my birthday pass without a word. It hurts me that I expected any different.

After inspection, we get all spiffed up to step out into the city. We are at the train station, looking sharp in our off-duty uniforms with our belts, gloves, and bags. Ruby lends me her lipstick for the occasion, and all of us look real nice. Even with our fine-looking hair, under our arms we've got our helmets.

Makes no difference that the London Blitz has been over for a couple of years. We don't play around with those V-1s, which are still flying at least a couple of times a day. Folks have got to put out their smokes and pull down the shades in every house and on every train every single time, so we won't take chances. In our bags we got flashlights, or "torches," like they call them here. It gets mighty dark on a train during a blackout.

Ruby's all excited about what we're going to do. "First, Marey," she say, "we're going to Buckingham Palace to see the changing of the guard. Then we're going to ride us one of those double-decker buses and see everything—even St. Paul's Cathedral, right where they were bombed the hardest. It'll be just like that picture from *Life* magazine—how it's the one big thing standing when everything else fell flat!"

"Oh, Ruby Bowie, you are precious," I hear someone say all sweet. Oh, no. My stomach twists. "What's cooking, girls?" Gloria Madden says, tilting her head to show off her hair. "Fancy meeting you here!"

"I didn't think you got a pass!" Peaches says, smiling at Gloria. "You coming with us?"

"Not today," Gloria says, cutting her eyes at me, and my stomach relaxes. "I know you've got to show Ruby and Marey the big-city sights and all. That's not my scene. I've got people to meet."

Annie rolls her eyes and sighs. Gloria Madden has got some nerve.

"Oh, you're going to see your captain?" Peaches whispers, and Annie leans in.

"What? Captain? Gloria Madden, what are you up to, seeing an officer?"

"I don't tell my business to just anyone," Gloria says, fluttering her lashes like she's crazy. "Can't talk—that's my train!"

I make a face, but I don't let Peaches see me. Gloria Madden is nothing but uppity Eastern trash, but for some reason, those two are thicker than thieves these days. There's no accounting for taste, I guess.

I don't have too much time to worry 'cause the conductor is waving us in, and we all board. This is not the first time I have been back on the train since we got to Birmingham, but this will be my longest trip. For once, the sun is even shining, and it really feels like we might halfway thaw out one of these days.

In the train folks just sit—colored and whites. Folks smoke and talk, and the country rolls on by. I keep looking up, waiting for somebody to send us into the segregated car, but nobody does. Everybody huddles in their coats and folks nod, seeing our uniforms.

England is green, green, green, and it looks like there is just nothing but nice little hills for miles. Annie says some of those "hills" are airplane hangars with planes in them, all camouflaged against the enemy. It's so pretty I wish I had a picture of all of those little hills.

Soon we see houses here and there, and then a few more, and then they are all stuck together, wall to wall, brick houses stained black from smoke, with chimneys all lined in a row. Next thing they holler is, "London Bridge

Station!" and Annie says, "That's us." I fumble for my gloves and look around, my stomach jumpy. Today, I might see the king of England; wouldn't that be something to write Feen about?

First thing Annie wants to do is find some postcards to mail to her folks back home. Ruby and I follow her into a little shop where everybody is nice as they can be. The folks don't look at us like they do in Birmingham; nobody cares if we are colored or not. Afterward, we squabble about what to do next.

"Let's see the Tower of London," Annie say.

"I don't want to go where they cut off all them folks' heads," I tell her. "Let's see the king."

"Nobody sees the king." Annie laughs at me good. "We get to see the guards change."

"I want to go to Piccadilly Circus," Ruby say.

"They got a circus here?"

"That's just what they call a circle in the street," Annie tells me, smiling. "It's way downtown, with lots of clubs and all of that."

"Let's go." Ruby grins, her eyes all full of mischief. "It's not too early to eat, is it?"

We end up at a little lunch spot where Ruby gets us some sandwiches and tea. Then we strut up and down the street, looking at the shops and the clubs. Folks look at us and smile, especially at me, since I am craning to look at everything. Downtown at Piccadilly is one big noisy place, and London's the biggest city I've ever seen. Folks are walking, jeeps are driving servicemen and officers around, and people are riding bicycles. I hear a growling sound, and I look up, grabbing my helmet. A lady says, "That's no Jerry, luv. That's the tram!"

Of course, one or two soldiers—navy—try to talk to Annie, but she isn't having that. A girl with three brothers knows how to give them that Look, so they leave her be. We walk a bit more, and the sun breaks through for real. I am almost happy. A fat little boy in short pants and a big hat says "Cheerio," to us and waves. His little cheeks are round like Peaches's, and she gives him a chocolate bar.

I buy Feen some hair clips in a tin box. After Ruby buys a book for her sister back home, we go to a pub called the Hawk 'n' Dove. I look around at the mirror and all the bottles and smile. Mama would be fit to be tied if she knew I was in a place like this!

"What'll it be, ladies?" The bartender is looking at us expectantly, his white rag rubbing up and down that clean bar. He looks like he could work for Lieutenant Scott, the way he's wiping up what shines already.

"Scotch and water," Ruby say, calm as you please. My mouth *drops*.

"Gin and tonic," Annie say, and the bartender nods and turns away.

Peaches nudge me. "Girl, you're catching flies. Come on. What'll you have?"

"Lemonade?" My voice is high.

Peaches giggles. "Two Pimm's Cups, please."

I turn on her, shocked. "A lemonade, I said."

"Come *on*, Marey girl. You're in *London*!"

"What's a Pimm's Cup?" asks Ruby. "Is it good?"

"Sure! It's just a teensy bit of gin; it's mostly fruit, some cucumbers, and—"

"It's got lemonade in it, miss," the bartender says, looking like he is trying not to laugh.

My face is tight and hot. Reverend Morgan says "Wine is a mocker," and I am already feeling shamed.

"If you don't like it, Marey Lee, you don't have to drink it," Ruby says, real soft.

I nod, just a little, and the bartender slide me that drink. It is just a little glass, not big. It has fruit in it, and cucumbers, like Peach say.

Probably it can't be that bad if it has fruit.

That stuff Mama drinks is malt whiskey straight from the bottle. It is not like I never tasted that, but liquor is the devil's own brew, I know what Reverend Morgan say, and Mama's stuff sure enough burned me like hellfire. I made certain Feen never got into Mama's whiskey.

But this isn't all liquor. And Mama hasn't had a thing to say to me for months.

And when I take a sip, it's not too bad at all.

23.

NOW

"I'm so jealous." Tali sighs. "I want to go to London."

As long as we've been driving, it feels like we could have driven there twice now. We're going to be in this car forever.

Mare's only been driving something like five or six hours a day, and since she doesn't like to drive when it's hot, and she doesn't like to drive when it's dark, and she likes to follow signs that say Amazing Roadside Attraction, 45 Miles! to see what they are, we've been crisscrossing the map, back and forth, hours off of any main roadways. We've seen cliff dwellings and conservation areas. We've seen Native reservations, natural wonders, and national parks. Every night, Mare shells out for fancier and fancier hotels and complains more and more about her "barking dogs" and her aching back. At the rate we're going, this trip *will* take all summer.

I didn't think I had a problem with being on an all-summer road trip in theory, but in reality, it is getting kind of hard. For one thing, who would have thought I'd get sick of pie for breakfast? Or sick of truck stops and diner food? Tali's been looking in phone books in every place we stop so she can find some off-the-highway restaurants that have table-cloths and decent salads. Mare insists we stop at every fruit stand and farmers' market in search of fresh foods that haven't wilted under a heat lamp. Tali's even started jogging when we get to the hotels at night. Even if it's just doing laps in the parking lot of a motel, she thinks it's necessary. "All this sitting is giving me a huge butt," she says. If she wasn't so obnoxious, I might run along with her. So far, I'm doing sit-ups when she's not around. If only my phys ed coach could see me now.

We stopped in Tombstone, Arizona, last week to have lunch at the O.K. Café. Mare just *had* to have a buffalo burger and get a load of the World's Largest Rosebush—which, okay, is huge, but it's a rosebush.

"Octavia, come stand next to Tali," Mare instructed me, aiming her phone at the massive shrub. "I've got to get a picture."

It's cool and all, but come on! It's an overgrown plant—who cares?

Ever since Tali's started talking to Brent Moore, she's been all about "recording our trip." She takes a picture of her breakfast every morning on her cell and texts Brent about the best barbecue in Texas, the state flower, the state bird, blah, blah, blah. To be honest, now that she's happier, she's gotten a lot easier to take. She and Mare aren't fighting every day, and she has something nice to say to me once in a while.

Even with all of the peace and love going on, I'll be glad

to be done with central Texas. It is flat, with oil derricks and miles and miles of plain old nothing. We just drive and drive, and Mare still doesn't seem to have a particular destination in mind. I look at the map sometimes and have no idea where we are or if my grandmother made up this whole reunion thing.

Today, Tali wants to ride shotgun, so I am sitting in the backseat, kind of dozing as I watch the flat, dry landscape blur by. We slow down to enter yet another nameless small town, marked only by its two stop signs and a flashing signal light where railroad tracks cross the main drag through town. A girl our age holding a fat, dimpled baby waits on the sidewalk beside us as a freight train rumbles past.

"Oh, look at his wittle cheeks! He is *so* cute," Tali says, wrinkling her nose and waving. Mare just snorts.

"Babies," she says, and shakes her head. "Now, that there's nothing but trouble, a baby having another baby."

Tali frowns. "She's not that young. She's got to be what, nineteen? Twenty?"

"That's what I said. A *baby*. Girl's got no business with one of those."

"What, so you don't like babies now? You had Dad!"

"And having him was the biggest mistake in my life."

"What?"

Just then the all-clear bell clangs as the last car of the train rumbles past. The black-and-white-striped crossing arm rises, and Mare lets the girl, juggling the infant on her hip, cross the road. She puts the car in drive and accelerates across the train tracks.

"You said Dad was a mistake," Tali prompts when it looks like Mare isn't going to say any more.

"Mm-hmm," Mare replies.

"Well, *why*?" Tali insists. "Unless you don't want to say," she adds lamely, suddenly seeming to realize her tone is bordering on rude.

"Doesn't bother me to say," Mare answers easily. "Some of us just don't have no business having babies, and that's all there is to it. After the war, a bunch of us got back into civilian life and didn't know how to act. We got used to just seeing a job to do and getting it done, and the people around us got nervous. Folks thought we were manly since we didn't wait on a man to take out the garbage or drive a car. A lot of us got married 'cause we couldn't think of anything else."

Tali makes a face. "Why couldn't you just live with somebody?" she asks. At Mare's raised eyebrows, she adds, "I meant a girl somebody—so you could have your own place and stuff."

"I did live with someone—my girl Peaches. We had a little place in Westside Courts, and we caught the streetcar downtown like everyone else, but back in those days, sometimes it wasn't enough to just have a good job and a place."

"So, you got married and had Dad?"

"I got mixed up with Christopher Marcus and thought I ought to marry him, if only to hush up folks sayin' Peach and me were sweet on each other." Mare glances at Tali sideways.

"So, Peaches was gay?" I ask. "So what? I mean, once you weren't in the army where they could kick you out, what was the big deal?"

Mare gives her sharp laugh and looks back at me. "You are downright broad-minded, Octavia Boylen. Not everyone is like that, especially not back in the day."

"Not everybody's like that even now," Tali says.

"You know, Peach told me she'd move out just to keep me from marrying that fool, but I thought a baby had to have his daddy, and I couldn't wait to be Mrs. Christopher Marcus. I was all of twenty-three." Mare clicks her tongue in disgust. "First time he came home smelling like cheap gin with lipstick on his neck, I saw sense. I packed up your daddy in a hurry and went right on back to my old place. Peach hadn't even had time to change the furniture around."

"Did Dad ever get to see his father?"

Mare shakes her head. "Back then child support was still kind of new. If a woman left, most folks didn't think her husband owed her anything at all, and a lot of us were ashamed to drag our troubles into court. I cut loose from Mr. Marcus and never looked back."

"Weird . . . somewhere we have other relatives," Tali says in a faraway voice.

Mare snorts again. "The ones you got to put up with aren't enough for you?"

"It's a good thing Peaches had your back," I say thoughtfully.

"Yes, indeed." Mare nods, signaling to exit the freeway. "Peach Carter has *always* had my back, and I wouldn't have made it without her. No, ma'am." Mare slows as we exit and signals for a left turn, heading out into the countryside.

"Where are we going *now*?" The sight of another anonymous town pulls the words out of my mouth before I remember that I promised myself I wouldn't ask that today.

"Paris," Mare says, and her mouth tightens the way mine does when I'm trying not to laugh.

"Paris. Okay." I don't even try to sound convinced. "Mare, why can't you be serious?"

"Paris, Texas. Lord," Tali groans. "It's real, Octavia. They made their own Eiffel Tower. With a hat."

That sounds too goofy to be true. "They did not."

"Just wait," Tali mutters, and slides down in her seat.

"You know, I actually got over to France to see the Eiffel Tower," Mare says musingly. "It was all right, but it wasn't much compared to the Arc de Triomphe. Now, that arch is beautiful. You know, folks flew their planes right on through there on V-day."

"Did you see them?"

Mare shakes her head. "Was in the wrong place for seeing that. But I did see dancing in the streets, planes flying with all their lights on, and bonfires on just about every corner on V-day. Hmph. That was something."

"This is something, too," Tali announces as we turn into the parking lot at Memorial Park. "Something completely lame."

The spindly replica of the tower rises high against a backdrop of puffy white thunderheads. The outsized red cowboy hat topping it catches the light proudly.

"Well." Mare sighs. "This isn't bad. But next time we'll go to the one in Las Vegas."

"Really?" Tali sits up. "Are you serious, Mare? We're going to Vegas?"

"There's an Eiffel Tower in Las Vegas?"

"That's for on the way home." Mare grins and puts the car back in drive.

Hey peeps,

Yes, we are STILL in Texas. And yes, that is a big dumb cowboy hat on top of a fake Eiffel Tower. Mare wants to see EVERY SINGLE WEIRD THING in every state. And she says on the way home, she's taking us to VEGAS! Can you believe it?!

😊😊😊😊😊

I'm completely sick of being in a car. I'm almost desperate enough to drive myself. Mare told us about how she learned to drive a jeep in the army. They just barely gave them any lessons—an afternoon—then they got their license if they didn't kill anyone. NO WONDER she drives like she does. It totally explains EVERYTHING!!!!!

Wish you were here!
😊 Octavia

P.S. Did you guys get the shirts I sent you from Roswell yet? I have one, too, only my alien is pink. What's actually kind of freaky is that the minute Mare saw MY shirt, she had to get one, too . . . which is why I'M NOT WEARING MINE!

Rye Preston & Eremasi Sariki
4174 Eileen Drive
Martinez, CA 94553

24.

then

The joint is jumpin'. Folks are squeezed up tight, laughing, hollering, drinking, and jitterbugging. Somebody is singing, but back at our table in the corner, we are too far away to see. Peaches has already been and gone, but Annie, Ruby, and me are still seeing the sights. We've got two hours yet till the last train.

It's so warm in here I could take off my jacket, but I don't want to lose it. Folks are jammed in every bit of space in here, in all kinds of stripes and all kinds of uniforms.

"Hey! Annie Brown!" somebody hollers, and Annie looks up at a couple of colored men in blue uniforms pushing through the crowd. The one looking at Annie is tall and long-legged, his jaw long and sharp and his nose straight with a bump in it like it was broken. The other colored boy is wider in the shoulders, shorter and heavier, and he looking at nothing but his drink, holding it high so it won't spill.

"Jake Pennington! Man, what are *you* doing here?" Annie jumps up and puts down her drink. She starts laughing

and hugging this man, and Ruby and me just sit there, jaws
dropped. Haven't hardly seen Annie lit up like this in
months.

"Red Cross left a unit here."

"Red Cross?" Annie has to holler to be heard.

"Yeah . . . Got a field kitchen, and we do coffee duty all
over. Who are your friends?"

"This is Ruby Bowie and Marey Lee Boylen," Annie
shouts. "Ladies, this is Jake Pennington and his friend . . ."

"Bob. Bob Carver." The shorter boy reach out to shake
my hand, and I almost don't give it to him. My stomach is all
jumpy. Strong drink *and* strange men. Mama would likely
have a fit if she could see me now!

"Can I buy you girls something to drink?" Jake looks at us,
smiling and friendly. His teeth are really white, and he has
got that citified conked hair, all waved and smooth like Cab
Calloway's.

"I am fine, thank you," I say, real polite, but Ruby kicks
me under the table.

"You can get us a couple of those Pimm's Cups, thanks,"
she says, and Bob sets down his drink and says he'll go.

Annie is just grinning, she's so happy. "You hear from
Abe and Marvin? I hear they're in France," she says. She and
Jake put their heads together so they don't have to yell and
gossip about all the folks from back home. Ruby looks up
and smiles when she sees Bob holding up our drinks. And
here come some more folks behind him—three more colored
boys in the blue Red Cross uniform and two white girls!

My eyes just get wide. I can't hardly keep my mouth closed.

Two of the colored boys look around and grin, swaggering. One of them has got his arm around one of the girls' waists. He's built like the Brown Bomber, that Joe Louis fellow, the boxer with the big old arms. The other colored boy is really tall, taller than most everybody I have ever seen. He's looking around at folks, grinning like a fool, trying to start some mess. The third boy doesn't hardly look at us; he looking back over his shoulders, looking at the tables, trying to find somebody. He's got his hat tilted over his eyes.

"Hey! Here's our gang. This little guy is Tiny Luke Green. And Andrew Rudley and his cousin, James." Bob slides our cups onto the table.

Tiny looks down and hollers something about, "Pleased to meet ya," and James can't hardly get his head turned toward us long enough to do more than give us half a wave. Andrew is too busy hugging up on that girl to pay anybody any attention.

"Cheers, everyone. I'm Adele," the other white girl says, sticking out her hand to Annie, who takes it right away. Adele's light brown hair is parted on the side and curled up over her ears, and her brown eyes go sharp, looking at Ruby and me staring at her. Her skin is what they call that "peaches and cream," and her cheeks are suddenly real pink.

Ruby swallows and takes the girl's hand, shaking it fast. "Ruby," she says, so quiet you can't hardly hear. Her face doesn't show a sign of what she's thinking.

"Call me Delly," she says, and I stand up to shake her hand. Mine is cold.

"Hello . . . Delly." I swallow. "Marey Lee Boylen, private, first class."

"This is Barbara," Andrew Rudley says, putting his arm around the other girl.

"Ta, girls," Barbara says, looking like a cat in the cream. She doesn't put out her hand to nobody. She turns around and pouts up her lips. "Andy, I want to dance."

"All right, then," he says, and up they get and onto the floor. Pretty soon they're all wrapped up around each other, Barbara with that little cat smile on her face.

I still can't believe my eyes.

Folks order up their drinks, grab chairs, and settle around our table. Tiny leans over talking to Bob and James. Ruby won't hardly look at me, but I can see her sitting there, all stiff. Annie looks at the dance floor, then she looks at Jake, curious.

"The white folks don't give Andrew any trouble?"

Jake shakes his head and laughs out loud, his big white teeth showing. "Are you kidding? You see this nose? Some white GI busted it my first week here, thought he could push me around since I was just by myself. Andy doesn't care about 'trouble' anymore; a guy can buy 'trouble' with some folks here just for walking around."

Annie purses up her mouth and shakes her head. "Isn't that the truth," she says. Then she sighs and talks about something else. "So, how many in your unit?"

Jake picks up his drink. "We've got eight," he says. "They moved the other units out closer to the front, but we're the mop-up team. We work with one of the Clubmobiles; we're the only colored unit with the Red Cross in London. . . ." He keeps on, saying something else, but I am not listening. I am looking at that white girl Barbara and thinking. She looks like somebody I have seen before—red, red lips, big green eyes, trying to look like some kind of movie star.

"Wonder where he got her?" Ruby leans over toward me. I wonder, too. I wonder where Andrew Rudley comes from to make him think he can strut around with a white girl like that. Folks in the South get strung up for just look-ing at a white girl. Maybe Andrew Rudley has forgotten who he is.

"What makes you think he's got her at all?" I ask Ruby behind my hand. "From where I sit, that cat's got an armload of nothing. You think she'd step out with him back home?"

"She'd better not," Ruby says quickly. "She'd just bet-ter *not*."

"It doesn't make me no difference who that boy steps out with," I say.

"It makes one to me," says Ruby. She looks put out. "There are few enough colored men around here. She doesn't need to be stepping out with ours."

Bob looks at Delly, then at Ruby, nervous. He thinks Ruby and me shouldn't say stuff like that in front of a white girl, but I know she is not hearing anything from *us*. Tiny is leaning over her, lighting up her cigarette and talking real sweet and low.

"Ruby." Bob's finally made up his mind. "You wanna dance?"

"Fine," she says, and gets right up, mouth still tight.

Tiny grabs Delly and heads after them, and Jake asks if Annie wants another drink. James looks at me, but I look down at the table. I can't dance no jitterbug, and anyway, I still have got my drink. Lessons with Annie and Peaches don't mean I can dance with a real boy, not yet.

They change the record to play something soft. "Tommy Dorsey's 'Marie,'" James says. "You're Marey Lee, right? Close enough. Come on and dance."

My mouth just dries out. Me? I can't. What if I open my mouth and he hears how country I am? What if I step on his feet?

"If you can't beat 'em, join 'em, huh?" James is still waiting.

"Sure. Okay." I can barely talk, but Annie gives me a thumbs-up.

The dance floor is no bigger than a postage stamp. James is tall and handsome, a real knockout, and he's a good dancer, too. He hums in my ear, and I can smell his hair pomade as he puts his arms around me.

We swing through not just one dance, but two. James asks me where I am from and says he is from Dayton, Ohio. He tells me he was a salesman back home, makes two hundred dollars a week already and he is only twenty-five. I don't say too much. I just listen. I know a smooth talker when I hear one. When we get back to the table, Ruby is smiling, and I can't keep a grin off my face.

Before I get time to catch my breath, Bob asks me to dance, and Jake asks Annie. James takes Ruby, and then we switch. I dance with James one more time.

"Hate to break up the party, girls, but we've got a train to catch," Annie says. "This curfew-on-leave thing is for the birds." Ruby and me groan, but Annie keeps at us till we get up.

"I wouldn't mind you lot stopping with me," Delly says, looking around at us. "We live just past Oxford, if you don't mind an extra railway stop."

"Thanks, Delly," Annie says. "We've got to be back tonight, but maybe we'll take you up on that tomorrow?"

"I'll take a rain check on that drink," Ruby says, and she stands up. Bob smiles at her with his whole face, a different kind of smile than before.

"Maybe I'll see *you* tomorrow?"

"Maybe," Ruby says, like she doesn't care.

I look at James. "Thanks for the dance," I say, trying to sound grown.

"Think nothing of it," says James, waving his hand. "Maybe I'll see ya around."

After some more talk, Jake, Bob, and Tiny walk us to the station. Bob walks with Ruby, while Tiny and Jake take turns telling us their fool stories. There are a lot of uniforms out, and folks are singing and laughing too loud. I can smell cheap whiskey and perfume, and I see folks weaving out there on the sidewalk, rolling like a ship in a high wind. One painted dolly grabs hold of Jake and says, "Hey, soldier! Slow down!"

"Hurry up," I hear Annie say. "We can't miss this train!"

Jake grabs her, and they run on ahead. I do my best to follow on, close as I can.

We walk on through a big old crowd in front of another juke joint, and Tiny steps in front, trying to clear the way for me. I slip sideways between folks, ducking under his arm. The crowd shoves, and Tiny jostles me, then straightens up.

"Watch it, boy!"

It is a slow moonshine drawl, but I hear the crack of an overseer's whip behind those three words. My stomach hits my backbone. I spin around, trying to find a face.

He is close to us, just another khaki uniform and a pair of broad shoulders. His face is hardly visible, but I can still see his mouth all twisted up. He hawks, and a gob of spit lands right next to our feet. He looks at Tiny, spoiling for a fight.

"There's no 'boy' around here," Tiny say, real slow, his voice real calm. "We don't want any trouble." Tiny puts his hand on my back, and he pushes, just a little. I know what to do. I start moving. Fast. Sister Dials always says folks who get liquored up don't make no kind of sense. It is best not to try and reason with them. Neither of us wants trouble, especially since Bob and Jake are somewhere ahead of us and I've got a train to catch. I step up my pace, and Tiny does, too.

We get another couple of feet before we know for sure that boy is following us. Him and some other folks I can't see. I look up at Tiny, and his face has gone empty, like his mind is somewhere else. He has got his hand on my shoulder, and he doesn't say anything.

"Tiny," I say.

"Don't talk, walk," he says, and I keep my mouth shut and my eyes on the ground.

Don't know why I want to look back. I've seen these folks before. All of us have seen them before, don't care where we've been, and hate always looks the same. It has got the same face, the same voice, the same mouth all twisted up sour, trying to say all those poison-mean things.

I trip over something in the road, take a little hop, and walk faster. My ankle throbs.

"You all right?" Tiny grabs my elbow.

"Just fine," I say, but my voice is tight. "Tiny . . ."

"Can you walk faster?"

I can.

"Yeah, you better run, you uppity nigra." I hear the voice again, sneering. "We strung up a big ugly nigra like you back home."

Now all I can think about is rope prickling raw against my skin. About colored boys who been dragged through the street and strung up for looking sideways at a white girl. About all of us who have ever been chased, been beat, been tarred. I wonder about Tiny. What is he thinking? How could he convince himself that white folks weren't nothing to think about here? My heart is about to burst right out of my chest, it beats so hard.

Tiny walks faster, and I try to keep up.

"We're going to get you to that train," Tiny says, pretending like that is the only thing that has got me worried. "Don't you fret, Private Boylen."

I keep my head down. It is supposed to be safe to walk after dark with a man, but walking with a colored man with white folks after him means I might be better off on my own. Leastways, then nobody would be chasing me about to kill me.

"Forgot who you are, nigra—found out you can get a white girl here. Been seeing you and them other coons of yours stepping out with them English whores."

Tiny's face is like polished rock. His nose is flared, like air is hard to take in.

"What's her name, nigra? You call that whore by your mama's name?"

Tiny stops cold. His hand on my back pushes, hard.

"No!" I blurt. "Tiny, don't—"

"*Run.*"

I run.

Before I get two steps, I hear a solid *whump*, and somebody grunts, hard, like the air just got knocked right out of them. Folks on the street start screaming, and I start hollering for Jake and Bob, feet flying. Next thing I know, Ruby has got me by the arm, telling me to calm down.

"They got Tiny." I can't hardly talk. "Tiny. They gonna beat him to death."

Bob grabs my arm. "How many?"

"I don't know—maybe five?" I can't stop shaking.

"I'll see you, Ruby," Bob says. He looks behind us, looks back at Ruby, trying to decide. "I've got to go," he says, and he runs.

I hear whistles, and Ruby grabs my hand. "MPs."

"I've got to go back. I can tell them what happened. I can—"

Ruby grips my arm. "We've got to go. We can't miss that train."

I look back. "Ruby! The MPs will haul them *all* in, and—"

Ruby shakes her head, but she won't say nothing, not about Bob, not about nobody. We run to the station, and our train is already there. We climb on, wrap up tight in our coats, and walk through the cars, looking for Annie.

"Are you girls all right?" she says when we find her. "I thought I'd lost you."

Ruby just flops down on a seat like her strings have been cut. She rubs her face while I tell Annie what went on.

Annie nods her head. "Jake said it, all right. Colored soldiers are fighting two wars over here." She sighs and looks out at the dark as the whistle sounds and the train jerks and starts to move. "One of these wars it doesn't look like they've got any chance to win."

"It's their own fault this time," Ruby say, suddenly hot. "Why are they stepping out with English girls? They're bringing trouble on themselves."

Annie shakes her head. "No. We're all American soldiers. We're here fighting for democracy; isn't that what they tell us? They've got the right to step out with anyone. And the English don't take kindly to anyone telling them what to do, so they won't stop seeing them."

"Specially not that Delly." Ruby smiles a little. "She is something, the way she just spoke right up, cool as anything, and invited us over. She doesn't know us from a hole in the ground!"

"I'm going to stay with her tomorrow night," Annie says, then she looks at Ruby and me. "You girls should come, too."

"I don't know," I say. I am not sure about Delly at all. Tiny sure likes her, though. It don't bother me who Tiny steps out with, but it seems to me he'd better be real sure she's worth all the aggravation before he starts beating folks over her.

"It's just one night," Annie says. "Come on, girls."

Seems the English have they own ideas about us "blacks," about our colored soldiers, and about us. All I know of the English is that they talk fast and pretend that don't nothing bother them, not war, not bombs, not nothing. It might be all right to stay with this Delly, to get a look at what Tiny sees in her. And anyway, it is only one night.

Back at base, we all hold out our passes, and the MP checks us in. Ruby starts humming a song, and I remember James singing in my ear. Seems like so much has happened since then. Too much.

Well, my first time in London, and I have drunk alcohol, danced with men, and run away from a fight. This has been some kind of birthday.

25.

then

Delly's house looks like all the other ones in Reading—brick and brown. In the front room at Delly's house, they've got a "sixpenny fireplace," like the gas stoves Ruby says they have got in the Red Cross hotel. They also have a picture of the old English king. Delly's mama, Mrs. Georgina Dye, sits in that front room and sews up something with a lamp on her, keeping her eye on the street, where Delly's little brothers play. She has got blackout curtains pinned up at the side, too.

If she was but taller and a little broader in the beam, she would look just like Sister Dials, sitting up there, talking about, "Adele! Introduce your friends," like we are somebody special.

In our shoulder bags we have brought gifts. Doris got us some C rations—beef stew in cans and such—and Mrs. Dye is glad like we brought her diamonds and gold. Ruby brings a stash of chocolate bars from back home, and I bring three oranges and K rations. K rations have got a

can of Spam or cheese, a few crackers, cookies or candy, a
few cigarettes, and powdered coffee. Mrs. Dye want to
open up that powdered coffee for us 'cause she say Americans
like their coffee, but we told her we would have tea
just fine.

We eat "tea," like a late lunch, I guess, and sit down to
what Delly and her mama and her little brothers eat. The
house stinks like cabbage; Mrs. Dye seems to like her
Brussels sprouts. Ruby scrunches up her face at the smell,
but I have smelled worse when Mama butchered a hog.

Tea is thin sandwiches with margarine and peppery
"cress," which don't taste like nothing different from
creasy greens back home. Course, at home, nobody puts
greens in a sandwich. They have also got carrot, cabbage,
and sweet pickle grated up on white bread for a treat,
which is all right, I guess.

Mrs. Dye says we have "bangers and mash" for later
on. Haven't never had anything like that, but Annie say
it is only mashed potatoes and sausages that pop open
when you cook them. Annie says the sausages are made
out of pork, but Ruby says they taste like sawdust and cotton to her. I am sure glad we brought a little something.
Folks here don't have no kind of good food in this war.

Delly asks where we want to go tonight. Ruby looks at
me and says she wants to go see Piccadilly Circus.

"Let's go to Rainbow Corner, then," Delly says.
Rainbow Corner is a big old Red Cross club right downtown so popular that even the movie stars go, like Irving

Berlin and James Stewart. Ruby looks up at Delly like she's crazy. We *know* we have got no business there.

"Better not," Annie finally tells her, smiling a little. "The club for the colored servicemen is in Winchester."

"But that's so far!" Delly says, frowning. "We can't go all that way!"

Annie shrugs and straightens up her collar. We none of us say nothing for a minute, thinking about last night and Tiny and Bob. "We *could* go back to that little joint we were at last night," Ruby says, like she don't care, but Annie is already shaking her head.

"Bob won't be there," Annie says, real quiet. "Likely the MPs took the whole lot of them in for disorderly conduct, and we won't see them for days."

Delly sighs. Some boys from Tiny's unit already have let her in on the news. "Well," she says finally, "mustn't sit here and sigh all night." She smiles and asks Ruby something about growing up in Texas.

Ruby still looks at Delly like she don't know about her, but Delly doesn't bother me none. English girls are not like regular white girls, and Delly is not like anyone. She talks and talks about how she went to "university" before the war; she asks me about folks back home, about Mama and Feen. She asks if any of us got a young man back home, and she tells us about her school friend who went off to the Royal Air Force. She hasn't heard what happened to him, and there's been no letter from him in a long while. That's why she volunteers with the Red Cross

after she gets off from the factory. Delly works on Station
Road, making Spitfire planes.

Delly pins up her hair while we are getting ready to go
out. "Marey," she says. "You're too quiet. Where do you
want to go?"

Ruby looks at me, trying to say something without
talking. I am in the hot seat. "Well . . . we could see a film."

"Aren't you sick of films by now? Let's go to the theater!" Annie argues.

"Oh, the theater!" Delly say. Her face gets red. "I . . .
Won't that be rather expensive?"

"Have they got a balcony?" Ruby asks, but Annie
shake her head.

"We don't need a balcony. We can get some fish and
chips after so Mrs. Dye doesn't have to go through any
trouble, too," Annie says.

"It's no trouble," Delly says, smiling.

"Don't think of the cost; we'll treat," Annie says to
Delly. "It's a good idea."

Ruby nods hard, but me and Annie know she is only
trying to get out of eating boiled sausages and Brussels
sprouts.

"Isn't there a theater near that little joint where we
were last night?" Ruby asks, and Annie roll her eyes.

"Girl, didn't your mama teach you not to run after
men?" she teases her.

Ruby narrows her eyes at Annie. "Do you see me
running?"

"I don't know about a playhouse," I say, but Annie shushes me.

"This is culture, Marey. Shakespeare was from England. You'll like it."

In the end, we take the train and then a cab—for ten shillings—downtown. Delly's mama shakes her head at the money we spend, but Annie says we are seeing the sights. Ten shillings is about two dollars, and we all put some in for that.

At the theater, folks are sitting in seats way up top and down in the front. We sit in the cheaper seats, but we can see enough. Everything is soft, and the curtains look like velvet way up there. We don't have much time to spend looking around, though, because the lights get low, and then we see a man wearing black, with white makeup on his face, holding a sword.

"Who's there?" he says, and his voice rolls all the way back up to where we sitting.

The only play I ever saw is the play we do every year at Sunday school, and that doesn't hold a candle to this. Here folks go crazy and make speeches, and everybody wear robes and costumes and makeup and talk like the Bible folks in the King James. This girl named Ophelia flat loses her mind, and there are ghosts, all kinds of fighting and stabbing. Folks die like flies, and at the end, hardly anybody is left. *Hamlet* wasn't nothing like this when we studied it at school.

After the show, there is no light on the street, and the shops have got drapes drawn and candles lit. There is a line for cabs, so Delly say we should take the Tube.

Annie frowns. "Are you sure?" she says. "The Underground must be pitch-black!"

Delly say we will stick together and be just fine.

The Tube is a train underground, just like it says. Delly tells us that only last year folks were sleeping down there, trying to get out from under the bombs. "Whole families lived there who had lost their homes," she says. "Most of them were evacuated to Reading, till we were full." She shakes her head, and I can barely see her pale skin in the dark. "Some folks still live down here."

We link arms and walk, and Delly keeps her torch pointed at the ground so we can see. Ruby is on one side of Delly, and Annie's on the other, and Ruby is whistling while she walks, which I know her mama says is not lady-like, but we are feeling fine.

"Hey, where you girls going so fast?" somebody call out.

"Party's not over!" somebody else hollers. "Where ya goin', girls?"

"Nothing like a drunk GI." Annie sighs. We walk a little faster.

There is no light at the railway station in Reading, either, but the station man has got a torch. We walk down the road, keeping quiet. Then Delly links her arm through Ruby's arm and she say, "So, now what are we going to do?"

"What do you mean?" Ruby laughs.

"I'm not tired yet," Delly says, and we all laugh at her. "Let's go to the pub."

Delly is crazy, but I like her.

When we get back, Mrs. Dye is waiting for us just like

Sister Dials would have been, her hair rolled up in pipe cleaners, listening to the wireless. Annie says she should not have waited, but Mrs. Dye wants to hear about London. Delly mixes up some powdered milk on the stove, and Ruby takes out one of her chocolate bars and melts it in there. We girls talk, sipping our cocoa, and I think of Feen. Tonight feels almost like we are sisters at home.

26.

NOW

"How long did Tiny have to stay in jail?" I ask. "It's so unfair that he had to go at all."

"Was a whole lot that wasn't fair then." Mare sighs. "I don't remember how long they kept them—three or four days, I guess. Like Jake said, it happened all the time, so he and Bob just took it in stride."

"It seems so weird that interracial dating was such a big deal," Tali muses. "It's so common now."

"Depends on where you are," Mare says, glancing over her shoulder to change lanes. "Some folks still aren't that comfortable with it."

"I guess." We're quiet for a moment. "Do you think Tiny married Adele?" I ask.

Mare smiles a little. "That Delly. If I recall, she married her school friend from the Royal Air Force. Tiny went on to the Pacific."

We follow Interstate 10 all the way into Houston, and suddenly we emerge in the middle of a city. After endless highways between clusters of small towns, Houston looks massive, full of quickly moving Texans heading in every direction, blowing their horns and driving assertively.

In the middle of the afternoon, the road is a sea of cars, and we wait in bumper-to-bumper traffic in the downtown area. Mare is tapping her nails against the steering wheel impatiently.

"What's going on here?" I ask as we creep forward a car length, heading toward the business district. "How could there be so much traffic in the middle of the day?"

"It's probably for Juneteenth," Mare says. "Folks come in for that from all over."

"Must be a big deal around here." I lean over the seat. "Most people at home don't do anything on Juneteenth, except maybe have a barbecue."

"Oh, shut up about barbecue," Tali moans. "I'm starving."

"We're going to pick up something in a little bit," Mare says. Then she adds, "Juneteenth is more of a Texas thing, since here it's an actual state holiday." She brakes for a stoplight, and waves of pedestrians in shorts and flip-flops cross. "Truth is, it ought to be a holiday everywhere."

"Why? Isn't it just for when the slaves in Texas were freed?"

"Yes and no." Mare pulls forward again. "It's actually a celebration of *all* slaves being freed; it's just that the South heard the Emancipation Proclamation only very slowly. Even though the slaves were freed on January 1 in 1863, Southerners first heard about it in Galveston in 1865—"

"Wait, what?" Tali interrupts. "It took them two and a half years to get a clue?"

"Well, it wasn't like slave owners just *told* their slaves they were free, now was it? News didn't travel fast back then, and it's not like the slaves were sending letters, since most of them couldn't read nor write. Only when the Union marched on Galveston was the truth told."

We digest that in silence. "So, Mare? Where are we going?" I ask when it's clear she's not going to give us any hints.

"Nowhere in particular," Mare says, scanning the road. "See if you can find a market somewhere, will you, babe?"

"A grocery store?"

"I see a Central Market up there." Tali points across the road. "Are we getting deli sandwiches?"

"If that's what you want," Mare answers. "I'm in the mood for cheese straws myself."

"I just want salsa and chips," I say, "unless the salsa doesn't look right. Then I'll just get a sandwich."

Mare glances across at Tali, and the two of them shake their heads.

"What?" I exclaim. "You have to be careful about salsa. We're in Texas."

"Anybody else want some melon?" Tali opens her door and stretches, suddenly energetic. "I'm going to see if there's any in the fridge section already cut. Should we get anything special?"

"Get what you want. Just be back in the car in"—Mare checks her watch—"'bout fifteen minutes."

"Why?" Tali looks surprised.

"We're going to keep moving," Mare says, and closes the driver's side door.

"What are we doing in Texas? I thought the reunion was in Alabama—"

"Come *on*." Tali grabs my arm. "Haven't you figured out by now she never tells you anything? Let's just go."

It is hard to leave the blissfully air-conditioned store to cross the blisteringly hot parking lot to the car, but we manage it. Mare has made it there ahead of us with a big bag of cheese straws and a diet cola. Tali brings her a half sandwich, and I have a package of string cheese, grapes, a bag of lime tortilla chips, and some chipotle salsa, which I hope isn't too hot.

Mare drives through town looking at signs, frowning.

"Are you looking for a freeway entrance?" I ask, worried. "I think you took a wrong turn, Mare."

"Not looking for that," Mare says. "I'm looking for a sign for Emancipation Park."

"Oh." I load a chip with salsa and speak around a mouthful. "It's an actual park?"

Mare nods. "The freed slaves all put their money together to buy a piece of land for their Juneteenth celebrations. It's an actual place within this city somewhere."

"What's the street?" Tali asks.

"Dowling," Mare says, and then brakes abruptly. "There it is."

"Are you sure this is it?" I glance around the playground in front of us. "This is the famous park?"

"I didn't say it was famous," Mare objects, and takes the key out of the ignition. "I said the freed slaves put their money together and bought it."

"Well, shouldn't it be more . . . historical?" Tali opens the car door and points to a community center across a broad green lawn from us. "This place has a pool."

"History happens where it happens," Mare replies, and pops open the trunk. "Go find us a table, Tali."

Next to the basketball courts my sister finally finds an open table in partial shade. Accompanied by the shrieks of kids in the pool and the soft slap of tennis balls against rackets, we sit down to our feast. Mare brings a disposable tablecloth to spread out and adds her other purchases to the general buffet—a basket of raspberries, a liter of cold ginger ale and plastic champagne flutes, and a pink box from the Center Market bakery. The fresh molasses cookies are soft and chewy and perfect. We fall on the food like we haven't eaten in days.

"Well, here we are. Emancipation Park. It's not like I thought it would be, either," Mare adds, looking bemusedly around the busy city park, "but it'll do." She holds up her glass. "Cheers."

"Cheers." Tali lifts her glass, downs her ginger ale in a gulp.

Mare winces. "Tali, you're going to make yourself sick."

Tali grins. "No, Octavia's the one who sicks up ginger ale. Remember the time—"

"Tali, jeez."

Mare barks out a laugh. "Girl, please. Do you think anybody wants to hear that?"

"Well, I was just saying!"

"Well, don't! Nobody needs to hear any more stories about how many people I threw up on when we were little."

"Could we have dinner table conversation?" Mare rolls her eyes.

"We're on a picnic," Tali points out.

"Here—eat some of this salsa," I say, shoving a chip in Tali's face.

We are insulting each other's taste when I hear a guitar. I don't really pay any attention until Mare sort of stills, and Tali starts looking around. A few tables away from ours, a graying African American man is sitting on a table, strumming his guitar with a couple of little kids seated on the bench next to him leaning against his legs, eating sandwiches. All around the park it seems like conversations are quieter as the guitarist plays. Even the kids screaming in the pool aren't as loud.

The guitar player sings quietly to himself.

Deep river. My home is over Jordan.
Deep river, Lord, I want to cross over
Into campground.

I glance over at Mare, and she's rubbing her arms like she's got goose bumps. She sighs, a nostalgic expression in her eyes. "Folks back home used to sing this one all the time."

I imagine Sister Dials and all of Mare's home folk singing a song about peace and safety after traveling, of getting to a "campground," and then going back to work, riding on the back of a bus, keeping their heads down. I wonder how many of the WACs like Mare felt like just getting out of the United States was going to "campground." The thought makes me a little sad.

The guitar player keeps strumming as one of the little kids uses his pant leg as a napkin, rubbing his face until it is clean to his satisfaction. His grandfather or uncle or father doesn't seem to notice but keeps on singing, eyes closed, thick fingers picking slowly at the taut guitar strings.

Tali nudges my arm. "Here."

I take the plastic champagne glass, and Mare pours more ginger ale in hers.

We sip and savor the liquid trail of notes while the city bustles around us and little kids run and squeal. It's a perfect afternoon in the park, which we are free to enjoy.

Hey Julie!
We're almost out of Texas, so our death march with AC is
almost over. Mare drove when we got into Houston, so I did
a little window-shopping. MAN, have you GOT TO get out
here sometime. The guys here are—wow. Why did we only
apply to U.C. schools? What's wrong with us!?!

And NO, I'm not being totally disloyal to Brent already;
I know what you're thinking. He's not OFFICIAL, okay?

My grandmother told us about these guys she met in
London during the war. Now, **that's** where we should go
to see some men!

 Tali

See you soon—I HOPE. This trip is taking my
LIFETIME. :/

Julie Guiao
29763 W. Sacramento Street
Martinez, CA 94553

27.

then

It is cold and no kind of spring, but since Easter, folks in Birmingham have got to turning over the ground. There are big galvanized cans on just about every other street, and folks toss their kitchen waste in there to slop the hogs and build up the fields for planting.

Skinny little Miss Victoria has got dirty knees all the time now. Her mama sets her to weeding, but every time she sees me, she's up and running, asking where I am going and what I am doing and don't I want to see her doll baby. Lord, that girl can *talk*.

"Didn't your mama send you to work in the garden?"

"I am," Victoria says. "I just want to see . . ."

"Gotta get to work, missy," I tell her. "See ya tomorrow, okay?"

"All right," she grumbles, and she stomps back to her dirt. But she is not grumbling too hard. I just happen to have a couple of sugar cubes in the pocket of my coveralls, and she already has got one in her mouth. She didn't want nothing else anyway.

Latrine gossip says we are fixing to move on from England. Doris Smith says the brass took a train to London to get our orders, and we are going back to Scotland. Peach say we are still going to Paris, but nowadays, she doesn't say it so loud as before. Mostly, she doesn't say much, at least not to me. She sure has got a lot of time on her hands to be with Miss Gloria Madden, though. She's met Gloria's captain in London, and would you believe that floozy set up Peaches with one of his friends? He's some boy who comes all the way from France on his leave to see her. All that way! No wonder she hopes we are going to Paris.

I sign in for the night shift at the Postal Directory Battalion, thinking I'll find Dovey and Phillipa later on. Phillipa has been trying to teach me how to shoot pool, and I just about got those angles worked out right. Phillipa says if we get good enough, we can play for money. Dovey's on operator shift; we all have to take our turn for two nights. Operators aren't supposed to listen in on a call, but that duty is dull, dull, dull, and we all listen in to keep awake. What I want to know from her is if HQ got our orders for sure. I don't suspect we going to Paris, France, ever.

Somebody has got a radio playing, and they're singing "I'm Beginning to See the Light." The CO, Captain Robinson, sitting at the desk, is yawning, going over the outgoing mail with her little razor blade. All of us have to make sure we tell no military secrets in our letters home, or the censor will cut it right out. "Loose lips sink ships," is what they say, like any of us know military secrets. What we know, we read in the paper.

The big news is that the infantry marched on the Germans and set free some prisoners of war. The Allies also freed about twenty thousand Jews and other folks the Germans have been starving to death in a camp called Buchenwald. The newsreel shows the folks have got arms look like sticks, and so many of them they found dead, they are calling it a Nazi death camp.

Seeing how the Nazis been treating folks, I am almost certain I was right to leave home. Somebody has got to fight for the folks who don't get help. No matter what, there's no call to starve folks like that. We have just *got* to beat the Nazis. If Hitler make it past our boys, there won't be no use for colored folks or *nobody* to go back to the States. The strong are supposed to help the weak and not to please ourselves, isn't that what the Book says? Right now we are the strong ones, and we have to win. We have to.

Somebody brings me another bag of post, and I have got my hands full of mail, looking at names, slipping 'em in the slots, checking the station number in that dim light, and squinting. I get to humming, and the work pass on in no time at all.

While I hear Duke Ellington on the radio, I think about Feen. Her neighborhood club is still collecting scrap metal, and Feen won a prize for collecting the most scrap of any colored girl in her neighborhood. She says Mama is real proud— and I am glad that she hears from Mama, even though it makes my gut knot up that she still don't have a word to say to me.

Feen say there is a Jap boy in her class. His name is

Tamekichi Takagi, but they call him Tommy. He is the boy who collected the most scrap in his neighborhood, but no neighborhood association is going to give no Jap a prize, not nowadays. Feen say he is as patriotic as anybody, but that don't make a difference.

Feen say Aunt Shirley says not to speak to him on the street in public. Folks say it is bad enough that she is colored, but no patriotic American should be seen talking to a Jap. Feen says it don't make her no difference whatsoever what kind of boy Tommy is. She says next time she sees him, she will buy him a Coke.

I have not been gone but a year, and already Feen seems like she's gotten busy and grew up. When did she get opinionated? I am proud of her. Aunt Shirley must be all right.

Mama still don't have nothing to say to me, but I am through waiting for Mama. The Dials girls sent me a little stationery for Easter, and I hear from Mrs. Ida Payne that Beatrice finally got on with the Red Cross. They sent her to work on one of them Clubmobiles somewhere in Belgium. Miss Ida say her girl, Bébé, has been seeing a major and had her picture in *Stars and Stripes*. Miss Ida says Beatrice calls herself a "Doughnut Dolly." Good ol' Beatrice finally got away from her mama.

Near midnight, I am tired out. My eyes are watering from keeping the blackout shades drawn and the lights down low. We all of us look up, startled, when we hear somebody running.

"Hey, Dovey!"

"What's up, Dovey?"

I crane my neck. "Girl? What's the matter? Who's minding the switchboard?"

Dovey's got her hands over her mouth, her eyes stretched wide.

"Dove!" I shove my stack of mail in the pocket of my utility and grab her arm. "What happened?"

On the late shift, it is just Women's Army Corps, no civilians and no Red Cross personnel. Dovey looks around the room making sure before she says it.

"I heard it on the switchboard. President Roosevelt is . . ."

I do not hear her say the word. Folks suck in air like there isn't going to be none left to breathe.

"You sure, Dovey?" I ask her, shaking her arm. "Girl, are you sure?"

Dovey starts crying. "I passed a call through to the major," she chokes.

And then folks start crying all over the place. I walk Dovey back and get her some water. We can't desert our posts, but nobody will know unless she don't stay put.

We stay at work but hardly get another thing done. Folks turn the radio up, but there is no news. What now? is the question we all ask.

President Roosevelt pulled us out of the Depression, made up jobs, and let folks get back some dignity. His wife has got more than respect for colored folks; she is known to be a friend in government. Harry Truman, the vice president, will be sworn in right quick, but hardly anybody around here really know a thing about him.

In the morning, while we stand in formation, HQ give us the official word: President Franklin Delano Roosevelt is dead.

It is April 12, 1945.

HQ gives out orders for the flag to be flown at half-mast for thirty days out of respect. The MPs wear black armbands, and we muster out in dress uniforms and caps, shoes shiny, to first one, then another memorial service. The major assigns some of us to attend services in Birmingham, so the U.S. Army is represented. We go on working, keeping our voices down.

Friday, I see Victoria hanging around the gate. I pat my pockets. Don't have no sugar for her; seems in all this I forget her little sweet tooth. I get ready to watch her poke out her mouth, but instead, she comes up to me, all solemn.

"This is for you," she says, and shoves something in my hand.

It is a wilted piece of tree, blue flowers all crushed, but it has a powerful smell.

"My mum said it's rosemary. For remembrance," Victoria say, still sober. "Mum says it's just terrible about your president."

For the first time, my eyes water. "Yeah. It is," I tell her.

Victoria makes to walk off, then she turns around. "Have you anyone else to be president over there?"

"We got somebody," I say, blinking hard.

"Good." Victoria nods her little head like she's made up her mind. "See you tomorrow, okay?"

I nod back.

Back home, it is still yesterday, yesterday before the president died.

Today, Doris says we got orders to go to France for sure.

The world has gone right on.

then

The news is that old devil Hitler done sent himself to hell, but none of us get too excited till we receive the official word from headquarters almost a week later. Then the whole base requests passes to cut loose in Birmingham, except those on necessary tasks.

Me, Ruby, Peaches, and Phillipa run up and down the streets in Birmingham. We take a number 7 bus to Victoria Square, where they have built up a big old fire, and we dance and sing. They have got a piano outside, and folks break out the whiskey they have been saving since rations started. For this party, nobody cares what color you are; everyone is happy. Folks are just kissing everybody they can reach. One of the real old men kisses me on my cheek with all his hairy whiskers. He says I am a "good gel."

Some of the men are just drunk, but it is a happy kind of drunk; nobody gets disorderly, and the MPs don't have to put nobody in jail. Folks just wave flags, singing "God Save the Queen," laughing and crying all at once.

We dance till our feet start aching, then we hobble on back. The double summer hours mean we got plenty of light, so we get to see every fire and every party and dance with pretty near just about everybody in the whole city of Birmingham. Nobody has got to use blackout curtains, and nobody puts those blinders over their headlights. The street is lit up as bright as day, since they got the old streetlights on. Folks are shining torches and lighting candles inside just about every window. Won't be no Germans and their planes dropping down the V-bombs anymore. I don't know how folks sleep with all this light, but on base, we are so tired we do all right.

Next day, the headline for the *London Daily News* says V-E DAY! IT'S OVER IN THE WEST! Phillipa makes sure she gets herself a newspaper to send back home. She reads out loud to us and says they are rounding up the Nazis for war trial and dragging them off to jail. Then she says she wants to go to London to see the other parties. Phillipa says this is "history," so she needs to see it. I say that girl just likes to get kissed by men with whiskers.

"Wonder if your friend Gloria and her captain going to get together and *celebrate*?" I say, and Peaches rolls her eyes.

"Let her tell it, she's already doing enough celebrating for all of us. That girl wants to make sure she goes home with a rock on her finger."

"It'll go with the rocks in her head," Ruby mutters under her breath, and I crack up.

"Troops are pulling out," Phillipa says, and we all get

quiet. "The Red Cross is boarding all branches of the service—they have already started sending out the wounded."

"I know." Peaches frowns. "Annie is shipping out on Friday."

Annie tried hard, but when she heard her friend from the POW camp had been shipped home, we knew she wasn't long for staying over here. Nobody blames her, but I will miss that Miss Connecticut something fierce. I cried almost as hard as I did when Feen left when Annie said she had to go.

Little old Miss Victoria cried, too, when I told her we have orders to ship out to France.

"But I want you to stay!" Victoria said, squinching up her eyes and glaring at me.

"We got to help find the Nazis hiding in France," I told her.

"I *hate* the Nazis," she said, and she stomped off home. Poor thing. I think she will miss my sugar cubes more than she will miss me, but even so, all of us are riled up with all the coming and going. Sure, the bombs have stopped, but nobody knows what comes next.

"Well, the war is over," Phillipa says. "They'll probably ship all of us out soon."

Nobody says anything for a while as we think about that. My throat is tight, so I speak up just to end the silence. "Poor Peaches. She ain't never going to get to no Paris, France."

"Yes, I will," Peaches says, and she throws her shoe at me. "You may laugh, Marey Lee Boylen, but I am going to Paris."

"The war isn't over anyway, not yet," Ruby says, and flops

back on her bunk. "The Japs haven't surrendered, so it's not over till it's over."

"Are you thinking they'll take colored WACs out to the Pacific?" Phillipa looks up.

"I don't know," Ruby says, and she shrugs. "I'm just talking."

I look over at Ruby, then get myself busy with my ironing. I know Ruby has been worrying that they will send Bob out to the Red Cross in the Pacific, and she wants to follow him. Everybody has got homes to go to, gentlemen friends to see, families who want them to get home safe. When they ship us home, what am I going to do? I have got to make a plan.

We don't get much time to wonder. Just after we see Annie off to the station, the lieutenant posts orders, and suddenly we are all scrambling. Been here for so long it doesn't seem right that we have got to leave so fast, but we are marching out to get on a train to France. We don't have any Paris in our plans, though. Orders say we going somewhere Captain Ferguson says is "Roo-ah." Most folks say the word like "ruin." It is spelled "Rouen," so we don't know what to call it.

"We better brush up on our French," Phillipa says, and I laugh. No one in my unit speaks more than one or two words of French; at Fort Oglethorpe they taught us Spanish and French, but we didn't have enough time to learn more than "hello" and "goodbye" and "How much?"

"Doesn't anybody have a French dictionary?" Peaches

asks. "How are we going to be able to tell them what kind of perfume we want?"

But pretty soon none of us worry about French folks and their French words or even French perfume. We get some real news: they have got colored troops in France!

"Lord, girl, they've got men out there?" Doris Smith asks, patting her hair. "We won't know how to act!"

"Sister, get me off this train!" Ina White says, and we all have a laugh.

Suddenly folks who didn't put a stitch more effort than needed into getting into uniform are trying to powder their noses and check the way their hats tilt in every mirror. Girls act like they don't have common sense, batting their lashes and looking all around.

France is a whole different story than Birmingham. For one thing, the postal directory area and our quarters are in one big building. We have got floors 2 and 3, and the post office is down on the ground floor. We find our footlockers okay and then our bunks, which are some of the ugliest we have seen yet.

First off, our so-called beds aren't anything but canvas cloth nailed across a wood frame. Folks complain about splinters nearly first thing. But worse than the wood against our backs, we got straw ticks—big burlap sacks—to fill and those are supposed to be the mattresses.

"We have to go into a barn and fill up a sack and sleep on straw?" are the first words out of Phillipa's mouth. "And we have to make our pillows ourselves? You've got to be kidding me!"

"Good thing Annie isn't here," Ruby says. "She'd be fit to be tied."

We are fit to be tied, too, not that it does us much good. Doris says the supply trucks haven't come, and it isn't the GI way to complain, so we've got to put up and shut up.

That first night, we sack out early, we are all so tired, but reveille doesn't wake up anybody; all of us is already up, sore, and buzzing like mad wasps. That scratchy straw is something else!

During the next week, we hit our stride and get sorted as fast as we can. We walk through our post and find the laundry, base supply, recreation, and mess hall. When we turn out for duty, we got one more surprise—we have got some three hundred German prisoners of war here. Captain says we have them to wrestle the heavy bags and to clean up, and that is just fine. But we don't have much need for them when we have two hundred French folks from the village set up to work with us, too. So it is Jerry POWs, French civilians, and us, all in one big old building.

The chief of mail, Captain Kearney, say it is for troop morale the 6888th Battalion moved closer to the front at Normandy, since some troops got to stay and rebuild roads and such that got bombed, and others are still rooting out the Nazis and bringing them in. I can see the sense in that: all the troops deserve to get their mail, and fast. But this just doesn't feel right. Nobody can talk to each other in plain English, and there are a lot of regular army guards and folks walking around with guns. The French folk get frustrated, since they don't even say the alphabet like us. Working the post directory is for the first time real hard work, but at least it is not so cold and dark as in Birmingham. We know the work, but it is not easy with all these languages.

My second shift on duty is the early shift, and our squad is paired up with two French girls for each one of us WACs. CO says we have got to teach them how to help us.

I get a skinny little black-haired girl named Édith and an older woman with hacked-off brown hair who says her name is Geneviève, except they say "A-dit" and "Jon-veev." Geneviève and me start off working on simple things—I got to teach her the American alphabet, which is work, but she works hard. Édith knows a little English, and we get a little work done, and after a lot of time waving our hands and pointing, they both understand that Robert and Rob, Bobby, Bert, Bob, and Robby might all be the same boy. By then it's time for lunch.

The battalion feeds the French a meal a day as part of the pay for them working, so we march to the mess hall together, pass by the steam tables, and find our places. We get meat, some soup, some vegetables, mashed potatoes made from dehydrated potatoes, and a bit of bread and butter. Édith and Geneviève don't say a thing when we sit down, so I don't neither and we just take a break from trying to communicate till we go back on duty. But the French girls don't look too good. Soon as we get back to work, Édith, the skinny one, turns a funny color like old oatmeal and—wham!—falls right on top of me, just about.

"Édith!" Geneviève drops all her mail and jumps up. Geneviève tries to pick Édith up, talking French to her, patting her hands, but Geneviève herself is shaking like a leaf, and she's all shiny with sweat on her face.

"No . . . don't!" I look around. "Somebody help me here!" I turn back to Geneviève. "Don't mess with Édith, hear? Wait. Uh . . . *je . . . vous* . . . uh . . . aid."

Geneviève try to say something, and then—*plop*—her eyes roll back in her head, and she passes right out on the floor.

"Medic!"

It is more than just me hollering. Some of us are trying to hold folks up, and some of us are about to panic. Dorothy Rogers looks like she's about to be sick.

"Don't touch 'em!" Dorothy steps back from the folks on the floor. "They've got some kind of disease for sure. They got lice!"

"Medics, coming through," somebody hollers, and folks carrying stretchers come running.

"What's the matter with them anyway?" Maryanne Oliver asks.

"Malnutrition," our CO says. "Mess hall food is too rich."

Maryanne looks at me, and she squats down and starts patting folks' hands.

"It's all right," she says. "You'll feel better. It's all right. . . ."

I look up at Dorothy, and she can't look me in the face. Lice. Please.

It's a crying shame when a body doesn't know what to do

when it get a little food. And our mess isn't nothing like fancy food. We have got dehydrated potatoes and Spam like always. But the mess officer say they have got to cut the French folks' rations and feed them twice a shift, or they'd be sick like this every day.

I write to Feen, remembering this. We are lucky, so, so lucky. Back home things might be tight sometimes, and we might not have too much we call luxuries, but we haven't ever starved, not starved skinny sick like this.

✳ ✳ ✳

"Psst!" I see Charline Spencer wave her hand at me next morning as she is about to go off shift.

"What?"

"Did you hear?" Charline grinning at me.

"Hear what?" I say.

"The men are here!"

I look out toward the gate, and I see the battalion commander; Major Addams, our CO; First Lieutenant Scott; and some MPs walking in front of the gate. I crane my neck and look up. In the officers' quarters, heads are sticking out the windows, and folks are looking down.

"Ooh! Are they gonna let them in?"

Charline shrugs, her eyes sparking mischief. "Don't know. They brought mattresses for every enlisted woman here, so some of 'em are going to have to get in here."

"Mattresses? We don't have to sleep on those nasty straw ticks anymore?"

"Nope," Charline says. "We've finally got some real beds around here."

"Isn't that something? The Six-triple-eight has men bringing us beds!" I glance at the officers walking back and forth in front of the gate. "The CO looks worried," I say.

"They say there are seven hundred and twenty-five enlisted men for each enlisted woman and thirty-one male officers for each female officer."

My mouth drops. "Seven hundred and . . . Well, that's plenty of men to go around, sure enough."

"You going out there to see?"

I laugh. "Girl, I have got to get on duty. Can't desert my post!"

"There's always a first time," Charline says, and we both laugh. Nobody wants the kind of trouble that comes with being AWOL, but we have some really curious women up in this post today. Most of us find all kinds of excuses to walk out from the post directory building all shift long, just to take a smoke or a breath of air and find a reason to look out toward the gates.

29.

NOW

"So this is why you were telling us about boys in the back of cars," Tali teases. "You must have gone out with a different guy every week!"

Mare laughs. "I did not. Sometimes it was two different guys in a week!"

I laugh but don't say much. I'm a little envious of the long-time-ago Mare. I can't imagine having that many guys interested in me just because I'm there. Actually, I can't imagine any guys interested in me at all.

Mare hustles us through Houston to Beaumont, where she books us into a hotel suite with mahogany beds, leather couches, complimentary laundry service, terry cloth bathrobes (that we can't take with us), and a minibar. Mare leaves us to look around and get unpacked while she goes to get a massage and a manicure. We're on our own for dinner; Mare says that after days on the road, she just wants to catch up on her sleep in a decent bed.

"Check this out!" Tali sings out from the bathroom. I join

her and marvel at the size of the tub. There is a small TV screen across from it.

"Sweet!"

"I know! And the toilet seat has a heater thingy."

"Okay, that's gross."

"Well, I'm using it anyway." Tali shoos me out of the bathroom. "Move out of the way. I'm getting ready for dinner."

"We could just get room service and watch a movie," I remind her.

"No way! Did you see that restaurant downstairs? And the waiters? No way I'm staying in here. We're going down to find some men—and I'm doing your makeup."

I am excited that Tali wants to hang out with me, and it only takes us about two and a half hours to get ready. She won't let me wear shorts, so I pair her blue plaid skirt and its matching baby tee with my yellow flip-flops, and Tali wears a little sundress that leaves her shoulders and long legs bare. I keep tugging on the hem of the T-shirt, wishing it were just a little longer, while Tali tries to adjust her dress to hit above the knee.

Tali won't let me put my hair in a ponytail but gels it and makes quick twists in it while it is still damp. The curls look good, but a bit wild. And with the makeup we are wearing, in the mirror we both look older. *Way* older.

"We are total babes." Tali grins, her expression triumphant.

"Yeah, we are," I agree, staring in shock. My eyes look huge, and it seems like my face is all lashes and big hair and shiny lipstick. With her short hair all gelled into points and wearing shimmering eye makeup, Tali almost isn't recognizable. "Don't ditch me, okay? If some guy comes to talk to you?"

"What do you mean, ditch you?" Tali exclaims. "They're totally going to be talking to you, too. Come on!"

Tali drags me down to the hotel restaurant, and we are seated at a high table with stools. I look around at the long polished bar with a mirror behind it. Someone is playing quiet music on a piano, and people sit talking and laughing. I look over the top of my menu at my reflection and can't keep a grin off my face.

"Can I get you ladies the wine list?" The server is completely gorgeous, with dark green eyes and a smooth Texas drawl.

My mouth opens, but Tali's ready with a quick answer.

"No, thanks. She'll have a coffee Italian soda, and I'll have Kahlúa and cream, please."

"My pleasure. Back in a moment." The server melts away.

I gulp. *"Tali—!!"*

"Shhh!" Tali grips my hand with her nails and smiles around the room. "Shut up, Octavia."

"But—"

"He could have asked for ID, right? So it's not like it's a big deal." Her nails dig in.

"Tali, Mare's going to kill us."

"Kahlúa has as much alcohol in it as, like, vanilla. It's not like Mare doesn't have a drink every night. She started drinking when she was practically my age, too."

My stomach lurches, and I stare down at my lap. The sophisticated little adventure we were having suddenly feels lonely and upsetting. While Tali is looking around the room, smiling at people, I pull away and twist my fingers together tightly.

Tali and Suzanne have all kinds of things they do that are cool and fun. They dressed up in old prom dresses from the thrift store and went grocery shopping one weekend, and they came back laughing at how people looked at them. They go to poetry slams, and once they joined a picket line in front of the state hospital because they were bored and wanted to carry signs and yell things at cars. I used to wish that Tali would take me on one of her adventures, but now that I'm here, I'm not sure what to do. When we were little, whenever Tali and I did something, I was always the lookout, the one who would tell her if Mom was coming while she dragged over the chair and took the box of sugar cubes down from the cabinet. Now I don't know if I'm supposed to watch so she doesn't get caught or help her pretend she's not a minor ordering a drink.

"Octavia." Tali's voice is a whisper. "Check out the hottie."

I glance up and follow my sister's eyes toward the broad-shouldered guy in cowboy boots and tight black jeans. He swaggers into the restaurant, his eyes scanning faces like he's looking for someone. When he sees Tali, he nods slightly and keeps looking around.

"Yikes," I say, looking at his huge arms and chest. "Do you think he takes steroids?"

Tali drops her forehead into her hands. "Octavia . . . ," she groans. "Wrong answer."

"I'm just saying!" I insist, miffed. "Either he takes steroids or he's been in prison. I mean, who else has all day to just work out?"

"Ladies, your drinks." Our server is back, sliding a tall glass half filled with dark and light liquid and ice in front of me. Tali's drink looks almost the same, except her glass is shorter and wider and her straw is small and red, not red-and-white-striped like mine. From his tray, the server also slides a small glass of water in front of each of us and a basket of bread.

"Someone will be right with you to take your order."

"Thank you," Tali says serenely, and picks up her menu again, turning to see where the man with the cowboy boots is going.

I hesitate. "Tali? Do you think—"

"Cowboy coming this way! Now don't say anything, Octavia, nothing. I mean it. Don't ruin—"

"Look at you two, looking all grown." Mare suddenly appears at our table in a whiff of perfume. I stare at her wig, which tonight is long wispy curls, the color of copper. She is wearing a striking fuchsia dress, with a manicure to match.

"Mare!" I swivel speechlessly between my sister and my grandmother.

"I thought you were going to bed," Tali blurts.

"Well, that massage left me feeling so good I thought I'd

see if I could catch you girls for dinner. . . ." Mare's voice trails off as her eyes take in our drinks.

"Mare," Tali begins.

"Did you already order?" Mare's voice is even.

"Not yet."

"Do you know what you want? Octavia?" My grandmother's eyes drill into mine.

"I'm not really hungry," I say faintly. "You can look at my menu."

We are so quiet now I can hear the conversations from other tables and the tinkle of piano music. The cute guy with the tight jeans sits down at the table closest to ours, but Tali, burying her face in the menu, doesn't even notice.

The server comes, and Mare orders a seafood omelet and a salad. Tali orders a basket of onion rings and a grilled panino sandwich. I choose a small plate of nachos and guacamole. When my stomach gurgles, I reach for my drink and take a sip.

"Good?" Mare glances over at me.

I consider, then nod. "I've never had the coffee syrup. You want a sip?"

"Lord, no." Mare shudders. "I want to go to sleep tonight."

"Well, there's only a little coffee in the *syrup*." Tali rolls her eyes. "It's flavoring."

"A little is still some." Mare takes a sip from the water glass closest to her and nails my sister with her eyes. "Don't fool yourself, Talitha."

We have a quiet dinner. Mare shares the hash browns

that come with her omelet with me, and she scoops my guacamole onto her omelet. Tali moodily munches her panino
crusts, looking sullen. My grandmother doesn't say anything when Tali finally touches her glass and pulls it toward
her, sipping it carefully while eyeing Mare for a reaction.
When the server comes by for Mare to sign for our meal,
she scans the charges, then signs slowly. I push back from
the table and head for the elevator, relieved that the ordeal
is over.

"You owe me eight dollars," Mare says to Tali, who is
walking behind me.

"Eight dollars? My drink was only four!"

"That's the markup for working my nerves," Mare
says flatly. "I am not paying for you to break the law,
Talitha Marie, and if you're going to pull this kind of bull,
you can just go on home, and Octavia and I will go on without you."

"I wasn't pulling anything. Mare, I am almost eighteen.
It was just some Kahlúa. It's not that big a deal."

"Eighteen isn't twenty-one, Miss Thing," Mare shoots
back, then drops her voice and says something I can't hear.
The elevator bell chimes before Tali can answer.

I push the number for our floor and wait as Tali walks in
and stands with her arms crossed, her expression smoldering,
stubborn, and hard. Mare comes in and smiles, looking relaxed as a family wheels in their luggage and their dog carrier.
They stare at us curiously.

"We're starting off nice and early tomorrow, girls. You

going to watch movies all night, or are you going to be ready?" Mare nudges my shoulder.

"I'll be ready." I relax a little.

"Good." Mare smiles and jiggles the car keys in her pocket. "Very good."

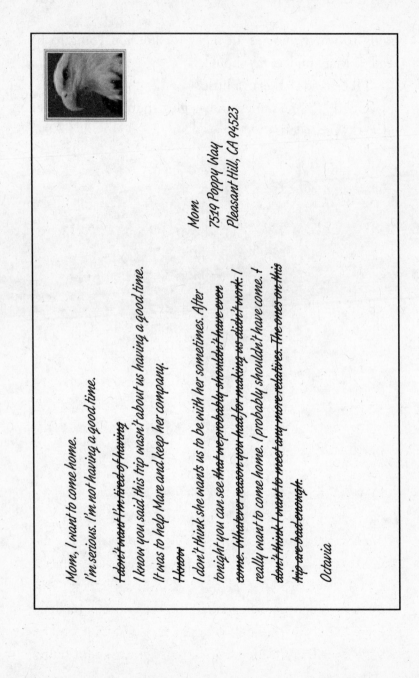

Mom, I want to come home.
I'm serious. I'm not having a good time.

~~I don't want t I'm tired of having~~
I know you said this trip wasn't about us having a good time.
It was to help Mare and keep her company.

~~I mom~~
I don't think she wants us to be with her sometimes. After
tonight you can see that we probably shouldn't have ever
come. Whatever reason you had for making us didn't work. I
really want to come home. I probably shouldn't have come. I
don't think I want to meet any more relatives. The ones on this
trip are bad enough.

Octavia

Mom
7549 Poppy Way
Pleasant Hill, CA 94523

30.

then

"So, have you ever been to New Orleans?"

The V-Disc records are too loud, and we are packed in the recreation hall sardine tight. It's an enlisted WAC party, and we invited all the men around to join us.

"Never been anywhere till I joined up," I say, and sip my drink. Peach dragged me to this thing, talking about I just have to meet this fella and if I don't like him, it might be that she has got another friend for me, but I don't see neither one of them. Now this lanky Louisiana boy has been holding up the wall next to me, just talking. If Peaches don't hurry up, I'm going. I've got less than an hour before I'm on duty, and she was supposed to be here fifteen minutes ago.

"My family came from down New Orleans way, but my grandparents moved us on to Chicago." The boy keeps talking, and I look at him sidelong, with his copper color skin and his high cheekbones. Mama would call him a redbone because of his skin. His hair is light, crinkled brown, and he has got eyes like a calico cat—almost green and a funny yellow-brown. Behind the GI-issue horn-rimmed black glasses, you can hardly see those eyes unless you look really close. No wonder he says he works in the chemical division. They don't let anybody that blind shoot.

"My great-grandfather was Greek, they say"—he goes on with his history like somebody asked—"which is why my mother named me George. She called me after that grandfather, George Eneas Hoag. The guys call me Diego, though."

I put down my cup. "Well, George, you want to dance or what?"

George blinks like a turtle behind those glasses. "Well, sure. Sure," he says. He has a big slow grin.

"Don't step on my shoes," I tell him as he puts his hand on my back and we walk out onto the floor. "I don't mean to take the time to polish them again before I go on duty."

"Do you like working in the post office?"

I sigh. "You sound like that reporter from Chicago we had in here yesterday, talking about, 'How do you like this place?' and getting all in the way. Don't know why these newsmen are still here. The war's in the Pacific; that's where they ought to be."

"What else did he ask?" George hasn't stepped on my shoes yet.

"Oh, all kinds of dumb stuff, like don't we want to stay on in Europe since there's so much discrimination back home and don't we all like it here."

George frowns. "It's nice here, but back home's where we

ought to be. Besides, once the Nazis are all chased down, the French folks will want their country back."

I look up, nodding in agreement. "That's what I say. They're real grateful, and Geneviève and all the others I work with at the post office are nice and all, but I just can't see staying here forever."

George clears his throat. It is hard to holler over the new record and have a serious talk, but he ducks his head in close, right next to my ear. "Have you been around Rouen yet?" George say "Roo-ah," like the French.

I shake my head and pull back, embarrassed to feel his breath on my ear. Where is Peaches? If this boy asks me to go out with him on a pass, I'm gonna wring her little neck. He is tall and skinny, and I don't see myself getting friendly with a cat in specs.

"I met some farmers," George starts to say, and I just about cross my eyes.

"George, nearly everybody is a farmer around here," I tell him. "I aim to get out of the country and into Paris on my leave."

George smiles a little. "Well, sometime maybe you'll get around in the country," he says, clearing his throat again. "They're starting to harvest a few things."

The song ends, and I step back. "That's real nice," I say. "Look, George, thanks for the dance, but I got duty at oh-eight-hundred, and I'd better run."

"May I see you again, Miss Boylen?" George asks me, and my stomach knots. I am going to hurt that Peaches Carter.

"Why, sure, George, but right now I'd really better rush off." I put out my hand. "Goodbye."

Ooh, that Peaches. Just as I stomp out the door of the rec hall, Peaches runs in, looking all upset. "Gosh, Marey, I forgot—"

"I've got duty, Peaches Carter," I say. "You see that lanky cat with the crooked tie over there? I told him you'd save him a dance." Peach follows my finger to where George is standing against the wall again. "He's just what the doctor ordered," I say, and move to push past her.

Peaches doesn't hardly give him a glance. "Marey, wait. I'm sorry to stand you up. Something's happened." She sighs, her face sad. "If you see Gloria, will you tell her—"

Heat pushes into my face. "Peaches. I don't expect to see your little friend Gloria Madden anywhere near me anytime soon. I don't have time to be your errand girl, all right? I'll see you later."

Peaches's expression gets all pinched up. "All right," she says. "You be that way."

I walk off, feeling irritable and hot. There is just time to stop by the mess hall.

When we are on KP, we see that our food comes out of dark green cans, and it is the same stuff as always. When we first got to France, we had all kinds of good food. Fried chicken, mashed potatoes, fresh carrots. Ruby says it was to make up for them straw ticks on our beds, but Ina says the supply sergeant said we was getting hospital issue. They figured that all women in one place must mean nurses, even though nobody told them that. This man's army still forgets there are more than men around these days. Well, soon as the supply depot figured out we weren't running a hospital, they busted us back to C rations—pork and beans, dehydrated eggs, and Spam, Spam, and more Spam.

I am sick to death of Spam. Today, I am sick of the entire U.S. Women's Army Corps.

Édith practice her English on me while we work. "I would like *une bif* . . . a *bifteck*," she say.

"I want a beefsteak," I tell her. "And some collard greens and fried green tomatoes. And a baked potato."

Édith looks at me and smiles, but I can tell I lost her a while back. "Um, I want . . . *une pomme* . . ."

"Ah. *Pomme de terre?*"

I shrug. Sounds good to me.

Somebody turns the radio on, and we listen to them read the news. The GIs in the Pacific are still having a rough time with the Japanese, and they have been pushing and being pushed back for a while now. The Allied nations are calling for the Japs to surrender. Ruby still talks about heading out for the Pacific, but I don't know about that. A couple of GIs ran across a land mine last month, and there were some bad injuries. I have had my fill of bombs in England, and anyway, Captain says she has a feeling it will be all over soon.

"Hey, Marey." Maryanne Oliver leans against the counter. "You hear Lieutenant Bothwell is opening up security training?"

I shrug. "I saw something about that. You going?"

Maryanne nods. "They've got a British lieutenant to teach us jujitsu."

I widen my eyes. "Ju-what?"

"Jujitsu. It's Japanese. Bothwell says it's a way to fight. Doesn't matter how small you are; they can teach you how to take down somebody even bigger."

I shake my head. "Can you beat that? We Americans are gonna fight like the Japs?"

Maryanne shrugs. "Our commanding officer requested we be issued sidearms when we go on duty, but the brass told her no woman's gonna be carrying firearms in this man's army. The villagers complain we've got men at the gates at all hours, and the captain says we have to call regular MPs too many times for help with the drunk and disorderly. We've got to do something."

"All right, I'll go," I tell Maryanne, "but nobody will believe we're learning Japanese fighting. I can't wait to tell my sister, Feen, about this one."

May 20, 1945

Dear Miss Feen,

It is hard to believe that you are finishing another year of school. I was sick and tired of school by the time it got warm, and right now I am just as tired of working inside. We are in a parade next week to honor Joan of Arc—at least then we will be outside!

When you see your friend Tommy, ask him
if he has ever heard of a thing called jujitsu. It
is a Japanese style of fighting. When I have got
MP duty and some man tries to come on base
drunk and disorderly, all I have to do is holler,
"Ha!" and grab his arm and flip him over, like
they taught us. He'll go away for sure if I do it
right. We all have got bruises now from
practicing!

I can't wait to teach you jujitsu fighting. It
sure keeps the boys in line! Aunt Shirley's not
letting you step out with boys yet, is she? You
remember to make them act like gentlemen,
hear?

You might laugh, but I am wheeling and
dealing here in France. Doris works for
supply, and she has been all around the
countryside, trying to find out what folks want
and what they will trade. That girl can't be
bothered with perfume nor trying to find no
antiques in France. She is trading "damaged
goods" from supply for vegetables. We are so
sick of Spam we are ready to give it away, just
about. The folks here are so starved for meat
that they can't get enough of Spam. Smokes
are great to trade—for fresh eggs, beets, peas,

carrots, and cabbage. We don't have space to dig a garden, but we make up a good mess of beet greens. It is almost as good as the greens at home, but nobody has lard or drippings for flavoring.

Don't you tell Sister Dials, but there is a skinny GI who call himself "seeing me." His name is George Hoag, and he went to the University of Chicago. He doesn't bring me flowers. George brought me a bag of sweet peas, just out the field. He is as thin as a rail and wears spectacles, and he can't hold a tune if he whistles. But you know how I like peas, so George is okay by me. At least he doesn't step on my shoes when we dance. Two girls in my unit are getting married this summer. Can't see the point of that, since folks might just get sent on to the Pacific and shot up over there, but there's no talking sense to some folks. One of the girls brought her blanket to a French lady who dyed it and turned it into a real fancy wool coat. She'll look real sharp when the chaplain does her service. I might just get one of those blanket coats!

I am glad to hear you are working at the hospital. You have to tell me all about your Dr.

*Dickens. It beats all to know that there is now
a colored women's doctor in Philadelphia. I
hope you learn all you can from her.*

Your loving sister,
Marey

31.

then

The 6888th is getting homesick. First Annie went, then in June, Dovey's young man asked her to marry him. They left at the beginning of August, just after we started bombing the Japs. Charline says she doesn't see why she shouldn't go find herself a man now that the war's over, and she went on back to Tennessee. Dorothy Rogers is going home at the end of this week, so there won't be anybody left but Ruby, Ina White, Maryanne Oliver, and me from our squad. Phillipa's squad lost Linda Travis and Junella Morgan, too. Out of eight hundred enlisted women, about half of them have gone back to the United States.

The CO says that just 'cause there are fewer folks don't mean we don't have to do the same amount of work. We still have to run mail for every U.S. citizen in the European theater—army, navy, marine corps, civilians, and Red Cross personnel. We still have got work to do.

After shift, I am walking to my bunk when out of the clear blue, Gloria Madden comes up to me and grabs my arm.

"Marey, can I talk to you?" Gloria is talking fast, looking around like she's scared somebody will see her.

I move my arm out of her claws. "What do you want, Gloria?" I ask. "Don't you have somebody to be looking down your nose at somewhere?"

Gloria shakes her head. "Shut up, Marey. Listen to me. I can't find Pamela."

I raise my eyebrow. "Peaches?"

Gloria sighs. "Peaches, Pamela, whatever. Have you seen her?"

I put my hand on my chin and pretend to think about it hard. "Well—let me think about it—no. Now scram."

Gloria grabs my arm again. She whispers, "Marey, I think she's AWOL."

My stomach clenches, and goose bumps go up my arms. "AWOL? No, not her!"

Gloria nods, and suddenly her face gets blotchy and her eyes get red. "We had an argument," she says, and she sniffs. "I was just telling her what was being said; I swear that's all. How was I to know she would get so mad that Roger Johnson told everyone she was the kind of girl who didn't kiss men? It's just talk, that's all! She didn't have to get so mad!"

"Gloria Madden, you were carrying tales about Peach?" I ask, stepping in close. If she did, I will *slap* her face, here and now.

"I know what you think of me, Marey Lee Boylen, but even I'm not *that* low." Gloria wipes her red eyes angrily. "Roger stepped out on Peach with some French girl when she wouldn't take him seriously, and he told his squad it wasn't his fault, that she was a man hater. It's just talk, and they all do that, and who cares? There's plenty of other boys to go around, I say. Anyway, Pamela blew up at me yesterday, and I haven't seen her since. She didn't sign out in the pass book, she missed roll call this morning, and"—Gloria's voice rises—"it's all my fault!"

Lord. Peaches has done had it now.

"Did the CO say something to you?" Now I'm the one holding Gloria's arm.

"She asked if anybody's seen her. The MPs at the gate are waiting for her. She hasn't shown up for her shift. . . ." Gloria sniffs. "Marey, you think something happened to her?"

"Peaches Carter doesn't take any mess," I say. "She'll come back when she gets ready."

"Maybe she went to meet somebody," Gloria say, but I roll my eyes.

"I don't think Peaches want to be bothered with a *man* right now, do you?"

Gloria says to tell her if I hear anything and she'll do the same. I walk on, shivering.

Around base I ask everybody I know, but no one knows where Peach has gone. It looks like she really is AWOL, which means big trouble with a capital *T*. If it weren't for the fact that the Germans surrendered, Peaches could be *shot* for deserting her duty in a time of war. My stomach hurts when I think about that. Peaches is gonna be sent home for sure.

The sun is barely thinking about coming up over the

horizon at 0400 the next morning when I meet Gloria just as she is going off shift. She shakes her head at me before I can ask.

"She missed her shift."

My stomach is cold and heavy all morning long. I lose my place filing letters, like I don't even know the alphabet. Then, right before lunch, I knock a whole stack of packages on the floor. Geneviève pats my arm when I start sniffling, but I am not crying over the stupid packages. Peaches has been my friend ever since we landed at the receiving battalion at Fort Des Moines. She rode me till I could make my bed and swore she'd charge me a nickel every time I said "ain't" till I almost never say it no more. If I hadn't let Gloria Madden bust us up, maybe she would have told me what was wrong instead of going off like she doesn't have a friend in the world would worry about her if she was gone.

After dinner, Ruby finds me on my bunk.

"Marey, she's back."

I sit right up, fast. "Where is she? I ought to tell her a thing or two about going off and leaving me with Gloria Madden, of all people."

"I didn't get to say boo to her. The MPs marched her straight to the battalion commander's office."

"Oh, Ruby. They are going to court-martial her for sure."

Ruby shakes her head. "I just wish I knew why she did it, Marey!"

I slide down off my bunk and sigh. "I'd better go tell Gloria."

Not a one of us talked to Peaches till she marched into the mess hall at lunch the next day. Gloria saw her and hesitated, but I stood up and went straight on over to her.

"Peaches Carter. You all right, girl?"

Peach look real tired, but she smiles. "Well, Staff Sergeant Hill 'bout tore a strip out of my hide, but I'm all right." Peaches sit down at a table, and I sit next to her.

"What happened?"

"Nothing," Peaches said. "That's what's so dumb. Nothing happened at all."

"What do you mean, nothing? We were worried sick!"

"Well, the MPs marched me straight to the CO's office and made me stand at attention until Staff Sergeant Hill and Sergeant Scott were good and ready to see me," Peach began, and I wince. All of us know that Staff Sergeant Hill has a humdinger of a temper once she gets going.

"I waited almost half an hour, standing stiff, and the MPs wouldn't say a word. Then—*bang!*—the door flies open and Staff Sergeant Hill starts shouting. She says she's going to see to it that I get a court-martial and get sent home. She says the Women's Army has enough problems trying to keep the honor of the corps without girls like me going off and acting like floozies in Paris, making everybody look bad."

Peaches is talking quietly, but almost everyone in the mess hall is leaning close, trying to listen. "Staff Sergeant Hill made me kind of angry, but Sergeant Scott was worse. She said she was disappointed in me. And then they took me to Major Addams," Peaches went on, "and I thought I was done for. She just sat there and stared at me for the longest time, and then she said, 'Explain yourself.' So I did." Peaches swallows and looks down for a moment.

"I said that I was fed up with all of you girls and that I wasn't meeting up with a boy or bringing dishonor on the corps. I told the major the truth—that I checked into the hotel and stayed by myself for two days."

I open my mouth, hurt, then close it. Peaches means she was fed up with me, too, and I remember what I said to her last time I saw her. She had every right to be fed up with me.

"The battalion commander sent an MP off in a jeep right then to check my story. It's a good thing that mademoiselle remembered me," Peaches adds. "She told Lieutenant Scott that I checked in and I stayed put the whole time. Major Addams let me off the hook then. She said, 'I understand, Carter, but don't you *ever* pull a stunt like this again.'"

"And that's it!?" My eyes are wide.

"Well-l-l, not quite," Peaches says with a wry smile. "I got punishment detail. I'm gigged and have KP for four weeks solid after my mail shift, and I have all my passes revoked for the next thirty days. But no court-martial anyway. Staff Sergeant Hill is still fit to be tied about that."

"I wouldn't have even known you were gone, except Gloria came and said so," I say finally. "You still mad at me?"

Peaches shrugs. "No more than I was with anybody else. I just got fed up, you know?"

"Yeah. I get fed up with all of us sometimes." I sigh. "I

should have been a better friend to you, Peaches Carter. I do apologize for telling you off about George the other night."

Peaches shakes her head. "This wasn't about a thing you did, Marey Lee."

"Wasn't a thing I did to help you, neither." I look over at Gloria's table. Her head is hanging down low, and she is picking at her food. Though I have heard more poison coming out of that girl's mouth than anything, I feel a little shamed at that pitiful sight.

"Peach. You gonna go talk to Miss Gloria?"

"I will. Later." Peaches sighs. "I've got to eat and get ready to go on duty, even though they kept me up last night, then I've got my four hours of KP." She smiles tiredly, then lowers her voice, her expression mischievous. "It was worth it, though. You know they've got room service in the hotels in Rouen?"

***

The last weekend in August, Ruby and me go on leave, and George takes us around Rouen to meet his farmers. We ride in a car with a driver, a "chauffeur," they call him, who has two little old kids sitting up there with him. I gave them some of the sugar cubes I carry, just like I used to give that scallywag Miss Victoria. George sees me giving the little ones sweets and asks me if I like kids. Ruby just about pokes a hole in my ribs with her elbow.

Bob has been writing Ruby and wants to know should he join back up or wait for her. Ruby says she doesn't know what to say, but I say she does. I hope next time Bob asks her if she likes kids.

George comes to see me every week. Peas are out of season now, so he brings me carrots, which are real pretty on the top. Ruby say my eyes will get real good in the dark if I keep eating George Hoag's carrots. Miss Ruby May Bowie had best keep her funny little comments to herself.

✳ ✳ ✳

"Marey!" Peaches comes screaming into the mess hall while I am mopping. "Marey!"

"Hold up, Peach. Don't you track up my floor," I warn her. She runs through the wet and leaves footprints anyway.

"Marey Lee Boylen," Peach say. "I don't care two figs about your floor. Guess what?"

"What?" I say, mopping around her feet.

"Guess," Peach says, and now she can't hardly stand still. "We're going to Paris!"

I just about drop my mop. "Paris? Peach, not again!"

"I told you! I told you we'd go! We've got our orders. The CO just posted them, and Ina told me the news. We are going to Paris, France!"

And this time, Peach has got it right—we really going to Paris. Who would have believed it! I guess just about anything in the world can happen now!

32.

NOW

Somewhere in my dreams, I am mopping around the Eiffel Tower when Tali's voice finally penetrates through the fog.

"Octavia! Wake up!"

"Mmmph?"

"C'mon, Tave, get up."

"What time is it?"

"Um . . . after four."

I scrub my face on my pillow and turn onto my side, trying to hold on to my dream of Paris. "Are you all right?"

"I'm fine. Get up."

I blink quickly as Tali turns on the light in the bathroom. She is standing next to the door, dressed. "Where are you going?"

"Just down to the car," Tali reassures me. "I need to do something."

"Okay," I say, still murky with sleep. "Why do I need to wake up?"

"Because you're going with me."

"Oh."

It isn't until I am out of bed and buttoning my jeans that my brain clears itself from the last little bits of my dream and I start to think. What I think doesn't make me happy.

"Tali. We're not . . . You're not going to do something stupid like leave Mare, are you? Because I am *so* not going with you if that's what you're doing."

Tali sighs heavily. "No, stupid, I don't have a death wish. We're not going to leave Mare. I'm trying to help you. Mare's going to make you drive today. You need some practice."

"What? Tali—"

"We're not going to leave the parking lot. I swear. And she *gave* you the keys before she went to bed, didn't she? She practically said to practice."

Wide-awake now, I groan and pull on my sweatshirt. I have a feeling this is going to be a very, very long day.

Last night, Mare told Tali to phone Mom and Dad and let them know how the trip was going. Mare stood right in our room while she did it, so Tali pretty much had to tell our parents the whole story about the Kahlúa, even though she told Mare it was "not that big a deal." Well, Tali was wrong. Dad just about had a full-grown cow when he heard, and after he got done yelling at Tali, he told Mare to put Tali and me on a plane home immediately. Then Mare took offense, and they got into this huge argument where Dad accused Mare of being a bad influence on us with her drinking and said that she should just come home and try to act like a woman her age for a change, and then *Mom* got on the other

extension and said we all needed a time-out before unfor-
givable things were said in anger, and that she trusted Mare
to discipline her grandchild, and that she'd see us all when
we got home. Then she made Dad hang up.

I thought, from the expression on her face, that Tali figured she'd pretty well gotten off the hook, except that Mare
handed me the car keys and said, "Well, since your sister
won't be needing these tomorrow, I guess I'd better give them
to you. Get some rest." And she'd gone to her room and
closed the door.

It went quiet after that. I sat on the bed with my mouth
open in shock. Tali locked herself in the bathroom, and I immediately tried calling Mom again, but the call went straight
on to voice mail. Nothing was settled by the time I went to
bed, and I was the most unsettled of all.

Mare *knows* I can't drive. She *knows* I'm scared. Right before I finally got to sleep, I made up my mind to make Mare
stop using me to get back at my sister. And now it's morning
and Tali is dragging me to the elevator and shoving me
inside.

"Tali . . ."

"The back of the parking lot is totally empty, Tave. It'll
be cool."

"But, Tali, if I hit someone's car—"

"I'll say I was driving, okay? Stop worrying."

Stop worrying. Right.

The morning air is a cold slap. Though sunrise is only a
little while away, it's still dark, and I am very aware of the

dark shapes of vehicles as we weave our way to where Tali parked. I feel my muscles tense as we find the car, surrounded by trucks and vans in front of it and on either side. I'm going to have to back out.

"It's not that hard," Tali assures me as she opens the passenger door. "You just do it."

"'Just do it.'" I imitate her in a snide voice. "Is that how Dad taught you how to drive?"

Tali sighs. "Actually, yeah. That's what he said. I ended up driving with Mom before I actually learned."

"Oh." I scootch up the seat and adjust the tilt of the steering wheel. "I guess he gets it from Mare. I don't know why she thinks I can just *do* this."

"Because she does." Tali shrugs, a blurry shape in the dimness. "Adjust your mirrors."

The car is ready before I am. "Tali . . . ," I begin.

"Turn on the engine, turn on your headlights, check behind you, put the car in reverse, keep your foot on the brake, and take off the emergency brake," Tali instructs in a bored monotone.

"Tali, I can't!" I say. "I flunked the written test already."

"That's only because you didn't write anything down. Just move, Octavia. Do something, even if it's wrong."

I bite down on my bottom lip and turn the key. The car responds to me, and Tali only has to remind me to turn on my headlights twice as I inch my foot off the brake. The car rolls an inch, and I slam on the brakes.

"Tali!"

"Octavia, you're fine."

"I know I'm fine," I say tightly, glaring into the mirror and inching out another few feet. That wasn't why I hit the brakes. How did she know why I failed my test? How could Mom tell her?

"You can start turning now," my sister says five minutes later when the car is well free of the ones next to it. "If you don't, you're going to hit that light pole."

"Fine," I say shortly.

"You're doing really well, you know."

I feel a surge of anger at Tali's condescending words. "It's not that hard," I tell her, and press the accelerator. And then the car touches against something solid. I hit the brakes again. "What was that?!"

"Turn the wheel," Tali says quickly. "Don't worry about it. Just turn the wheel and put the car in drive. Slowly—really slowly—pull forward."

I flick a glance in the mirror and see the light post right behind us. "How could you let me hit it?" I wail, my eyes filling with tears. "Tali, Mare's going to—"

"Don't worry about it. There's a rubber strip on her bumper; you probably just bounced. Don't worry about it. Put the car in drive."

Sniffling, I carefully pull forward, feeling a distant surprise at how the car swings straight in the little lane between the lines of vehicles. I glance in the mirror again and frown at the light pole. "Should I get out? Do you want to see how bad it is?"

"In a little bit," Tali says. "Drive to the end of this row

and head for the back of the lot. You need to practice back-ing out again."

My muscles are zinging with tension, but I turn left, sig-naling carefully despite the emptiness of the lot, and drive to the open space furthest away from the hotel. Tali tells me how to back in, to back out, to get out of a space using three turns, and to park straight against a line. Almost two hours go by before she says we should probably go back inside.

"Now don't tell Mare you practiced," Tali reminds me as we wait for the elevator.

"She's going to see the scratch," I argue. Though the rub-ber caught most of the impact of the light pole, the cement base made a small scratch beneath the license plate.

"No, she won't," Tali assures me. "She has nail polish that matches the color of the car almost exactly. I'll just patch it up, and if she notices, we'll make it up to her when we get home. Okay?"

"Okay." I can't keep a little smile off my face. I drove. I *drove*! I didn't totally wreck the car, and I drove!

"But, Tali?" I say, suddenly feeling a stab of unhappiness.

"Yeah?"

"When did Mom tell you about my test?"

Tali turns to face me. "What test? Oh. Octavia, Mom didn't tell me you flunked. You did. Just now."

"But—"

"I didn't even know you had taken a driving test. But I'm right, huh? You didn't write anything down on the paper, did you?"

"Well . . . no, but—"

"See, that's why I wanted you to get some practice. Mare doesn't know you like I do. I knew once we got to the car, you would freeze like a deer in headlights. At least now you got the first time out of the way, right?"

"Tali," I say as we walk down the hall. "Thanks a lot. I really owe you one, big-time."

My sister yawns as she slides her key card into the slot on our door, effectively shrugging away the moment. She peels off her sweatshirt. "I'm going back to bed. Don't bother me until sixty seconds before we go."

Suzanne,

We've left Texas, and since the next state is Louisiana, I guess I'll be in Cali pretty soon, because we've pretty much crossed the whole country. Unless my grandma's reunion is somewhere in Mexico, we've got to go home at some point.

There are a lot of hot guys pretty much all over the U.S., so I'm completely over getting upset about Brent. Next year is going to be the last year we're in high school, and I'd rather not spend it mad at you. I didn't know you liked Brent, or I would never have said anything, and I wouldn't have been talking to him every day. Just say the word, and I can blow him off next time he calls, if you want.

Mañana, chica,

☮ Tali

Suzanne Labruncherie
16 Sandpiper Circle
Walnut Creek, CA 94549

33.

then

George Hoag takes the train to visit me in Paris and says he thinks he needs to get on back home to the United States soon. He's been saying that just about every week since the Japs surrendered. Now that the war is over, most folks have stopped worrying, but George, he never does do anything like everybody else. He is all kinds of uptight, fretting that he won't have a job back home unless he gets there, fast.

"They told us about the GI Bill of Rights and that the folks from U.S. Employment Service are supposed to help us find work," George says. We are sitting in Service Club No. 2, the club for colored soldiers, watching folks play Ping-Pong. I am holding my paddle, waiting my turn.

"You want to go back to school?"

"Maybe." George is quiet. "Plenty of jobs in Illinois, though. I could teach chemistry until I figure out what to do."

"You could." George even looks like a teacher with those specs.

"Could go back to the University of Chicago and get a master's degree. Not too many colored research scientists, but the future's in science, that's what folks say."

"Mm-hmm." I watch the ball blur as it is hit back and forth.

"I'll find out soon enough, I guess. We're shipping out beginning of November."

"Mm-hmm . . . November?" I turn around with my mouth open. I hadn't thought that George would leave before me. "Guess you'll be glad to get home so you can stop worrying."

"Guess I will." George polishes his glasses on his handkerchief.

"Not me," I say. "I'm gonna be on the last ship out of here. I don't aim to leave Paris till they drag me home, kicking. You ever stayed someplace as fancy as the Hotel Bohy-Lafayette? Not me, and I don't expect I ever will again. I have got to live it up as much as I can before I go."

George frowns, his forehead wrinkling. "You might come back someday."

I shake my head. "Nah. When I go home, I . . . I won't ever get back someplace nice as this again." After Paris, Bay Slough isn't a place I can go back to. Even though sometimes I dream about that red Alabama dirt and can almost hear Feen's voice talking in her letters, I know Mama hasn't forgiven me, and Marey Lee Boylen is going to have to just carry on by her own self once the U.S. Army gets through with her. I am in a nice hotel, and right now I am making good money and saving it, though what I will buy with it, after Paris, I do not know. I do know this: I will never feel right working for Miss Ida again, and Bay Slough is not my home. Where is home, then? And how will I find it?

George nods toward the Ping-Pong table, his expression thoughtful. "Your turn, Marey."

"Oh." I push back my thoughts and turn toward the table. Ina White is waiting for me, grinning. Just because last week she beat me three games out of five, she thinks she is going to take me again. "Pride goeth before destruction, Ina White, just you remember that. George, you want to play winner?"

George clears his throat. "I'll take a rain check. Got to get back to base." He puts down his Ping-Pong paddle and stands abruptly, his lanky tall back stiff and straight. "I'll be seeing ya, Marey Lee."

"Oh." Confused, I hold out my hand, and George shakes it briefly, almost hurriedly, as if he has somewhere else to be. "Well, sure. I guess you've got things to do. See you, George."

I don't get time to think too long about why George just up and left. Ina waves her paddle from across the table, and I get ready for her serve. Ina puts a mean spin on that ball, but she can't get past me. We play five games, and this time, I win 4–1. Ina wants to play again.

"You can't win 'em all," I tease. "I'll play you tomorrow. Some of us have work to do."

I head for the mess hall—which is a dining room, since we're staying in a hotel. So far, Paris, France, is all right with me. I am learning me a little more of the language. I can say the word "hotel"—it's "o-tell," since the French don't use the sound of *h*. I can say "good day" and "good night." Peach can say just about anything. She can even call a taxicab and tell the driver where she want to go, though nobody with sense uses a taxicab if they can help it. The cabdrivers in Paris have no understanding of "slow" and "stop." Every time I get in a cab, I have to commend my soul to the Lord, but Peach is taking to France like water takes to ducks. She says she might stay for good.

"Hey, I saw your friend George walking around downtown like a lost soul." Phillipa Barnes gets in the chow line behind me. "I hear his unit's shipping out."

"That's what he said," I say, and hold out my plate so our French cook can fill it up. Since our barracks is a hotel, we have hotel cooks making up our rations. Don't know anybody else who can make plain old potatoes and meat loaf taste so fine. The only thing the French cooks can't make sense of is corn bread. They mix up cornmeal into these little yellow cakes. It tastes pretty good, but it is not hardly real corn bread.

I sit down next to Phillipa at a table. "Guess the Six-triple-eight will be just about the last ones out here, huh? They're even sending some of the Red Cross girls home."

"Get a load of that," Phillipa says. She grins and points at Gloria Madden, who has just come in and is waving her hand at anyone who will look. "At the rate girls are getting hitched to the boys shipping out, there won't be enough work for anybody to stay much longer."

Gloria sees us and comes over, smiling all over her face. "Look! I'm getting married!"

"Well, what do you know. Gloria Madden finally got her captain."

Gloria holds out her ring, turning it so it sparkles. "He's not a captain, Marey Lee. I gave up that creep a long time ago. My Freddy's a first lieutenant stationed right here in Paris. We're going to say our vows at Sacred Heart and stay here in the city. Can you believe it?"

I can believe it, all right. Gloria Madden was born with a silver spoon in her mouth.

"Don't know anybody who doesn't want to live in Paris!" I say.

"Hey, what about George?" Gloria says.

I tilt my head. "What about him?"

"Well, has he said anything to you?"

"Anything about what?" My face feels warm.

"Well, you-all have been seeing each other for two months! Is he a man or a mouse?"

Phillipa rolls her eyes. "Now, Gloria, don't you start. You girls with rings think everybody wants one!"

I shed Gloria and her big diamond just as soon as I can, saying I have to go on shift. We've got a motor pool that takes us on to the post exchange, and so I pick up my jacket and straighten my hat and make sure I am on time for my driver. Downstairs in the lobby, I check my mail slot and give a whoop. A letter!

It's not from Feen. The writing is sloped and loopy, and then I look at the address: Bay Slough.

Could Mama—

My hands are sweaty, and I can barely make myself open the letter. A little slip of newspaper is on top. I fish it out and look it over. It says:

A wedding was solemnized Tuesday morning in St. John the Baptist AME Church when Mrs. Edna Mae BOYLEN, Bay Slough, was united in marriage to Ernest Joseph PETERSON, son of Mrs. Sophie PETERSON and the late Bernard PETERSON, Huntsville. Rev. Emmanuel Morgan officiated. The bride dressed in pale blue and her corsage was of white roses, and she carried a white Bible. She was attended by the groom's cousin, Mrs. Cecelia JACKSON, who wore a corsage of pink roses. The groom was supported by his brother-in-law, William WHITE of Huntsville. Mrs. PETERSON, mother of the groom, wore a corsage of white camellias. After

     the ceremony a wedding breakfast
was served at the home of Mrs.
Elizabeth Ann DIALS.

A *wedding*?!
Good Lord above, Mama up and married someone.
I fumble for the letter.

October 25, 1945

    *Sister Dials thought you would want to see
this.*
    *Your sister, Josephine, was not able to
attend but will be home to visit when the school
term ends at Christmas.*
    *I expect you will be home soon. Ms. Ida
say your old job will be waiting.*

I remain,
Mrs. Edna Boylen Peterson

    I look at the unfamiliar, loopy handwriting, trying to
calm my mind. Mama didn't write this; I know Sister Dials
wrote this letter herself. I know she is trying to let me know
how things stand back home. Mama married somebody not
even Feen has ever said a thing about. My mind is running
in circles. What about Toby? Was Sister Dials wrong? Was
the man Mama was keeping company with all this time this
Mr. Ernest Peterson and not that no-'count Toby?

Maybe Mama knew the truth about Toby all this time.

Maybe I had no call to run off and leave like I did.

"Boylen, you coming or what?" Georgette Todd, our driver, is leaning her head out of the window of our transport vehicle.

"I'm coming," I say. I get into the car, folding up that letter smaller and smaller.

I walk into the postal exchange and do my shift, and I don't remember any of it.

34.

then

"You want me to look in on your sister?"

"If you can," I say, staring down at my cup. George brought me to this little café to tell me goodbye, but I have something to get off my chest first. "She won't need to know. You could say you're a Fuller Brush salesman if anybody asks. Just . . . see how she looks, would you, George?"

"I don't mind looking in on her, Marey Lee. You know that. But you could send a telegram from Western Union and find out how she is faster than I'll ever get there."

I shake my head. "Can't. If Mama knows . . ." I stop.

"Hold up now. You want me to look in on your sister without your mama finding out?" George pushes up his glasses and leans forward, pinning me with those funny calico cat eyes. "Marey, what—"

"Never mind," I mumble, remembering Feen's wide, scared eyes and her hunched body when Toby had been messing with her. "You wouldn't know what to look for anyway."

I'm worried. Mama's sent for Feen to come home, maybe

just for a visit, but maybe for longer. None of Mama's so-called uncles ever got her to marry them, not with me and Feen around. What if Mr. Ernest Joseph Peterson didn't want to be nobody's daddy? What if he is worthless, like Toby? Mama doesn't pay enough attention to Feen, not like she should. I should go home. I should watch after my sister, like Mama said.

I never intended to go back to Bay Slough, Alabama, no way, no how. I know what I ought to do; Mama didn't raise me to shirk my duty, but my chest squeezes every time I think of leaving Paris. Mama said to look after Feen. What about looking after me?

"Marey," George is saying, leaning his elbows on the table, "is your sister in trouble?"

"What? No. No, it isn't like that, no. Listen, George, for-get it, okay? Like as not, Feen is just fine. I just"—I shrug and try to smile—"worry about that crazy girl, you know?"

"I'll look in on your sister, Marey Lee," George says serious-like, and he reaches across the table to pat my hand. "I've got sisters, too, you know. If anybody asks, I'd like to be able to tell folks"—George clears his throat and glances out at the street—"that . . . that I'm a friend of yours."

I lean back and breathe a sigh of relief, but my sigh is sad-ness, too. George will do what I ask, since it's me who's asked him. He'll go, and I'll have someone else to look in on Feen, but a body would have to be blind not to see it: George Hoag is doing it because he's sweet on me.

He is a good man, the type who would work hard and

look after a body, but I can't let him get notions. I have got Feen to take care of until she is grown; she's all I can handle right now.

"I hope nobody asks you, George Hoag, but you sure are a friend of mine. Heck, you're one of the best friends I got. I sure won't have anybody bringing me peas once you're gone."

I think George will laugh, but his face gets more serious. "And I'll have those peas waiting on you, Marey Lee, when you get back home to the States. You just tell me when."

"It's November, George Hoag. Didn't your farmers teach you anything? You got plenty of time to worry about all kinds of things before you go worrying about getting me peas."

George just smiles a little. "Just you let me know when, Miss Boylen," is all he says.

George and his unit ship out the next week, and when we say goodbye, it seems like then the gray, cold weather blows in to stay. I am feeling pretty low. The wet weather has given me a head cold, and I am almost tired enough to go on sick call. I don't really know what is wrong with me, except everybody seems to be waiting for something. I am waiting to hear from Feen.

"I guess they're going to ship us all out pretty soon," Ina White says. Everyone is piled on her bed, huddled in their blankets and bathrobes. The hotel is fancy, but the rooms are damp in this cold. "Once Major Addams is gone, there really isn't any more Six-triple-eight, is there?"

"I'm ready to ship out," Maryanne says, her voice tired. "Mama wrote and says my grandpop's been doing poorly. I should get home."

Peaches sighs. "My folks want me home, too. They offered me a job at the secretarial college in Atlanta, and Dad thinks I ought to come back and take it."

"Bob says . . . ," Ruby begins, then ducks her head.

"He says what?" Peaches bumps Ruby's shoulder. "That boy finally pop the question?"

"I'm gonna say yes," Ruby says, and looks up at me. I can't help but laugh out loud.

"Ruby May Bowie! You never said!"

For a minute, everybody is talking all on top of each other, asking Ruby for the date and congratulating her and all, but Ruby looks at me again. "I told him yes on a condition," she say, and everybody hushes.

"What?"

"That Marey Lee came home to be my maid of honor," Ruby says, and she grins. "How long do we have to wait, Miss Boylen?"

"Now, that's not right!" I say as everyone laughs. "You know I said I'd be on the last transport out of here!"

"Oh, I know it," Ruby say. "I was counting on George to help me make my case, but he didn't have much luck, did he?"

I throw a pillow across the room. "Keep it up, girl, and I won't go home at all!"

"Gloria's wedding is going to be something," Peaches says. "Her fiancé's best friend has a buddy in the 301st Squadron. Do you know, he gave them a parachute and Gloria's found a seamstress to make it over into a dress?"

"Gloria'd take the blackout shades down off a window if

she thought it would make her look good. Remember how mad she was about how her uniform fit back in basic?"

"Now we'll all be needing to wear some of those big old French hats, won't we?" Ina laughs. "I hope they give us plenty of room for luggage when we ship out!"

"I want shoes," Ruby sighs. "Before I go home, I'm going to buy me three pair of those high-heeled shoes!"

"Marey, what do you want?" Maryanne asks suddenly. "You'd look good in a fox stole."

"Can't see buying a thing like that." I shrug. "Don't have nowhere to wear it and nobody to see me."

"George Hoag would step out with you somewhere," Peaches say, but I have had enough.

"George Hoag couldn't care less about a body's clothes. Girl, don't you start with me about George again!"

"But, Marey girl, you're giving that poor boy an awfully hard time." Ina grins. "He did wait around here like a faithful hound till you'd get off shift. He didn't ever come to see anybody but you. Didn't he ever declare himself?"

"He said he'd like to call himself my friend, and I said he was that," I say truthfully, ignoring the hoots of laughter that follow. "Anyhow, I don't want to talk about it, so I'm gone."

"Oh, Marey Lee, don't go yet," Ruby groans as I stand and pull my blanket around me. "It's early. We won't tease you anymore."

"I've got to pin up my hair."

"Don't be like that," she says, and pulls me back down to

the bed. "We just like to mess with you. That George Hoag sure didn't look at another girl once he met you."

"I don't want to talk about George!"

Peaches leans forward and grabs my hand. "Marey Lee! What did he do to you?" She looks mad now, like a mama goose about to hiss and run somebody off.

"He didn't do nothing," I say, and rub my forehead.

"Marey Lee Boylen," Ruby say. "Come on now, girl."

"I asked him to look in on my sister," I say finally. My hands are shaking. "I haven't heard a word from her in over a month—since my mama got married. And once . . ."

Once, one of Mama's "uncles" she brought home almost got her. Once, one night when Mama was drunk again. Once . . .

I look around the ring of faces, but the words don't push past my tongue. I can't tell them about Mama and the way she hides in her bottle. I can't tell them about Toby, his grasping hands and greedy eyes. I can't tell about leaving home when didn't nobody want me to stay.

"Once, I promised her I'd look after her when I was grown," I say finally. "I promised. . . ."

"We can send a telegram," Ina says immediately, but I just shake my head, too tired to explain, feeling my throat squeezed up tight with tears.

"Isn't there somebody who can take it to your sister without letting your mama know?" Ruby is quick, quicker than I am.

"Does she have a teacher she can trust?"

"You got someone at church you can trust?"

Don't know how I could have forgotten about Sister Dials.

Just before the 0300 shift at the postal exchange begins, Ruby goes with me to the post radio and telegraph station.

```
WESTERN UNION
NIGHT LETTER = MRS. BETTY ANN
DIALS = BAY SLOUGH ALABAMA=

PLS TELL SISTER A FRIEND
GEORGE HOAG WILL LOOK IN ON
HER HE WILL SEND A MESSAGE IF
SHE NEEDS ANYTHING SHE IS TO
TELL HIM.=

MAREY LEE BOYLEN PFC
```

I hope this is enough.

35.

NOW

Louisiana is hot, flat, and humid. The lines of moss-draped trees mark the edges of the interstate, and there are rain runoff ditches on the sides of the road where Mare says alligators and nutrias live.

"What's a nutria?" I ask, keeping my eyes on the road.

"A giant rat." The machine-gun laugh rattles in her chest.

Sometimes I can't tell when Mare's telling lies or not. But now that Mare is telling Tali and me stories again about her last days in Paris, I don't care.

We weren't back in our hotel room ten minutes this morning before Mare hammered on our door. And I mean *hammered.* She stood there with her suitcase next to her, surprised to see us already awake and dressed, and her eyes got all narrow when she looked at my sister.

"Well, look who's all bright-eyed and bushy-tailed this morning," she said.

"Whatever that means," Tali said, crossing her arms defensively.

"Are we going now?" I asked, hoping to keep them from locking hands on each other's throats.

"We're already checked out. You got the keys, Octavia?"

"Yes, ma'am. But, Mare—"

"Come on, then."

Mare had marched down to the lobby, and if she noticed that the car was a little further from the hotel, she didn't mention it. I was just relieved she didn't ask me to drive right then.

Tali slouched into the backseat, leaving me to ride shotgun, and we had started off—the three of us wound up, on edge, and silent.

"Traffic," Mare had hissed as we entered the freeway.

"People do have to go to work." I shrugged, but Mare just glared.

"What do you know about work, either one of you?" she snapped. "Not a doggone thing."

"Oh, here we go," muttered Tali.

Mare's mood persisted even after we stopped for breakfast just over the Louisiana state line. She was disappointed that the little diner didn't carry fresh beignets and then was greatly annoyed when she had to tell me what they are.

"They're like doughnuts without holes," Tali said disinterestedly. "They're not *that* good."

"They're a part of Louisiana tradition," Mare insisted.

Tali shrugged and ordered a Belgian waffle.

For once, the idea of pie didn't make me glad. Tense and unhappy, I couldn't eat more than toast. Mare kept looking at us, glowering like she wondered why she had brought us along. Tali ignored her, cutting her waffle into tiny squares. And I felt stuck in the middle.

The angry silence lasts all the way past Lake Charles, when Mare abruptly pulls over to the side of the almost empty two-lane highway.

"You ready to take the wheel?" she asks, looking at me over her large round sunglasses.

The minute our eyes meet, I can't answer. My tongue dries to a thick plank of wood.

Mare sighs. "If you don't want to . . . ," she begins.

"She can do it," Tali says from the backseat.

"I don't recall asking anyone else's opinion," Mare says flatly. "Octavia? It's up to you."

The silence stretches. A truck flies by, making the car rock slightly in the wind of its passing. My hands grip the edge of the seat. In my mind, I can see jackrabbits running across the freeway and the words of my driving test swimming across the narrow white test form. I had thought I was ready then, but I wasn't. I think I am ready now, but what if I'm not? If only—

"Well, do something, Octavia," Tali groans. "Don't just sit there again."

The word "again" stings against my memory like Tali intends. I take off my seat belt and open the car door. Already, the morning sun is beating down fiercely, and the stew of swampy smells from the rain runoff ditch adds to the already thick humidity. Swatting a huge mosquito, I hurry around the car while Mare scoots over into the passenger seat. I shut the door and belt in.

Adjust the seat. Adjust the mirror. Check for traffic. Put the car into drive. Go.

The moment the car moves, I stomp down on the brake hard, flinging everyone forward.

"Sorry, sorry, sorry," I chant nervously, waiting tensely until my leg muscles can unlock. I glance into the mirror again, crane around to double-check for cars. With a deep breath, I press the gas too quickly, and with a lurch and a roar, we are on the highway.

"Octavia," Tali begins. "Just—"

"Hush." Mare turns stiffly. I can see she is gripping the armrest. "Leave her be."

We stay in the slow lane. I can feel Tali moving restlessly behind me, barely restraining impatience as cars pass us. Mare talks quietly as I drive, telling me about the lives of the Acadians in this part of Louisiana, the Cajuns from New Brunswick, Canada, some of whom still live in the Atchafalaya River Basin, still hunt and fish and can vanish into the trees. I can let my hands and my arms and my back relax as Mare spins stories from the gray-green trees all around us.

"You can go faster than thirty," my sister sighs as three cars pass me one after another.

"Now, you're doing fine, Octavia. Hush, Miss Thing."

"I'm the one who taught her how to drive," Tali scoffs. "All you were going to do was throw her in the water and see if she could swim."

"That's how I learned," Mare says tersely.

"That's how you taught Dad, too," Tali reminds her. "And he says he almost drowned."

"Well, your father"—Mare shrugs dismissively—"exaggerates. He turned out all right."

"He also told us about the time you made him smoke a whole pack of cigarettes so he threw up." Tali snickers. "He told us about the time you nailed shut his bedroom window because he kept sneaking out at night."

Mare sighs. "And he wonders why I never had another child." She glances wryly at Tali. "Just think. I might have had a daughter."

"You did not just say that! You did not just disrespect me like that!"

Tali's wounded dramatics finally brings what we have both been waiting for—Mare's rattling, wheezing laughter. It seems the air in the car moves more freely as Tali continues to complain and Mare keeps smiling.

"Tali really did teach me," I say. I can't keep a smile from my face. "She let me practice with her. This morning."

"Well, I hope so," Mare says. "It's what I did for *my* sister. Feen about wore me out, jumping and jerking, riding the brakes. George said he was going to teach her, but I got there first. By the time he got around to it, she was ready to take the exam." Mare sounds proud.

I am thrilled that George is going to continue to be part of Mare's story. I imagine how it must have been when he looked in on Feen. Was she impressed with her sister's beau?

"When are you going to take the test again?" Tali interrupts my train of thought.

"When I get home, I guess," I say.

"Do it," my sister commands. "If we both ask, Mom and Dad might get us a car."

"Now, you two don't hardly need a car," Mare says, shaking her head. "You know how old I was before I even got a driver's license?"

"But that was back in the day, Mare," Tali says, grinning. "Nowadays, people need to get to the mall."

"Maybe so." Mare sighs. "Maybe so. You young girls are fast and sassy these days, and maybe you do need a car. I don't know."

I look over at Mare in surprise. "Really?" It's not like her to be so mellow.

"Watch the road!" Mare and Tali shout in unison.

"I am!"

As I straighten the car from drifting off into the ditch on the side of the highway, Mare keeps talking. "When I was your age, it was the same. You girls want cars; well, we wanted gentlemen friends and adult lives. Can't try and get everything you want all at once, though. Most of the time, the good things are worth a wait."

Tali groans loudly. "Is this where you tell us not to have sex?"

Mare laughs, a single harsh sound. "No. This is where I tell you if you have another drink on this trip, I will send your narrow behind back home."

"What? I won't," Tali protests, a little hurt. "I'm not an alcoholic or anything. I was just . . . I don't know, trying it."

Mare sighs. "You know, your father thinks I'm a bad influence on you. I'm not too sure he's not right."

"He's not right," Tali says stubbornly. "It wasn't like it was your idea."

"It's not something you would have done if your parents were here, is it?"

"No, but they don't drink. . . ." Tali trails off uncomfortably. "Fine." She sighs. "Mare, I'm sorry. What's my punishment?"

"You've already got it," Mare says easily.

"What?"

"Your sister is driving. All day today, anytime she wants to, Octavia gets to drive."

"And?"

"And that's it," Mare says, and turns back to me. "Did I tell you about how your father learned to drive?"

"Didn't he just learn in school?"

"Oh, no, he didn't think he needed anything like driving school. He went south to work one summer, ended up in Fresno, and told them he could drive a tractor."

"What?" I blink. Dad had a lot of nerve.

"Octavia," Tali interrupts. "Speed *up*. Mare, don't talk to her; she slows down."

"Your sister's doing just fine, Miss Thing. Hush up and take your punishment."

"My punishment?! Oh, *no*. No! This is SO wrong!"

I can't help it. I laugh. It bursts out of my stomach, a single, loud noise, and rattles from my throat in a staccato chortle.

The road ahead of us is long, straight, and flat, and we have miles and miles to go.

Guys, guess what—GUESS WHAT!?!?!?!

I drove on the road today for TWO HOURS!!!! We're in
Louisiana, and it's all flat, so that was cool. The only bad thing
was that there are these HUGE ditches on the side of the road
and I almost drove into one, but that was because I was
looking at it. Tali said just not to look.

Mare says all anybody has to do if they want to drive is get
behind the wheel and try it. That's how she taught her sister.
And my dad. I can see why they started teaching driver's ed in
schools in California. It was probably all because of Mare.

Next state is Alabama. I'll let you know if I have any hot
cousins you should meet.

Ciao!

😊 Octavia

Eremasi Sariki & Rye Preston
6 Waverly Place, Apt. B
Martinez, CA 94553

36.

then

"Maryanne! Ina says we've got orders!"

"We're shipping out of here?" Maryanne drops her stack of reports and balls up her fists.

"The Six-triple-eight is going home!"

Maryanne raises her arms and cheers. We knew we weren't staying on in Paris, France, forever, and the European theater of operations will soon be closed for business for good.

Major Addams shipped out just about right after they made her lieutenant colonel. Most of the Red Cross folks settled themselves working with orphanages or moved on to the Pacific to help out the Japanese now after the surrender. The boys have been shipping out of the ETO one unit after another, and now it's down to the Postal Directory Battalion to come on out and close the door behind us. Folks are gonna have to do without the U.S. Women's Army Corps now.

In the lobby of the hotel, folks are talking all over each other. Somebody brought out a bottle of French champagne, and we all get a sip. It is a party that started when the captain first posted the papers, and it will go on till we march out.

Most folks are glad to be going 'cause things have been changing. For one thing, Uncle Sam has time now to be sending out postal inspectors, and it seems our efficiency is down at the Paris postal exchange since the French folks have been helping. It also seems things have gone missing from the post, and the inspectors say we have to do searches before folks leave for the night.

Nobody likes that. We don't like treating the French like they're lying to us, and they get all riled up when we follow orders. And our orders are to search and seize. On the captain's orders, we turn out pockets, dump out handbags, check up under hats and through hair, and we find every little place folks might hide something, and I do mean every little place, everywhere. And we find things, too. Tubes of scent, fountain pens, chewing gum, money, smokes. We confiscate it and send folks away. We can hardly be social with the French after that.

The weather is just as tired as we are. The streets are all slippery puddles, and it is raw cold around here. Things that were exciting to look at—the bistros where French kids drank down watered wine like they were grown, the shops where they lay out the food with no covering on it, all the dance hall shows and the cathedrals and all—none of that seems interesting anymore. Everywhere some fool writes Kilroy Was Here, somebody else scrawls Yankee, Go Home! This man's army has just worn its welcome out.

* * *

I might have saved my time, sending that telegram. I get a letter from George a few days later, telling me he is just now getting away from the U.S. Army. He landed at Camp Shanks, then they sent him on to a "separation center" in Fort Bragg, North Carolina, where he got part of his mustering-out pay—they gave him a hundred dollars in cash—got the details of the GI Bill of Rights explained to him, gave up all his uniform clothes except the ones he was wearing home, and then got asked to sign up for another hitch in the service! When they finally understood that no meant no, they gave him his orders releasing him from active duty and he hopped a bus for New Orleans, where he stayed a day and a night with his relatives back there. Then he got himself directly on a train to Alabama to see after my sister.

After all that, I get a letter from Feen the following week:

November 30, 1945

Dear Marey,

I am sorry I have not written. I didn't want to be the one to give you the shock, but Sister Dials says you have already heard that Mama is married. I see you sent word to see how I am. I am fine. Mr. Peterson smiles a lot and tries to make Mama laugh, and that is fine with me. He is nothing like the other one.

Miss Ida asks if I would like to work for

her. She needs a girl to help out around the place, and I can replace her girl who cooks, too, since money is tight. I could live in, she says, and would not have to finish school or go back to Philadelphia.

With the war over, many GIs have returned. Will you come back soon? I am trying to figure out what I should do.

I hope to see you.

Your sister,
Josey Boylen

Feen didn't hardly say a thing about what's going on, and that doesn't make my worry any less. Worrying don't rush the U.S. Army, though. Now that we have our orders to muster out, everything is "hurry up and wait." We have more medical checks and record and equipment checks than we know what to do with. The brass is checking and double-checking that we don't allow any equipment that should belong to the U.S. Women's Army Corps to get left behind. Packing up is all we do for weeks, and then it is time to board the train to Normandy, then board ship in Le Havre.

I send a telegram to Feen to let her know to expect me home. Last time it took us eleven days on ship to get here, and this time the ship is not so big and the weather is just as bad. The navy is sending colored nurses home on the same transport, so we will be bunking with strangers, but after all we have been through getting to the ETO, just knowing we'll find dry land at the other end is almost enough for me.

This time our bunks are down in the hold, and like the time before, they are triple decks. We hear the officers get two bunks to a room and a recreation lounge, but that is no surprise. It is stormy out on the Atlantic sea, but none of us in the Six-triple-eight are surprised by this, either. We have been through storms before.

Ruby got a bottom bunk this time, since she just about killed herself last time falling off the top. Peaches and me are above her, and all she can talk about is how Bob is coming for her at the separation center and how once she gets her orders, he is going to drive her home and meet her parents. Ina says she might sign up for another hitch, seeing as they might offer more money and another stripe on her sleeve. Maryanne thinks she will use her GI Bill of Rights money to go back to nursing school, but she says she can't think past getting home and going to sleep in a room she don't have to share with seven other people.

"You hear anything back about that teaching job in Atlanta?" I lean down and ask Peach.

"No," Peaches says slowly. "I wrote them back and told them not to hold it for me."

"Are you kidding?" Ruby leans out from her bunk. "Why not? I thought you wanted to teach."

Peaches shrugs. "I had a good time at secretarial college, but . . . I don't want to go home. Not yet anyway," she says, and she grins. Ruby looks at Peach like she's just said she doesn't love her mother anymore.

"But, Peaches, what are you going to do?"

"I don't know," Peaches admits. "Since we've been in Paris, I've felt so free I've almost forgotten what home is like. In France we ate in any bistro we wanted to, shopped in any store we wanted. Atlanta won't be like that."

"Won't be like that anywhere, not for colored folks," I say. "We only won the victory in the ETO, remember? Didn't anybody realize we wouldn't win the war back home."

"I got a letter from a fellow I met in London," Peaches says. "He was a dishwasher at a café before he joined, and then he trained as a truck driver. He drove with the Red Ball and took a shot in the leg, so they discharged him. He went home to Athens, down in Georgia, and he hasn't found a job yet."

"That's what George was worried about," I say.

Peach sighs. "The GI Bill of Rights guarantees service personnel all kinds of help, but in the South, you just might be out of luck. This gent went to the U.S. Employment Service folks, but they can't find him anything but dish washing, and he's supporting his mama. Got turned down for unemployment pay. That's the way it is back home, and"— Peaches shrugs—"I don't want any part of it."

"Have you got a plan, then?" Ruby knows Peaches too well to try to talk her out of anything.

"Oh, I don't know," Peach says. "I want to go west. How about Los Angeles?"

"Los Angeles? Peach, are you aiming for Hollywood?"

"I just might," she says. "I got used to seeing the lights in Paris, and now I want to see the lights on the ocean."

"You can see the ocean from the deck." I laugh. "And I'll shine a flashlight on it for ya. You don't need to go near any crazy movie folks for that."

"Well, then, I could go to San Francisco. I've heard there are jobs there," Peaches says. "You could come with me, Marey Lee. First go home and see about your sister, and then come on out west."

"Oh, I don't know a thing about San Francisco," I say, but I feel a funny flutter in the pit of my stomach.

"Bob says he has a job with Boeing in Seattle, working on airplane engines," Ruby says. "You girls ought to come on up to Seattle."

"I'm going to San Francisco," Peaches says, like she had this thought in her head all along. "I'm going to get myself a job, maybe use my GI Bill and take a few classes somewhere. I'm going to live by the ocean and . . ."

"Find yourself a good man and settle down." Ruby smiles.

"Well, no, not quite"—Peach smiles crookedly—"but something like that, maybe. And not the 'settle down' bit, either, not just yet. Girls, I've got a lot of partying left to do."

Peaches Carter makes me laugh like she always does, but her words start me to thinking. What if I did go to a city like San Francisco? What if I did find a job, find Feen a school, and have some kind of life? There are colored folks in cities like that, and art and music and poets and writers. Maybe Peaches is right. Maybe I don't have to go home and take up my job from Miss Ida. I may have to go back to Bay Slough to see about Feen, but I don't have to stay.

Maybe Feen and me could get a little place with Peach and invite folks to come see us. Maybe Ruby and Bob could visit, and Annie, when her young man can travel. Even Mrs. Freddie Hughes, Gloria, could come and see us as long as she didn't think she was the lady of my house. And after a while, maybe even George . . .

Don't get crazy, Marey Lee.

I like my San Francisco dream, but I know George Hoag won't be coming around much longer. He may think he is sweet on me now, but nobody from a big city like Chicago wants to wait on little country Marey Lee from Bay Slough, Alabama, once he knows she'll be dragging her little sister behind her.

I can't be bothered about that. I promised Feen I would take care of her. I won't break my word. George will find somebody else, some girl who's already been to college and all that.

First thing I have to do is get home and see about Feen. Mama, Miss Ida, George Hoag, San Francisco, and all the rest will just have to take care of itself.

❈ ❈ ❈

When we reach New York Harbor, every GI on that boat lets out a holler. All of us come out to the deck, hang on the rails, and cheer. Folks are laughing and crying, pointing to Lady Liberty holding up her torch. Posing for pictures and hugging their friends, everyone celebrates. We are home, home, home. We have just about made it.

For just a few minutes, isn't a soul on the ship upset. Even the craps games hold up for long enough to let folks set their eyes on the Statue of Liberty.

America.

Home.

I lean out and look, trying to see freedom.

The boat dips and bobs on the waves, and for the first time I want it to hurry up and get on. I have things to take care of and things to do.

37.

then

We stay at Camp Shanks for two or three days. Most of us are sick as dogs by the time we finish twelve days on the Atlantic, and the U.S. Women's Army Corps can't let no ailing woman stumble on home, no sir. They feed us up, give us hot showers and clean beds till just about everyone perks up some.

The PX at Camp Shanks makes us know for sure we are in the U.S. of A. They have all kinds of nonsense in there we suddenly can't do without—rose-scented soap, nylon stockings, chewing gum, hand lotion, and more. Ruby picks up one of those new ballpoint pens; it costs her $12.50! But she says she wants to get something nice for Bob. It doesn't write worth $12, but that is all right with Ruby.

Most folks take the time to use the telephones at the telephone center in the middle of the base. I wait with Ruby and watch her rush into the booth assigned to her when they get through to Dallas. It takes only a half an hour, and when she comes out, her eyes are shiny and she is all smiles.

"That was Mama," she says, smiling through tears. "She let out a holler when she heard my voice and just about scared my father out of his wits."

"They're coming to meet you?" I ask.

Ruby wipes her eyes. "They are. My father and Bob are driving down together."

Ruby is so happy she can't stand it. I wish I was that glad to be going home.

Since we don't have a telephone, I don't have a soul to call except maybe Miss Ida, who would surely put me through to Mama. I could ring her, but I don't want to be beholden to her for anything, not when I am not going to set foot in her house with a dust rag in my hand ever again.

Peaches doesn't have anybody at home waiting on word from her, either. Her mama is put out with her for not taking that job, so she expects her folks won't have too much to say that she wants to hear. When they tell us it is time to ship out to our separation centers, we are all ready. Ruby is going to Fort Bragg, North Carolina, and Peach, Dorothy, and Ina are going with her. Maryanne Oliver and I are on our way to Camp Blanding in Florida. From there, I will take a bus to Alabama. It won't take me long to get to Bay Slough.

"They hire colored stenographers in California, and we will make good money," Peach tells me one more time, putting on her gloves. "Now, I plan to stay on till Christmas with my folks, but I'll be on my way before the new year. Can't let them snatch up all the good jobs!"

"I will let you know about the wedding," Ruby says.

"Don't you forget, Marey Lee Boylen, it's going to be in June, and you've got to stand up for me!"

"I'll see you," Peach hollers. "Soon, Marey! Soon!"

Maryanne and I wait with our duffle bags for our camp to be called. Everyone is crying and laughing and hollering goodbye, but I can hardly speak. I have a feeling I won't ever see some of them again. And me, once I get split from Ruby and Peaches, 6888th Battalion, Company C, and the U.S. Women's Army Corps, I feel like I will disappear. If I am not careful, I might get on back to Bay Slough and never remember who I am.

I am Private First Class Marey Lee Boylen, from Bay Slough, Alabama.

And pretty soon I am going to be somebody better.

✳ ✳ ✳

Don't expect anybody to meet me at the station, so when I step down off the bus by the post office, I don't stop. Instead, I heft up my bags and walk on.

Nothing has changed too much in Bay Slough, but it sure looks small. The Pentecostal church on First Street looks tiny when I think about St. Paul's in London or Sacré-Coeur in Paris. Young's looks downright lonely standing by itself when I think of bistros and shops and stalls all bunched up and shoved together side by side down those narrow Paris streets.

Mist is hanging in the air, and cars rattle by as I walk out past the edge of town and turn down Fourth Street toward the colored section of Bay Slough. I see St. John the Baptist AME, painted white and standing proud, the wrought iron fence around its yard straight and tall. I think about Feen's Christmas play way back when and the social we had at Sister Dials's. I can't just walk on by when I see her front porch, but I don't expect a long-legged girl in a knee skirt and loafers to come tearing out her front door, screaming my name.

"Marey! Marey Lee!"

"Feen! Girl, look at you!"

"Yes, Lord," Sister Dials sings out. "She's come on home. Lord, she's come on home!"

We are all hugging and Sister Dials is singing, and I do a little two-step round with Feen hanging on. She is taller and a bit more woman-like, but for the most part, Feen seems just the same as always. Aunt Shirley must have bought her that pleated skirt and those loafers. She's pretty as ever.

I look at Feen and she stares at me, and we just grin big. "Welcome home," Feen says, pulling back and examining my uniform. "Marey Lee, you look real sharp! Get a load of all those muscles!"

Sister Dials is peering at my uniform, shaking her head. "Girl, wasn't nobody watching for you today but Miss Josephine here. It just goes to show you," she says. "Before they call, I will answer, isn't that what the Book says?"

"I am sure glad you were expecting me," I say to Feen, holding her arm as Sister Dials welcomes us into her warm front room. What happened to my "little" sister? Feen, hefting my duffle bag, is just as tall as I am.

"How is Mama?"

"Mama is fine," Feen says, but her smile fades a bit. "Mr. Peterson is a real joker. He keeps Mama laughing all the time."

"It was a real pretty service," says Sister Dials. She has put a plate of tea cakes in front of me and is pouring me a cup of her special coffee. I can smell the bitter chicory swirling up in the steam. "Your mama wanted to wait, but Mr. Peterson got a job out at the mill in Huntsville. He had to get back."

"So, he's going to stay on in Huntsville?" I say, pulling off my gloves and reaching for my cup. "He must be a man of some means, driving back and forth like that."

"Mama's selling the farm and moving on to Huntsville with him," Feen blurts. "I wanted to write you, but Sister Dials said you'd be better off not hearing till you got home."

The words knock me back. "Selling? Selling? But Mama always said Daddy bought that land with his sweat and blood and the farm was always going to be in the family. Mama said . . ."

"Your mama say she is pure tired of taking care of them hogs," Sister Dials offers. "She got a man to take care of her now."

"But . . ." My mouth moves. I can't find a thing to say.

"I thought if you got your job back from Miss Ida and put in a few more hours at Young's," Feen says slowly, "I could take in her washing, same as Mama did. I don't want to go back to Aunt Shirley's. I can find a domestic job, and between the two of us, we can maybe afford enough to rent the farm. Or maybe just a couple of rooms . . ."

"Josephine Louise Boylen," I say. "You are going to school. Don't talk foolishness."

"I don't want to go back to Philadelphia, not unless you're coming back with me," Feen says, and her eyes fill up. "Please, Marey Lee! I—"

"Hush, Feen. Didn't nobody say nothing about Philadelphia." I turn to include Sister Dials. "You might as well know I don't intend to stay here long. If Mama has plans for me, she might as well understand I have plans of my own."

"Well, now, Marey Lee," Sister Dials begins.

"But Mama doesn't have plans for you," Feen says, wringing her hands. "Mr. Peterson's already got a little house. It's just for Mama and him."

Even though I don't expect different, hearing the words makes my breath roar in my ears.

"Now don't go getting all riled up," Sister Dials says worriedly, reaching across to pat my leg. "You been walking on your own all this time, Marey Lee; your mama didn't think to . . . Well, like I told your friend that come by to look in on Feen, wasn't nothing here nobody needed to worry you about, and I meant that. Now, your mama knows the Lord God don't look well on them that don't take up the cross like he's given 'em. A mother's children are her cross, and . . ."

"Feen, stay here," I say, standing and pulling on my gloves. I shoulder my bag. "I'll be back."

"Now, Marey Lee Boylen, don't you go rearin' up on your hind legs in your mama's face," Sister Dials warns. "You are just like her—don't listen to nobody. . . ."

Feen looks up at me, and in her face I see fear—and hope. "I'll be right here, Marey."

❊ ❊ ❊

Staff Sergeant Hill shouts cadence in my memory as I march down the road. I don't have a word in my head but the left-right-left steps on the packed dirt road, my hands as empty as my mouth.

Almost two years and not a word. The paymaster sent her half my check every month, faithful as clockwork. I worked hard to make sure she didn't miss what I took in from Miss Ida's, made sure she didn't have cause to worry about that farm mortgage. But not a word.

The knob is in my hand before I know it. I wrench open the door and step inside the front room.

"Mama!"

The lamp is sitting in the same place, next to Mama's old upholstered armchair, where she would sit sewing every night. The house smells like greens and fatback and vinegar and sets my stomach to growling. I stay where I am.

"Mama, where—"

"Why you come up in here hollering, Marey Lee Boylen? Women's Army make you think didn't nobody teach you no better?"

My heart just about jumps out my chest when Mama appears in the doorway of the kitchen. A faded flowered apron is hung over her dress, and she is holding her wooden spoon. She looks some put out, but not surprised to see me at all.

"No, Mama. I'm sorry."

"Where Feen at? Hogs ain't gonna slop themselves."

I swallow, trying to wet my tongue. "Mama," I blurt, "why didn't you write?"

Before the words are out, I feel my face burn. Oh, why did I say that? Mama don't have time for a girl bawling after her about, "Why didn't you do this?" I don't need to listen to know what she has to say.

"Why I got to write to you? You are grown. Grown enough to go off and join the Women's Army without nobody's say-so." My mother turns back toward the kitchen. "See after them hogs, Marey Lee."

"Mama—" I follow her, standing a ways behind her. "Feen says you sold the farm."

"Mr. Peterson is kind enough to have bought me a house," Mama says, and her lips curve into a smug smile. "That man is something else. Mm-hmm." She laughs softly.

"You said we weren't ever going to sell. You said Daddy built this farm with his blood and sweat."

My mother sighs and looks over at me, crossing her arms. "That he did. And then his hardheaded girl child went off and left it all on me. I do what needs to be done. This farm ain't nothing but a noose round my neck."

Anger pulses in my temples. "Well, what about Josephine, Mama? You said we were always gonna have the farm. You said nobody would be able to take what was ours."

"As long as I am on this side of the grave, Josephine Boylen has got a roof over her head. She is doing fine in Philadelphia, and what I do for your sister ain't no business of yours." Mama shakes her spoon in my face. "You left out of here, Miss High and Mighty. Big old grown girl like you can take care of herself."

"You know why I left!" The words rush out, bitter on my tongue. "You sent Feen up north, and what was I supposed to do? Work for Miss Ida the rest of my days? Sister Dials says she saw Toby coming back around—"

"Ain't nobody talking about that no-'count man round here." Mama holds up her spoon in warning. "Didn't I say to see to the hogs? Or is you so grown you forgot how to mind?"

I stare my mother down, heat rising up in my skin. I am grown now. I don't have to listen to a thing this woman says to me, not a thing. I am about to open my mouth and tell her so.

Then I think about Feen's face looking up hopefully at me, and I bite my tongue hard.

"Yes, ma'am," I say, with military courtesy that would make Lieutenant Hundley proud. "I will see to them directly."

I will do what I'm told this one last time. For Feen's sake. Only for Feen's sake.

The slop buckets are in the same place on the back porch as always, stinking to high heaven, even in the cold. The hogs stink, too. The yard looks small and cluttered and dirty, and I look around at the field, the garden, the pigpen, the henhouse, remembering. Remembering everything.

The hogs squeal and fight over their slop like no one ever feeds them. I lift the buckets to tip them, and they seem almost light. I guess in the Women's Army Corps, I hauled heavier loads than this, with my pack and my mask. Mama doesn't know what I can do, but I do.

I know what I can do.

My mother hands me a rag to wipe my shoes when I bring in the buckets, but I don't need it. She looks at me, eyes traveling up my uniform and down to my shoes.

"Well, now." She clears her throat. "I got your money right here, Marey Lee."

"Ma'am?"

Mama pats her apron and pulls out an envelope. "This your money. I kept it for you."

"Mama, that money was for you and Feen! I—"

"I know what it was for, and I didn't have no need of it. You going to need it now. Here." Mama pushes the envelope into my hands and steps back, and for a minute, the ground doesn't feel too solid under me. I left without her say-so, and my mother doesn't want me back.

"Mama." My voice cracks under the weight of the words I don't speak. "I'm sorry."

Mama looks back toward the stove a moment, her shoulders stiff.

"Feen over at Sister Dials's, ain't she? Girl don't hardly ever set foot in this house if she can help it. Well, I'm just about to eat without her. You hungry?"

I take a deep breath. "I'm going west, Mama. To San Francisco. I've had some schooling in the army. I can type and use a stenographer machine. I plan to get a job, use my GI Bill of Rights, and go to college. And I plan to take Josephine with me."

My mother raises her brows, her chin going down as she eyes me. "Is that so? That fool girl's talking about staying on here, gonna call herself paying me rent."

"I'll see to it she stays in school, Mama. She's going to graduate. You'll be proud."

"That Miss Feen gonna do whatever pleases her," Mama says dismissively. "That girl thinks she grown."

"I'll take care of her." I hear myself almost begging. "It'll be good for her to get out of here. You know that Miss Ida is already talking about Feen going to work for her? Like she already has her life planned, like Feen has no plans of her own. Like she bought and paid for us and Feen, too? There's opportunity for coloreds in the West, Mama. I'm taking her with me."

My mother turns away, her mouth tight. "Go tell your sister stop pestering Sister Dials and get on home. I'm about to make the biscuits, and we best eat 'em hot."

"Yes, ma'am." My heart twists, but I know better than to keep talking.

"Marey Lee." Mama's voice stops me as my hand touches the door.

"Ma'am?"

"It's dark out. You watch yourself."

I pause, midstep. "Watch yourself," is what Mama has said every night, like I am a little old kid who doesn't know how to watch out for myself. "Watch yourself," she says, even though I am grown now, grown enough to have gone to war, heard bombs dropping all around me, and come home in one piece. "Watch yourself," Mama says, and in her own way, she is maybe saying watch out or telling me the world's a cold, hard place for a colored girl like me.

"Watch yourself," Mama says, even though she knows I do.

She taught me how to watch.

I don't tell her any of that. Everybody knows better than to argue with Edna Mae Boylen.

"Yes, ma'am," I say, tugging on my gloves. I grab my handbag and close the door.

38.

NOW

"So, you and Great-aunt Feen ended up in San Francisco?" I ask, wiping my mouth and wondering if Mare's going to finish her Mississippi mud pie. We are at a chic restaurant and casino in Gulfport, Mississippi, and we are all enjoying the air-conditioned dining room.

"Mm-hmm," Mare says, sipping her coffee. "They had military jobs all over. We moved on into the Fillmore District."

"The Fillmore?" Tali's voice is disbelieving.

"Oh, it was different back then, back before the city tore it all apart, trying to make it fit for rich folks and to give something back to the Japanese. The Fillmore was the spot back in the forties. The Harlem of the West, they called it." Mare gestures with her lighter.

"There was a jazz or a bebop band on every street—on a couple of streets it was two or three of them. You know I heard Ella Fitzgerald sing at the Long Bar between Post and Geary? There was Club Alabam, and the Blue Mirror, and across from the Blue Mirror, there was the Ebony Plaza Hotel, and in the basement, they had another club. There was all kinds of folks listening to swing and bebop and jazz. Oh, we had a good time."

"Did George Hoag ever find you?"

Mare grins across the table at me, looking suddenly sly. "What do *you* think?"

"I think you found him, but you blew him off and found somebody more exciting," Tali says, licking Key lime sauce off of her finger.

"Exciting? Girl, please. I had all the excitement I needed, living in the city and trying to make sure Peach didn't totally ruin my sister for decent living. No, ma'am, when George Hoag showed up again, I let him visit all he wanted. He had a good-paying job, and he had a car. That was what we needed right then. He was your aunt Feen's first husband."

"Aunt Feen?" I gasp. "Oh, Mare, no! Did it break your heart?"

Mare smiles and looks at my troubled face with pity. "Lord, no, girl! I finally got somebody to take care of my baby sister, like Mama always said. Once Feen got married, boy, Peach and I tore up that town. We had the time of our lives." She laughs at the expression on my face, at life in general, a deep, chortling belly laugh that has others in the restaurant looking up at us, smiles interrupting their meals and their conversations.

"So, whatever happened to your unit? To Peach and Ruby? To Bob?"

"What happened to your buddy Gloria?" Tali adds slyly.

"Well, Ruby and Bob still live in Seattle; they got kids and grandkids. Haven't seen them in years, but we write. That Gloria—she was Mrs. Frederick Hughes—divorced Mr. Hughes the next year after she married him and shacked up with a French count. Far as I know, she is still in Paris somewhere. Peach moved on to L.A." Now Mare grins. "Peach was an extra in one of those action flicks, calls herself a movie star now. That girl just tickles me. Old as she is, she's still trying to get in front of the camera."

"She didn't get married?"

Mare shakes her head. "Nah, not Peaches. Even when they made it legal that first time, she said she didn't feel the need. Peach has a houseful of friends, she has a job she loves in a city she loves, and she has her movies. She hasn't ever needed much else."

"Well, what about you?" I ask, then bite my tongue. The look Mare gives me makes my toes curl.

"What do you mean, 'what about you?' I'm sitting right here in your face, Octavia!"

"I mean, what did you do?" I ask, braving Mare's focused attention. "When you got to San Francisco, I mean. Afterward."

Mare looks slightly less ferocious now. "Well, I took

the civil service examination for the San Francisco County Welfare Department and I went back to school, of course. Wasn't nothing else I *could* do. Peach said I was setting Feen a bad example, not finishing school." Mare smiles at the memory.

"I worked nights at a club when I went to class in the day. I was a clerk and a secretary when I went to night school. They let me be a welfare officer when I was halfway through. Had to go up in that so-called temporary military housing and make sure folks were treating their kids right. Lord knows I had enough taking care of your daddy by then to know what to look for.

"I had summer school every summer till I finished my bachelor's degree, and by then I was a social worker, and worked my way to caseworker, and stayed on till they made me quit."

We sit in silence for a moment, listening to the far-off sounds of the slot machines and the roar of voices in the casino. Mare fiddles with her water glass, then breaks the silence.

"I stayed on in San Francisco, even when Mama passed. Your great-aunt Feen went to the service, saw all the folks, but I didn't go. Your daddy went back year after he graduated from college. I never did get back down to Bay Slough."

"So that's why we're going." Tali's voice seems loud, even though her words are soft.

Mare nods slowly. "This is the reunion, girls."

Shocked, I glance at Tali, but she's looking at Mare, nodding like she already knew.

A waitress bustles in and collects our plates, looking pointedly at the check, which Mare has left sitting. Mare tightens her lips and puts her lighter back into her bag, nostrils flaring in irritation.

"I s'pose we ought to get on," she says finally, and slides her oversized sunglasses over her narrow face, hiding her expression. "Do this one last thing so we can get up out of here."

❄ ❄ ❄

The first thing that catches me is the trees. They are live oaks, tall and black, draped with the green-gray Spanish moss that has become familiar since we've been in this part of the country.

The little cemetery is hidden on the back side of a neighborhood. The road is packed red dirt, and there isn't a manicured green lawn like in the cemeteries back home. Instead, there are little cement walls and plots bordered with little fences and overrun with vines.

Mare says we don't have to get out, but Tali and I climb out into the cloying heat after her. We each hold an arrangement of creamy white roses as she slips on a pair of flat shoes so she can walk safely in the uneven grass. Tali looks around nervously for snakes, but I look around at the number of flags on some of the larger tombstones. Confederate flags. I feel like I am in a place beyond time.

We walk, and Mare seems, for the first few moments, aimless. Her stride is short and tentative, little bird steps heading first one direction, then another. I match pace with her, realizing that we are the same height, but without these trees looming over us, she has always seemed so much taller. In the dappled light, her skin appears seamed and wrinkled. For the first time this trip, Mare seems to me fragile and frail and old.

"Did Aunt Feen give you a map?" I ask after we have walked in silence for at least ten minutes. The air itself seems to be burning silence, and we hear nothing else but our own footfalls, the calls of birds, and the lazy buzzing of bees.

"No," Mare says, but she says it with some of her usual tartness, and I feel a little reassured. "Don't need a map. Just head for a back corner—that's all you have to do. That's where they bury all the poor folks."

Tali flashes a look at me. "There's no stone?"

Mare shakes her head. "No headstone. Might not even be a body there after all this time. Gulf states flood every so often, you know."

My toes curl in my shoes. How can she just be so matter-of-fact? No bones? No stone? How can she stand not knowing?

We reach a fence. On the other side are what appear to be older graves, most of them covered over with leaves and grass. Mare stops and nods. "This is far enough." She takes my arrangement of roses and leans over the fence, setting the flowers near the closest grave site. Tali sets hers down next to it, and we stand for a moment.

Why did Mare wait so long to come? Was she scared, as scared as she must have been when she left home, or when the Germans chased her ship, or when the first bombs burst over her head in England? Could someone that incredibly brave really need Tali and me? For this?

Mare lets out a sigh. "Mama had a hard road without Daddy. She did the best she could. We all did." Mare looks at my sister and me, her face tight and crumpled with sadness. "Not everybody is cut out to be a mama, you know."

"No, ma'am," I say respectfully. I brush my hand across my damp forehead.

Tali squints at her through the gloom. "But you were great, Mare," she says. "Maybe she wasn't the best mother, but she had to be proud of you, Mare. She had to be. We are."

Mare turns away, her voice low. "I was so scared I'd turn out just like her. The war saved me from that, I guess." She stands a moment longer, her long nails tapping against the old wrought iron fence. "They thought I would come to a bad end, joining the Women's Army, but I guess I did all right. I finished raising Feen to be a nurse, raised your father, and got two hardheaded grandbabies in the bargain." Mare straightens and puts her arms around Tali and me in a rare show of affection. "It all turned out all right. Marey Lee Boylen didn't do half bad."

We bump heads and do a group hug, the sort that other people and their grandmothers probably do all the time. My grandmother's wiry arms are surprisingly strong, crushing us both in a loving grip. After a long moment, Mare steps away from us and tosses Tali the keys.

"I need to get *out* of this heat. Octavia, get out the map and find where 75 breaks off from Interstate 10. We need to keep going east," she says, walking briskly back toward where we parked. "I made hotel reservations in Tallahassee, and I want us to get settled in before it gets dark."

"Tallahassee? Where are we—" I bite my tongue as Mare looks back, her brows raised.

"This close to Florida and we can't hit a couple of amusement parks?" She grins. "Girl, when you get as old as I am, you and everybody else know where you're going next. I don't know about you, but before I get there, I mean to have a *good* time!"

"As long as your idea of a good time doesn't include taking pictures of me with mice," Tali mutters, shoving the keys in her pocket. "I'm not going to be seen with some oversized rodent."

"I think a set of those Mickey ears is the price of admission." Mare smiles evilly, and Tali groans.

"Ma-*re*! What if I see somebody cute?"

"Now, Mr. Mickey is cute!"

"Oh, please!"

My grandmother laughs, the throaty machine-gun rattle comforting in its familiarity. Somehow as she walks away from the graveyard, putting the past and the darkness behind her, she seems taller.

Greetings from Florida

Wish you were here.

Mom
7519 Poppy Way
Pleasant Hill, CA 94523

acknowledgments

Not one American woman stands tall without standing upon the shoulders of those who have gone before her. I'd like to gratefully acknowledge the writing of Charity Adams Earley, whose book, *One Woman's Army: A Black Officer Remembers the WAC* (1989), first informed me of the work of the 6888th in the European theater. Brenda L. Moore's *To Serve My Country, to Serve My Race: The Story of the Only African American WACs Stationed Overseas During World War II* (1997) also added to and shaped the details of this novel. Without these factual bones, I could not have begun to knit this body of fiction.

I further acknowledge the contribution of Mattie E. Treadwell's *The Women's Army Corps* (1954) and Bettie J. Morden's *The Women's Army Corps, 1945–1978* (1990), which has an introductory chapter on army women in World War II and provided me with color photographs of all the uniforms; Judith A. Bellafaire's *The Women's Army Corps* (1993), which has details of rank and regulations; and the Women's Army Corps Veterans' Association, whose Web site includes pages of WAC songs from World War II.

You'll find more about African Americans in World War II, like I did, through the contribution of the National Archives, which provides pictures of African Americans during the war. These were amazing to look through when I was needing inspiration and should make any American thoughtful—and grateful—for the work that African Americans did, even though it didn't seem to be appreciated by a segregated world.